Giving the
Devil His Due

A Charity Anthology by The Pixel Project

Edited by Rebecca Brewer

Stephen Graham Jones, "Hell on the Homefront", ©2008, originally published in *Cemetery Dance* 58.

Kenesha Williams, "Sweet Justice", ©2017, originally published in *Black Magic Women: Terrifying Tales by Scary Sisters* (Mocha Memoirs Press).

Linda D. Addison, "Finding Water to Catch Fire", @2016, originally published in *The Beauty of Death* anthology (Independent Legions Publishing, 2016).

Nisi Shawl, "The Tawny Bitch", @2003, originally published in *Mojo: Conjure Stories,* edited by Nalo Hopkinson, and reprinted in 2014 in *The Mammoth Book of Gaslit Romance*, edited by Ekaterina Sedia (Hachette Publishing Group, 2014).

Published in North America and Europe by Running Wild Press. Visit Running Wild Press at www.runningwildpress.com Educators, librarians, book clubs (as well as the eternally curious), go to www.runningwildpress.com for teaching tools.

ISBN (pbk) 978-1-955062-11-4
ISBN (ebook) 978-1-947041-90-5

This anthology is dedicated to

All the women and girls who have lost their lives to
gender-based violence;

All the women and girls who have rebuilt their lives from the wreckage
left by gender-based violence;

All the women and girls who are still battling or recovering from
gender-based violence in their lives;

and

All the activists and advocates dedicating the time they have on this
earth to forging a future where women and girls can live safely and
reach their full potential as human beings.

We *see* you.

We *hear* you.

We are *with* you.

All net proceeds from the anthology will go towards supporting The Pixel Project's anti-violence against women programs, campaigns, and resources.

Contents

Foreword

(Or Why Stories are Important in the Battle to End Violence Against Women)

The Pixel Project has long recognized the importance of stories in the battle to end violence against women (VAW). Be it hard-hitting documentaries, investigative reports by news media, memoirs by high-profile survivors, or our own advocacy work, which has empowered survivors and activists to share their experiences, stories are an awareness-raising tool that galvanizes many people to push for the eradication of this human rights atrocity.

However, many people remain resistant to real-life stories about VAW. Some react with denial and apathy, others with cynicism and hostility. We needed to tell these stories about VAW in a way that would get through to the holdouts. Thus, our Read For Pixels program was born in 2014 to harness the power of stories in pop culture by enlisting the help of award-winning and bestselling authors to reach out to people worldwide.

Right from the start, we knew that fictional stories can be part of the cultural narrative for perpetuating societal norms of sexism, misogyny, and VAW. Stories that tell the reader that women and girls are disposable and that female pain is acceptable collateral damage in service of mass entertainment. "But it's only fiction!" is the go-to fig-leaf refrain that is routinely trotted out to explain why VAW as a plot widget should remain an uncontested staple in pop culture. Yet the cumulative and insidious influence of such stories, many of which are extremely popular, is to make VAW palatable by trivializing and fetishizing the grim realities of the violence that blights the lives of over half the world's population.

The poisonous attitude that such fiction plays a part in reinforcing is so entrenched that, even in this post #MeToo era, when thousands of survivors worldwide have gone public with their stories, justice remains elusive for VAW survivors. In many societies, murdering a person on the street is considered a serious crime, yet it is deemed acceptable for a man to kill his wife at home. The courts of law and public opinion are heavily stacked against female victims, who are blamed and punished while men who commit rape, assault, coercive control, and femicide often get away with a mere slap on the wrist.

Giving the Devil His Due is our first effort to directly use fiction to counter these toxic narratives. The anthology brings together sixteen major names and rising stars in fantasy, science fiction, and horror who share our belief that stories can be a force for good, that if enough of us speak up to counter the misogynistic messages both in fiction and daily life, we might just be able to win over some reluctant hearts and minds over time.

To help everyone envision a future where VAW is rightfully treated as a heinous crime, the sixteen stories in this anthology invite readers to imagine alternative worlds where violent men receive their much-deserved comeuppance, proportionate to their crimes. Just deserts are served cold to the male abusers, rapists, and murderers of women and girls in the uncanniest of ways. Many of the authors have also included brief notes with their stories and why they wrote them, adding a deeply personal layer that shows that no one remains untouched by the effects of VAW.

While this book is thought-provoking reading, we also hope it will light that spark of courage in you to go out to start breaking the silence surrounding the violence. VAW is a difficult subject to broach with family and friends, so use this anthology as your very own conversation starter: gift it to your book-loving fellow geek for their birthday; ask your neighborhood librarian to order it; read it together with your weekly book club. Maybe even tuck a copy into the bag of a female friend whom you suspect is a domestic violence victim or a rape survivor so they know they are not alone.

Even if you get only one person to stop victim blaming or help a survivor access the support that they need, you will have taken your first step toward changing the world.

It's time to stop violence against women. Together.

Regina Yau
Founder and president, The Pixel Project
September 2021

Hell on the Homefront Too

Stephen Graham Jones

War changes a man. So does getting shot seventeen times by Germans. What Sandy had been hoping the war would change her husband Letch into was a dead man. Just so his outsides could match his insides. Or so his insides could be out. But seventeen German bullets wasn't enough. Letch came back to Decatur, Georgia, a hero. As far as the town was concerned, he was a miracle of science, too tough to die. Sandy knew different. He'd come back for her. And, now that he had medals and was a bona fide hero, the deputies weren't going to come out to the house anymore to stop him, she knew. Getting shot seventeen times was going to be his license to keep on doing to her what he'd already been doing for two years before Germany.

The day his bus rolled into town, Decatur PD caught her in Tallahassee, Florida, driving a truck she'd stolen from her uncle that morning. She was in her nightgown.

"You don't understand what he's like," she told Sheriff Karlson.

He chuckled good-naturedly and delivered her back to Letch. Standing on the porch in his pants and undershirt, Letch saluted the sheriff, then balled that same hand up, slung it into Sandy's face.

She crashed back into the clapboard wall.

Another Friday night in Georgia.

***

Two weeks later, she didn't even recognize herself. Mostly, Letch just hit her in the face, because it was hard to cook with broken arms, hard

1

to clean with cracked ribs. They knew this from before the war.

"Make any friends while I was off saving the country?" Letch asked from the kitchen table.

Sandy was standing at the sink, her bloodied nose dripping into the dishwater. This because she'd opened his beer instead of letting him do it himself.

"Just waiting for you," she said back.

Letch laughed through his nose.

The bullet holes had left puckers all along his left side and gouged out some of his jawline, made a furrow he was always touching now. What Sandy thought was that he wanted them to match now—wanted to make her face like his. What she asked him while he was passed out in the living room wasn't *Why didn't you die?* but *How can you still be alive?*

She was talking to herself, of course.

The one time he caught her watching him sleep, his finger jerked up to the scar on his cheek, and then he sat up, and Sandy knew that running wasn't any good, but she couldn't help it. She was in her nightgown again. He caught her by the mailbox and pushed her hard enough into it that her collarbone snapped. The metal also peeled some of the skin from her face. It flapped under her eye. She tried to hold it in place but Letch set his lips, knocked her hand down, then stepped back to hit her right there on the cheek.

Sandy didn't wake until morning. A dog was running its tongue all the way into her sinus cavity, it felt like. She rolled over onto her good side, threw up, and staggered inside. In the mirror, after rubbing it with alcohol, she could see the eggshell white of her cheekbone. She held her skin in place over it and knew better than to cry, because the salt from her tears would burn.

***

Letch didn't come back from the bars for three days after that, and when he did, it was just because his hand was making him sick. He made Sandy work on it with a pair of pliers. What she finally pulled out, she was pretty sure, was a splinter of bone from her cheek. It was too late, though. The hand was already infected, red streaks of blood poisoning climbing Letch's arm.

She rolled his sleeve down to his wrist, told him he'd be fine.

The next time he came home was a week later.

His hand smelled like rot, and his arm was going black.

"Does it hurt?" Sandy asked him.

"Looking at you, y'mean?" he said back.

This time, she spit on the bandage before cleaning his hand.

Four days later, her collarbone on the mend, Letch crashed his truck into the porch at two in the morning. The whole house shook.

Sandy pulled him from behind the wheel, opened his shirt. The rot—gangrene?—was all the way across his chest now, but, like in Germany, he still wouldn't die. She touched the skin and it was spongy, like meat that been in the sun too long. She left him there for the flies, and they came, blanketed him, but still his chest rose and fell. On the third day, no food, no beer, he coughed, turned his head to the side, and retched maggots onto the shoulder of his shirt.

Sandy sat on the porch and watched, a warm cloth on her collarbone.

"Seventeen bullets," she said to herself, and lit a candle to mask the smell of decay.

***

By the ninth day, Letch's whole body was black like he'd burned, and this time when he opened his mouth, full-grown bottle flies drifted up.

"You're dead," Sandy told him, from the porch.

Letch's shoulders hitched together and then he coughed, and it turned into a laugh. He pulled himself up with the bumper of the truck.

"Not so long as I got my baby," he told her, and lurched onto the porch railing.

Sandy stepped back, her eyes flared wide.

"Lay down, William Letch Cross," she said, trying her best to sound like a preacher.

"On top of you. . ." he said back, smiling, then pulled himself up onto the porch faster than she would have thought he could, being dead and all.

Up close he smelled even worse.

She pushed him away, ran inside, but he caught her by the hair, slammed her into the china closet. She fell, holding her collarbone in place. Letch walked behind her, like he just wanted to see where she was trying to crawl to.

"Yeah," he said, when she got to the stove, "that's right, baby. Daddy's hungry."

Sandy pulled herself up the door, to the burner, to the cast-iron skillet her mother had left her. It was full of pork chop grease still melted from breakfast. She slung it back onto Letch. He licked it off his face with his purple tongue, started fingering the rest in, his white, lidless eyes fixed on her.

"Not quite K-rations," he said, "but who am I to complain, right?"

"How many times you say you got shot over there?" Sandy asked.

Letch stopped licking the grease and just stared at her, said it: "Seventeen."

"Guess they don't know you like I do," Sandy said, and brought the match around, scratching the head on her belt.

The grease Letch was wearing went up like a torch. When he still wouldn't die, Sandy started in on him with the backside of the skillet, and because he was still laughing, she went outside for the axe, came back, slung it through him until the bit gouged through his torso, into the floor. Then she set her feet, aimed at the joints of his shoulders, his knees, his neck. Just to be sure, she burned them all until he was crumbs and ash and bits of bone. This she funneled into a tall metal thermos, the one Letch had come back from the war with. Then, her eyes closed tight, she reset her collarbone.

***

Two days later, at a diner in Tallahassee, all her clothes in the bed of her uncle's truck she'd stolen for the second time, the waitress bellied up to her side of the counter, an order pad in her hand.

"You okay, darling?" she said.

Sandy just stared at a dirty spot on the counter.

"Anybody comes asking for me—" she said.

The waitress narrowed her eyes, waiting.

"I went . . . I went *west*," Sandy finally finished.

"West," the waitress said, tapping her pencil on her pad. "Not down to Miami, right?"

Sandy bit her lower lip, nodded.

"He that bad?" the waitress said.

Sandy squeezed her eyes shut.

"California it is, then," the waitress said, shrugging, then, after one of the men in the far booths started tapping his spoon on the side of his water glass, she came back to Sandy, held up a stained pot, asked, "How you like your coffee there, hon?"

Sandy focused in on the thermos she'd brought in with her. It was sitting by the napkin dispenser.

"Like I like my men," she said, a new hardness in her eyes, like laughter.

"Black?" the waitress asked back, a lilt in her voice because she'd heard the joke.

"No," Sandy said, shaking her head, touching her collarbone, "in a cup."

5

Note from the Author

When I was seventeen, a friend showed up one day with a black eye. She was seventeen too, and the guy she was dating was twenty-two. I asked her what happened, and she said he just gets mad sometimes, it's nothing—I didn't need to worry about it, about her. I lost track of this friend after high school, but I never lost track of her excusing that guy. She's always in my head, saying that, I mean, so, in some of my stories, I give her a pan, or a machete, and I have the story turn out a different way.

— Stephen Graham Jones

The Steering Wheel Club

Kaaron Warren

Eddie sat in his car for a long time in front of his wife's house. His hands clutched the steering wheel, knuckles white. He barely blinked, and when he squeezed his eyes shut, the glare of the street lights meant there was no darkness even behind his eyelids.

He let out a breath. In the confines of the car, his breath stank: whisky, cigarettes, beer, tooth decay he had neither time nor inclination to get fixed. He laughed; a short bark. She wouldn't be nagging him about that anymore, would she? Not that or anything else.

She stirred next to him.

He unclenched his hands and looked at them.

Something caught in his throat. It was the same feeling he'd had on their wedding day, when he turned around and saw her coming down the aisle, beautiful when she was usually just pretty, walking towards him to say she'd love and obey.

He momentarily felt that same sense of excitement, love, and desire.

His phone rang, his mate Gerry. "How the fuck are ya?" Gerry said. "You were ber-lined last night." He HAD been blind drunk, so much so, it was only the last few hours he remembered. The irritation leading to fury.

"Mate," Eddie said, "what a night! If anyone asks, I crashed at yours. Right? Too pissed to get myself home."

Gerry laughed. "What's her name, mate?" and for a moment, Eddie wished that's all it was, that he'd fucked some slut and didn't want his wife finding out. That'd be easy. He'd done that enough before. He didn't even have to try; women loved his blue eyes, his smooth skin, his cheekbones. They loved his footballer muscles.

He started the car. "Thanks, mate."

Hanging up, he looked at his wife curled up in the passenger seat, her hands folded over her head. "Pretty as a picture," he said, and laughed. "Ready for a ladies' lunch with all your friends." She had no friends anymore; they all hated him. Fuck them. And her family were bastards; he would never have to talk to any of them again, thank fuck. A feeling rose, for a moment, a possible sadness, but he swallowed it down, necking a stubby of still-cold beer to wash it away.

Both her eyes were swollen shut, and fingermarks around her neck seemed to pulse at him.

He wasn't feeling much pain. She'd feel it. She'd suffer. She'd deserve every bit of it. He punched a song into the player, Public Image Limited: "This Is What You Want. . .This Is What You Get", a song he liked to play loud, so loud. She used to like the band; years ago, they'd seen them live.

He floored the accelerator. She reached over to try to stop him, both hands grasping at the wheel, climbing onto his lap like she used to long ago, reaching for his eyes with her long fingernails, and for a moment he was back there in that time, remembered it. And so he died with an erection.

***

Alex Thompson kept an eye on the auction sites. Most of the club's memorabilia came from these places or lucky finds at garage sales or charity shops. When he saw the steering wheel, described as carrying "visible bloodstains, fingernail impressions," he knew they needed it.

Alex had been a member of the Steering Wheel Club since its inception twenty-five years earlier. It was established as a place where men could gather and talk about cars without anyone telling them off or making them feel lesser. Over the years, they'd filled it with things that made them happy: framed front-page newspaper stories about classic race wins, and photos of race winners, as well as their collection of steering wheels. The idea was inspired by a defunct English club, and they'd talk about that, the famous drivers who'd attended it, and the steering wheels that decorated the walls there. Alex's club had close to a hundred of them now; wheels from famous drivers, including the "death crash" ones. Wheels from cars that had travelled across the Nullarbor Plain, and those that had travelled the entire National Highway. They had other wheels, too, infamous ones like the wheel from a van driven by a drunken mother, in an accident which killed seven children.

All of them carried a ghost of the driver, an echo of what was.

***

Alex wore driving gloves to buy the steering wheel, and tolerated the sideways glance the two men at the auto-wreckers gave each other. They weren't the brightest of souls.

"Lucky you got permission to sell off the parts," Alex said.

The men laughed. "We don't need permission, mate. Once the police have done their shit and it crosses the threshold, we can do what we want with it. It's part of our charter."

Alex itched to touch the wheel with his bare hands. "You're doing good work."

"Be glad to get rid of it." Most of the car was unsalvageable. "I don't believe in ghosts, but that wheel gives me the creeps."

Alex handed over a business card. "Let me know if you get any more like it. And you're welcome to come to the club one evening as my guests. See how it all looks." It was easy to be jovial with these men. They offered no challenge to him. They admired him because of how he presented himself, clean and confident.

He kept the wheel, wrapped in a towel, in the boot of his car until he could get to the club, not wanting to touch it until it was in place.

***

The club was in an old building on a backstreet, a converted mansion that had quirky shops on the ground floor. They rented the top floor. Alex loved the smell of it: motor oil, cigar smoke, good aftershave. The foyer was tiny and really only served as a place for them to put out flyers and promote motor events. Through the door to the main bar, well lit and with converted car seats as furniture. The walls were covered with memorabilia, and in the far corner was the arcade driving booth. Alex had picked up the booth years ago when a games arcade closed down, an "as is" game. They'd never tried connecting to sound or power, and there was something meditative about sitting in that booth. It wasn't soundproofed but at the same time felt all-encompassing.

Alex wasn't the only one who saw, or rather felt, ghosts in the club. They didn't talk about it, but some of the steering wheels carried something with them. You sat in there, positioned your hands, and you were transported, you felt what that driver felt. The exhilaration, the glorious fear.

Alex sat in the driver's seat of the game. He wanted to experience the existing steering wheel one more time before he swapped it for the new one he'd just bought. This one had come from an accident on the track, the car careening wildly out of control, crossing the boundaries and almost flying over the crowd. Eyewitnesses described it as being in slow motion, giving almost all of them time to run out of the way. There were injuries, people hurt in the rush, but just two deaths: the driver and an elderly man who had drunk himself into a stupor and, people hoped, had not known what was coming.

Alex put his hands on the wheel. The immediate sensation was a stomach-churning one, like you get on a high-flying ride at the fair. Then exhilaration and, Alex thought, a sense of relief. The members had all felt this and between them decided that perhaps the accident was deliberate, that the driver had chosen to die.

Most of them didn't believe the steering wheel (and others before it) was haunted. They thought it was Alex's stories, his fantasies, that made them seem alive.

The feeling had faded. Either the ghost was fading, or his echo at least, or Alex was becoming immune to it. Either way, it was time for a new experience.

Most of the steering wheels carried little or no echo. Some carried just a shiver. Others thrust you into the last moments, embedded you in the experience. He had high hopes for his new one. Useless Euan was the only man in the club. He stood with his light beer, sipping it as he always did.

"How's the wife?" Euan said.

"Oh, you know. She's a modern woman. Thinks cooking and fucking are provinces of China." The joke was that nobody believed this of Alex's wife. "I've got a new steering wheel. You can stick around and watch it go in."

More of a command than a request, but Euan said, "Sorry to love you and leave you; need to go coach my daughter's soccer team."

Alex offered to do the coaching for him. He offered this service often. Euan said, "Err, no, thanks," to which Alex said, "Your loss."

He didn't want to unveil the steering wheel until there were plenty of other members about, so with the club so quiet, he ducked home for dinner. He'd been neglecting his wife, and club food was notoriously bad, frozen food cooked in the microwave. He returned to the club after he'd eaten, expecting he'd have the chance to show off the steering wheel and fill them all in on the story of it. None of them were interested, though. It seemed they were having a wake; Paul Moss had lost his brother (not in a car accident, although Alex couldn't quite gather how he'd died) and Paul was drinking to excess, joined by the rest of them. They were raucous, laughing and joking, as disorderly as these men got. Alex set aside the new steering wheel, thinking now was not a good time to present it.

A group of women arrived, perhaps summoned by Paul, and Alex enjoyed their company. He slipped off his wedding ring and played the lonely widower. Women loved that. "I miss her. I just want to hold her," he said. He had the air of a military general, but he'd never been one. Pink-skinned, broad across the shoulders but also across the stomach, he smelled of soap. He was a keen hand-washer and fuss would be made if there was no soap in the bathroom, at home or there at the club.

There was no female bathroom. The rare lady visitors (always racing fans) used the men's, although the board had to draw the line at assignations happening in there. Plenty of private nooks and crannies for that stuff.

Alex didn't want to bring out the new wheel with the idiot women there. One of them climbed into the driving booth and play-acted but left it quickly, face white under her thick, ugly makeup.

"See a ghost?" Alex winked at her. She ignored him, which pissed him off. This was his club. Who did she think she was? He turned his anger into something else, though, an irresistible, passionate charm, and he wouldn't take no for an answer as he pressed her into the alcove that used to house a telephone, many years ago.

Paul Moss was crying in a corner, the drink and the grief meeting in the middle. The members stood around watching him for a while, disgusted. "Pathetic," they said. "Look at him."

Alex didn't have that last whisky. The idea of being physically incapable, of not being able to look after his physical needs, was one that filled him with horror.

He showered at the club, wanting to maintain the moral high ground at home. He had no delusions about the hypocrisy of this, but he didn't care. When once his wife had looked at him reproachfully, now she looked at him hopefully. That look made him livid; how dare she wish him a lover, a woman on the side, in the hope he might leave the marriage?

Alex got a lift home from Euan. He'd been fine to drive, had driven in that state before, but Euan was there to serve, so why not. On the way home, Alex called his wife.

"NORWICH," he said, winking at Euan, who barely suppressed a laugh.

"Nickers Off Ready When I Come Home," Euan said. The men always liked to say the actual words.

Alex didn't ask Euan in for a drink. While he knew the house would be spotless (it better be), he was so ashamed of his wife, he couldn't let anyone see her.

Not anymore.

She hadn't been out of the house in what, six months? He thought even if he let her go now, she wouldn't be able to. Luckily, she'd been a primary school teacher so she knew how to fix cuts and abrasions. Breaks she treated with painkillers. He didn't mind her when she was on those. He could blame the drugs for her unresponsiveness.

She was sitting up on the couch, wearing one of the dresses he liked. Bottle of wine open on the coffee table, and some kind of snack. The sight of all of it relieved him. He really didn't have the energy to put her in her place tonight if she'd done the wrong thing.

***

The next day, Alex got to the club early. A couple of members were already there or, given the state they were in, hadn't left. It was disgusting; Alex prided himself on his appearance and couldn't understand how others didn't. It was the mark of a man.

They watched as he laid the new wheel down and stretched out with tools to take off the old one.

"That was a good one. Loved it. One of the best." This from one of the club's greatest sycophants.

"It's no Le Mans '55," Alex said. He was still on the lookout for one of those.

"What's the story on this one, Alex?"

He told them about the good man who couldn't take it anymore, and about the crash that left nothing behind but this steering wheel and a tool box, and their wedding rings in the ashes. The last time they had one like this, it was the drunk mother, with all the kids in the car. They'd pulled that one out after a couple of days; even without touching it, they thought they could hear screaming. "I reckon you go first on this one, Alex. You scored it, you get first go." They all nodded. Most of them don't really like touching the wheels.

The old wheel came off easily. Holding it, he got that sense of vertigo, of flying, and it made him feel a little ill. He laid it carefully on the floor outside the booth. They'd hang it on the wall later, between the Austrian Grand Prix winner and the Bathurst 500 winner. He positioned the new steering wheel, still covered with a towel, and then fixed it in place. He really wanted the rest of them to piss off, leave him to it. He wanted privacy for this, wanted the experience, the first experience, to be uncluttered by these observers.

"Drinks, boys? I'm parched, I tell you. My shout."

That surprised them, and they trooped to the bar, where he bought them all a whisky and a beer each, before he slipped out back to the booth.

He sat in the driver's seat, breathing hard. He wasn't as young as he used to be, and even this level of exertion puffed him out. He lifted off the towel and placed it beside him on the floor. There was no passenger seat but there were pedals, something he'd insisted on when the booth was being converted. He put his foot on the brake (an old habit) and placed his hands on the steering wheel.

He felt powerful. He felt his chest filling with air, his lungs inflating, and he breathed out. His muscles tensed; he recognised this. It was anger, his muscles tensing as if some kind of chemical ran through his veins, and he could feel that lessening of thought, the *forget all else* blankness he knew so well himself. His knuckles ached. His heart beat with excitement, and he felt a deep sense of rightness, of satisfaction, but then his eyes filled with tears because there was sorrow as well. If he survived this, he'd never stop crying; he knew that. This was why the man had died. He wanted to stop crying.

Then something else, on top of that. It wasn't lust but he had an erection. It was a physical response, a muscle-memory action. Like the times he caught his wife sidelong, and for a moment remembered their early days, how he was taken back to those wild times and he wanted sex again.

It was that.

And speed, he felt speed, and then the coming of impact.

Then orgasm.

He tried to take his hands off the wheel, feeling the impact coming, not wanting to experience it, but it felt so good, he couldn't.

And it was impact and orgasm and impact and orgasm and impact, until something clicked, his hands froze, and he could no longer decide for himself to take them off the wheel. In his mind's eye he could see her, the other wife, thrusting her fingers into his eyes, reaching deep into his brain.

He became dimly aware of men around him. One of them was a doctor and they roused him, brought him back to life, but he couldn't lift a hand, could barely blink. He'd never experienced anything so powerful. "Elizabeth," he rasped, calling for his wife.

***

Elizabeth Thompson heard a key in the front door and ran her hands over her hair, flattening down any wild bits. She had a roast in the oven (it was Sunday) and she'd made a trifle for afterwards. She had to start early because she couldn't move quickly at the moment; every breath hurt her ribs.

"Hello?" It wasn't Alex. *It wasn't Alex.*

"Hello! Hello!" She tried to calm herself. She'd practised the words she'd need to use to save herself, so many times. How to get it across quickly? How not to sound insane? She'd considered simply asking for a lift somewhere, to the shops, making sure she had her handbag with wallet and passport, which he'd never taken from her, and her pills, ready to go with just that.

"Mrs Thompson?"

What could she say? What words could she use? Two men stood in the doorway, from the club, she thought, with their Hardie 500 T-shirts, their Peter Brock caps. What could she say to them, her husband's friends? Then she saw their faces; the pity, the shock, the horror, and she knew she wouldn't have to say anything at all.

The relief at not having to explain anything made her cry.

***

Paul ushered Mrs Thompson out the back door while Euan helped Alex in the front. He could barely walk and Euan didn't want to touch him. The doctor said take him home, put him to bed, but Euan wasn't touching this man any more than he had to. "What sort of cunt are you?" Euan said. "Ay? Who does that to a good woman? Who does that to anyone?"

He sat Alex in an armchair. Alex grabbed his wrist, starting to regain himself, starting to remember who he was. His eyes ached; he could feel that woman's fingers in them and was sure he was bleeding, but when he haltingly reached for his face, he found tears, not blood.

***

16

Euan and Paul returned that night with the steering wheel. Alex had managed to get himself a beer, and there were some crusts of bread at his feet. He was back in the armchair, fumbling with the remote, wanting to watch the racing, the race.

Euan unwrapped the steering wheel. "We all decided you can have this. None of us want it. We never have. And you're not welcome back at the club, Alex. And it'll be the nurses looking after you, not us. Not your wife."

Paul appeared from upstairs, carrying two heavy suitcases. "I think I got everything she wanted," he told Euan.

Euan placed Alex's hands on the wheel. Alex shook his head, half-shook it, but then the sensation over took him and there was nothing else.

***

Alex called for help but none came. No one organised the nurses or anyone else for him.

He died and orgasmed and cried and the impact and the fingers in his eyes, and he died and orgasmed and cried and the impact and the fingers in his eyes

He called for help

He would be found. In all of it, he knew he would be found, filthy, rotting, and they'd say, what sort of man dies like that, with no one to love him?

He died and orgasmed and cried and the impact and the fingers in his eyes, and he died and orgasmed and cried and the impact and the fingers in his eyes/guilt/sorrow/death/orgasm/

He wondered who would touch the wheel next and whether they would feel him, too. Would he be, at least, remembered there?

The pain was worse each time, and the fear. Now he got it. How this shit could build up. How it wasn't a single event, it was a series of them, and the more of them, the worse the next one would feel.

He felt the loss of the future. All he was supposed to be.

They would find him like this. That was worse than the pain and the fear, the guilt, the sorrow, the death/orgasm/death/orgasm, the blindness of her fingers in his eyes.

They would say, this nobody. This unloved man.

This powerless man.

This forgotten man.

Sweet Justice

Kenesha Williams

How does that song go, by that skinny blonde girl that writes all of those bad boyfriend songs? Oh yeah. *I knew you were trouble when you walked in.* That's the thought that entered my mind as soon as Detective Nelson walked into my office. Actually, it was a garage I turned into an office, but dammit, you get the point.

I really wasn't surprised when he walked into my office. I knew sooner or later, the police department would get their heads out their ass and come inquiring about my assistance with their latest spate of murders. I should have known they wouldn't come kowtowing until they absolutely had to, though. Especially since the last time we'd worked together, I'd thoroughly showed them up after they'd made countless excuses as to why they couldn't get results. But I knew they'd come knocking eventually, and I should have known that they'd use one of my biggest weaknesses against me, Detective Nelson.

Nelson had the swagger of Idris, the face of Morris, and the body of. . .well, the body of Morris Chestnut, too. He was six foot three of delicious, dangerous, and dirty manhood. The last time I saw him was when I threw my mom's favorite vase at his head as he was buck naked out of my shower. Luckily, it wasn't my favorite vase, because that bad boy cracked into at least a million tiny pieces. Unfortunately, it narrowly missed connecting with Detective Adam Nelson's handsome block head. He knew how I felt about commitment, and his fool ass asked me for the key to my house. He was lucky I gave him time to get dressed before I threw him out.

Understandably, he hadn't come by since then. But now, here he was, looking just as fine as he did the morning he narrowly escaped a busted head. He came in, hat in hand, inquiring about my help. The body count had been adding up for at least six months. The deaths had been swept under the rug until the assistant DA became one of those bodies. First pimps, started disappearing, and when they reappeared, it was as gnarled and dried corpses in back alleys that no one should have been down anyway.

No one knew what to make of the disappearances and subsequent reappearance of almost-mummified bodies, and no one really cared. "Good riddance" was the attitude. Then the johns started to disappear. There were a few frantic 911 calls from housewives looking for their husbands but still little fanfare. To be honest, some of the wives didn't want the husbands found. It seemed like once the detectives started looking hard at the victims, they found that those who were missing were abusive bastards and major assholes and therefore had many known enemies. In fact, it turned out the lot of them had more enemies than friends. And if you asked anyone who knew the ADA, they'd count him in with the bastards and assholes. But he was the ADA and therefore, important people were looking for justice or at the very least a miscreant to pin the charges on.

When they couldn't find a single shred of evidence, and someone on the force with sense looked at the clues they did have—shriveled body, no mortal wounds, unspecified cause of death —they called upon me and my unique gifts.

In plain terms, I was a Supernatural Private Investigator. My business card, however, just had my name, Maisha Star, PI. I know it sounds like a porn star's name, but it was the one my mother and father gave me. I kept the *supernatural* part to myself or to those who were on a need-to-know basis. Still, even without spelling out the unique part of my talents, word of mouth always kept me with a steady supply of clients and my mortgage paid on time.

Speaking of mortgages, although I wasn't happy that some weird magical killer was on the loose, it was getting close to bill time, and my last client had flaked on my payment. Actually, I killed him and like they say, dead men tell no tales, but they also pay no invoices. If we're being technical, I didn't kill the client, because you can't kill something that's already dead. I guess if we were being spot on, I re-killed the client who was trying to lure me to my death. I'm sure there was still a price on my head since he had failed miserably to carry out his orders, but such is the life of a Supernatural PI.

"Don't just stand there looking stupid, sit down," I said, and waved to the two guest chairs that sat in front of my mid-century modern wood desk. He did as he was told and continued to look everywhere but into my eyes.

He took in a big gulp of air as if he needed more wind in his sails to spit out whatever he had to say before we got down to business. I braced myself for the barrage of words but was surprised when all he said was "I'm sorry."

I leaned forward on my desk, wondering if I was imagining the words. "Excuse me?"

"I'm sorry. You told me how you felt about rushing into a commitment and then my stupid behind goes and asks for just that. And for that I'm sorry."

He said it all in one breath, like if he didn't say it all at once he wouldn't be able to say it at all. I sat back in my chair speechless, for once in my life. It took a lot of cojones to admit you made a mistake and I was honestly surprised by the apology.

"I'm sorry too. I should have talked to you about it instead of trying to inflict bodily harm." I smiled, and then laughed at the joke. Luckily, he laughed too and all the weird energy in the room dissipated.

21

"Alright, now that that's out of the way, what took y'all so long to contact me? Shouldn't take a big muckety-muck's death for the law to be seeking justice, right? All Lives Matter, huh?" I asked, disdain dripping from each word. Seems like as long as certain folks are victims, the police felt like maybe someone was doing their work for them, but now that the chickens had come home to roost, they wanted my help.

"You know I don't feel that way, Maisha," he said as he looked me in my eyes. I crossed my arms in front of me. Sure, I knew he didn't feel that way, but his brothers in blue were a different story. I was going to help out, of course. I was afraid that whoever was doing this was going to start attacking the working girls next, and I knew they'd get no kind of justice from the police.

"I know," I said. "So, what do you think is going on?" I asked. Although Adam didn't have the gift like I did, he had a pretty strong intuition that served him well on the force.

"It seems like someone's getting revenge, if you ask me. All these creeps dying." He leaned closer as if we weren't the only two in the room. "Between you and me, I'd heard that ADA Johansson sometimes let crimes go unnoticed if a pro gave him a little loving on the side. Also heard that he liked to play rough, too rough, and sometimes would push the boundaries of consent."

"So, he was a rapist. Is that what you're telling me?" I shook my head in anger. "That bastard! He deserved what he got."

"I'm not arguing with you. I just need to get this person off the streets. Who knows who they'll take next?"

I leaned as far back in my chair as I could without falling. I knew that Adam wasn't like the ADA or those dirty cops in California who'd been passing a teenage prostitute back and forth for years. But seeing what he represented vexed my spirit in ways he just didn't know. I was happy that I knew for myself that there was at least one good cop on the force. It still didn't make me feel any better, knowing how many bad ones there were. I thought maybe I could beg off on this case and wait for whoever was doing the killings to knock off a few more assholes, but that wouldn't be fair. Assholedom shouldn't be an automatic death sentence.

"So, will you help me?" he asked, giving me puppy-dog eyes all the while.

"Of course," I said, "but you owe me something."

***

I woke up with a start, feeling like I couldn't breathe. I was trapped under something large and immovable and began to panic. Then I heard a loud noise that could only be the sound of Adam's insufferable snoring. Realizing that he'd thrown his tree branch–like arm across my chest in the middle of the night and that's why I could barely move or breathe calmed me down. I threw off his arm and slid out of bed.

It was still early, and the alarm clock on my dresser glowed the time of three AM in fluorescent green. Seeing the clock's lights reminded me of something I'd noticed in one of the pictures Adam had shown me last night at one of the crime scenes. There was a bright fluorescent orange hoop earring that reminded me of something that Lisa Turtle might have worn on *Saved by the Bell* near the body. It was far enough away that the police didn't think anything of it, but something about it caught my attention. Had the idiots thought to bag it, I might have been able to use it to scry.

I walked to the bathroom and grabbed my fluffy white robe off the back of the door and looked in the mirror. My hair was flying all over the place because I hadn't even had time to grab my hair turban before Adam grabbed me and placed soft kisses all over my throat after I agreed to work on the case. He went straight for my weak spot, so I went straight for his, and after that, there was nothing but the shouting left. I hadn't had a romp like that since I kicked him out my house, so I wasn't complaining about the hair.

23

I looked around the bathroom, trying to remember where my turban would be, and remembered that I had placed it in the small shelf above the lavatory. I grabbed my turban, and something fell as if it were placed on top of it. I bent down to look to see what had fallen, grateful that both the seat and the lid were closed or it would have definitely been in the bowl. I reached behind the commode base and closed my hand around something small and circular. When I brought the item to my face, I knew what it would be but looked anyway; the bright fluorescent orange hoop earring lay in my palm.

I instinctively looked around the bathroom, as if someone might pop out at any moment, but no one did. I padded back to the bedroom and shook Adam awake. He lazily opened his eyes and grinned with a line of dried drool across his cheek, no doubt thinking I was waking him for round two. "No, it's not that," I said before he got any ideas. He frowned but sat up in the bed, awaiting my next words.

"Seems like the killer might have left us a clue."

***

The air in the alley smelled like squalor and death; even the antiseptic properties of the sun couldn't erase the putrescence. I thought coming back to the scene of the crime in the day would make the whole thing less grimy, but it had the opposite effect. Women who looked pretty under streetlights in the dark looked decidedly less so in the harsh rays of the sun's light. They looked like what they were, downtrodden women who needed a chance to make it in this world, by hook or by crook. Not that I could blame them one bit. And one of them was making her way through the men in blue on the beat one by one.

"Hey, miss," I shouted to the youngest-looking girl out here. She had her hair dyed an unnatural shade of red and wore a skirt in the same color hitched up to her hoo-ha. She looked young enough to be my daughter, if I were able to have one. I could tell she wasn't even nineteen under all the war paint she'd put on, but I understood the need to look fierce when facing an even fiercer opponent, life.

"Yeah," she said swaying towards me on spindly high heels. In another life, she could have been a runway model. In this one, she was some unkind man's cum receptacle. Life was funny like that.

She was now so close to me that I could see the color of her eyes. They were a light hazel that was striking against her ebony face. Her lips were full, and she turned them up in a way that said, *I've seen it all before*, but her eyes told another story. I don't know how long she'd been out here, but whatever she'd seen had spooked her. Just not enough for her to give up the corner. She didn't look like a junkie, so I was thinking runaway.

"You see a girl who wears jewelry like this?" I asked, holding up the orange hoop that I'd found this morning.

The girl held out her palm and I dropped the earring in her hand. My attempts at scrying with it back at the house had produced nothing. It was odd. Seemed like someone wanted me to find them, but they weren't giving me enough clues.

She looked at the earring and then held it back out to me in between her thumb and pointer finger. I noticed her chipped manicure, which told me she still tried to keep herself up. "Nah, don't know anyone who wears stuff like that. Looks old."

"Yeah, it does," I said mostly to myself. "If you see something, can you give me a call?" I held out my card to her, and she pinched it between those same two fingers. I saw her eyes squinch up to read it and could make out her lips moving as she read.

"Maisha Star, PI? What does that mean?"

"Means I investigate stuff that others can't."

"Yeah, like what, ghosts and stuff?"

"And stuff," I answered back.

"My grandma could see stuff like that," she tossed out, and then

25

closed her mouth tight like she'd said too much.

"Your grandma still with us?" I asked as nonchalantly as I could.

The girl ducked her head down and looked at the toes of her shoes as if they held life's mysteries. "Nah, she been long gone. I was ten when she died."

"And your parents?" I knew I was being nosy and was waiting for her to tell me to mind my own damn business, but I needed to know.

"I don't know. Mama left me with her mama, and I never knew who my daddy was. Don't think my mama knew, either." She looked around to see if anyone else had heard what she'd said. The streets were pretty empty, it being so early. Just her, me, and some other working girls either leaving to go back home or on their way to set up shop.

"It's pretty early, not too many. . .customers this early. You want to come with me and get some breakfast?" It was a hunch that I needed to follow up on. If her gran had the sight, maybe she did too. And hell, if I was being honest, there was something about the girl that I liked, that I wanted to protect.

Before she could answer, a black car pulled up to the curb behind her. "Babydoll," a man's voice called out from the car.

I watched as the girl's face crumpled while she faced me. She then whipped her head around, and I could hear the smile in her voice as she said, "Hey, baby". She had turned from schoolgirl to coquette in a matter of seconds. But the look on her face before she turned told me the man in the car was nothing but trouble. Trouble she knew, but trouble which she needed.

I walked over to the car where she was now leaning halfway into and cleared my throat. She was so deep in her negotiations, she jumped a little.

"So, about that breakfast," I said, throwing my arm over her shoulder, all the while peering into the car. There were two men in the car. The man at the wheel had a pockmarked face the color of left-out mayonnaise, and the man in the passenger seat next to him wasn't winning any beauty contests either. The third man in the back scooted further into the seat as if to remain hidden.

She gently shrugged my arm off of her and turned to face me with pleading eyes. I didn't know whether she wanted me to save her or if she wanted me to let her go with the men. But until she told me to shove off, I was going to be sticking right by her side.

"I'm good," she said through teeth clamped down so tight, the words sounded like the hissing of a snake. I took the hint and backed up a bit. Watching her get into the back seat with the man I couldn't see made my body buzz like an electric current. I got nothing but bad vibes and couldn't do a damn thing about it. I watched helplessly as the car drove off, but committed the license plate to memory. If Babydoll didn't come back by tomorrow morning, I was having Adam look up the plates and find out who it was registered to.

It's a shame. I didn't have to wait until the next morning to find Babydoll because the eleven o'clock news had her face plastered on it.

***

Young Woman, Age 17, Found Dead in Same Alley as District Attorney.

Those were the words on the bottom of the television screen. I was in so much shock that I couldn't even make out the words the reporter was saying. I watched the scene unfold on the television; they showed the alley I'd just been to earlier in the day, and on the ground was a white sheet covering what I could only assume was her body.

Hot tears slid down my face, and I used my balled-up fists to wipe my eyes. If the person who killed the cops killed Babydoll, they were going to have to personally deal with me. I know it was a cliché, but this time it was personal.

I walked like a zombie to my closet and pulled out a pair of shorts that I wore with tights last Halloween dressed as a Soul Train dancer. I carefully made up my face, spritzed on some rosewater perfume, and strapped a sheathed knife to my upper thigh. Mama was going hunting tonight.

***

The cops had now left the murder scene, and all that remained was the yellow police tape. It still didn't stop the johns and the ladies from doing their business. I craned my neck towards the alley, seeing if I could get a glimpse of Babydoll's spirit, but I didn't see a thing.

Seemed like maybe she wanted to move on. I was happy her soul was at rest, but I selfishly wanted to see her one last time. When I turned back towards the street, my eyes fell on a woman about a half a foot taller than me as well as a whole two feet wider. She looked me up and down and then sneered as if what she saw was lacking.

"You new?" she spat at me. I didn't know whether it was a question or a statement, so I just nodded. "Yeah, you look like it. You smell too clean, and you look too eager. Ain't gonna be nobody but the desperate and the depraved out tonight. The cops and the reporters spooked all the regular guys away. Watch out for yourself."

Before I could come up with a response, she swaggered away and melted into the scenery. I took my hands to my hair and pulled it in different directions, giving myself a roughed-up look. I didn't want to look like I was an easy mark. I sauntered up and down the street a bit, hoping I wouldn't make any enemies by taking some of the regular girls' customers.

It didn't take long for what I wanted to show up. Criminals are dumb. They always return to the scene of the crime. I don't know why they do, mainly for bragging rights, I guess, but it was a damn risky thing to do. The black car from this morning slowly circled the block. Just when I thought it had disappeared, I saw it round the corner again.

I stepped out from the shadows and made myself seen. I was hoping that pock-face had a need for another girl. Hopefully, they didn't just have a taste for young flesh. I was pushing forty but on a good day could pass for twenty-nine. My legs were good, my ass was round, and my tits hadn't succumbed to gravity. The car stopped in front of me, and the window rolled down.

"You looking for some fun," I sang out to pock-face. He looked me up and down like a slave on the auction block, and I held in a shudder as he appraised me from head to toe.

"Yeah, sure am," he said. I leaned into the open window and saw that his partner that rode shotgun was missing, but the man in the back was there.

"Sure am," I repeated.

I grabbed the door handle, but before I could open it, a hand touched mine. The hand was cold, dead cold. I turned to see a woman behind me. She was about my height with a mahogany complexion, and her hair was in a roller-set shag reminiscent of Claire on the *Cosby Show*. In her ear, the other orange hoop.

"I'll take it from here, sugar," she said in a Southern drawl that I couldn't place. She could have been from anywhere south of the Mason-Dixon line.

"Can we talk?" I asked.

"Yeah, y'all fight over who gets to come with us," the driver called out.

She blew him a kiss and then took my elbow in her hand and guided me closer to the alley. "You don't want none of that, sugar. They're into that kinky shit, and they don't believe in safe words," she said in a low voice.

"I think they killed my friend," I said as I ran my hands up and down my bare arms that were now shivering in the frigid air.

"Which is why you need to let me go with them, and you stay here." She kept the car in her eyesight, and I looked over at where it idled.

"Your earring?" I asked.

"You got the other one, right?" she countered.

"Ghost?"

She chuckled, and the breath she expelled was icier than the night air. "Something like that," she said with a grin. "Let's just say I'm a worker of justice. Much like you, Maisha. You go on home. I'll take care of everything."

I wanted to protest but knew that she could give these bastards a better home-going than I could with my knife. Plus, it'd be two on one. Not exactly a fair fight for me, but a spirit, well now, that would even up the odds a bit.

"Make it hurt," I said and then walked away.

"Oh, I will," I heard her say in the distance.

***

Mayor Found Slain in Upper Northwest Home. Body of Missing Woman, Justice Hawkins, Missing Since 1987, Found in Basement.

This time, I watched the chyron on the screen and smiled. The picture of the missing woman was the spitting image of the woman I'd met the night before with the icy breath and the Southern drawl. She wore a smile as big as the sun and as bright as the highlighter-orange hoops in her ears.

"Hot damn!" I exclaimed, waking up my cat at the foot of the bed as well as Adam, who was sound asleep on my right side.

"What happened?" he asked as he sprang up from his pillow.

"Justice happened," I said as I laid my head on his chest. I used the remote to turn off the news and then threw it off his side of the bed. "Sweet justice."

The Moon Goddess's Granddaughter

Lee Murray

New moon

It was the beginning of everything. It was a night full of promise and wonder, when beneath a marquee, a young couple—two young lovers—danced under the new moon, You, grand-daughter of the moon goddess Chang'e, were weightless in frothy white. It was the beginning of everything when your new husband twirled you across the boards, with his strong arms and confident stride, and his big hand pressed into the small of your back to guide you. You trilled at his touch, at this nuptial dance of the earth and the moon, of yin and yang, and East and West.

Your mother hovered at the edge of the dance floor, watching the billowing train as if it might trample underfoot, creases forming at the corners of her eyes like the folds in the fabric of your gown. Floating by on a dream, you noticed that her own dress, carefully selected to convey humility and grace, also picked out the silver threads in her dark hair. But by then, you had swept beyond her censure, carried away by your love to the centre of the dance floor, whirled and twirled in time to the music, until there were just the two of you, his breath gentle at your nape and his voice an intoxicating lullaby in your ear. He spoke softly, beautiful whisperings, of the realms he would conquer, the legacy he would create, and the things he would do with you by his side. Then the music stopped too soon—and a knife tolled, insistent, against a glass, demanding the revellers' attention. The dance must wait. You

31

clung to his wrist, your gown swirling at your feet. The murmurs died away and in that expectant hush, your father cleared his throat and made a fine speech, proclaiming the man at your side as his new son-in-law, and sealing the contract with the gift of your body. Heat rose in your throat at that—such an antiquated tradition with you so modern and your job a train-commute away in a glass-glinting high-rise in the city. Still, you couldn't help blushing, your skin turning as pink as the rosé served in the cut-crystal glasses. The guests cooed and clinked and sipped and supped. The young men slapped your new husband's back with exaggerated bravado, and the bachelorettes giggled, rushing in twos to the restrooms to draw up their battle plans. And beneath the marquee, under the dark skies of the new moon, your new husband raised his glass and drank to your life together.

First quarter

A daughter came, a child full of promise and wonder. So tiny, almost weightless. You carried your love in your arms, and in your heart, which fluttered with the immensity of the task, with this precious soul entrusted to you. It was the most important thing, too important to put a foot wrong, so you gave up the job in the glass-glinting high-rise in the city. No need for the daily train-commute, your husband said. It was a privilege to be able to stay at home and raise a child. It was what he wanted for his daughter—the right thing to do. It was what you wanted, too. Of course it was. A career was all very well, but a child was a gift from the heavens. So, you puréed apples, sang songs, and slept barely at all, smoky love-smudges appearing beneath your eyes. At night, when your daughter woke with colic and cramps, her cherub face crumpled and her chubby legs drawn up to her chest, you walked the house, up and down and up and down, your palm pressed to her back, and your cheek against hers, humming a lullaby, while milk-moonlight slipped past the edges of the curtains.

I have a meeting tomorrow, your husband grumbled. Any chance of some quiet?

Mindful of him, you closed the bedroom door, and walked some more, your daughter in your arms and your bare feet tread-quiet on the carpet. Over time, the smudges beneath your eyes deepened and you grew thin, although the baby thrived. Sometimes you forgot things, like seeing your friends, where you parked the car, and studying for an advanced degree.

One morning, your mother swept in—I'm fine, just a bit tired, you insisted—yet, stern-faced (and even more insistent), she took your daughter from you. Fierce, you went to take the baby back, but, clutching a clump of your mother's hair in one hand, your daughter shook her fist at you. Your warrior princess. You had to laugh. Your protests died away, and in that moment, you felt the heaviness of it all. So, you gave quarter to your mother and your daughter, and you went to the library and then to shop at the mall, and afterwards you sat on the beach, your toes in the warm sand, while you breathed in the salt air. When you returned, the smudges had faded, and your baby was asleep, her fists splayed above her head as the moonlight seeped through the curtains of her room.

You neglected our daughter, your husband said, when you came to bed. Don't do it again. For the first time, you glimpsed the shapeshifter's features superimposed on your lover's face, smelled its sweet rot on his breath. You tensed, heat rising in your throat, but the monster was as fleeting as yesterday's dreams, and you thought perhaps you'd imagined it.

The next day, because she was the most important thing, the only thing, you carried your daughter into the backyard and whirled and twirled her over the fresh-cut grass, her laughter spinning into the air like dandelion seeds.

Later, at bath time, your husband leaned against the bathroom door, his eyes on the dark liquid swirling in his glass, while your daughter splashed rainbow prisms in the tub. After a while, he put the glass down on the sink and crouched behind you, his arms about your waist. You stilled at his touch. This time, when he whispered into your nape, his words were a river of regret. You couldn't help but be carried away by his lullaby; how could you not?

A soap bubble burst, and you yielded.

Waxing gibbous

Full of promise and wonder, your daughter went off to school. A daughter-descendant of Chang'e the moon goddess, she did not look back as she swept through the gates, the light of your lives, her dark hair swaying and her lunch box bumping against her thigh. The gates closed behind her with an iron clang, tolling the end of the beginning—too soon, slow down—but in the playground, the children cooed and climbed and skipped and soared. You hovered at the edge of the schoolyard, creases at the corners of your eyes and your dark hair wisping around your face, and you couldn't help thinking of the realms she would conquer, the things she would do, and your heart fluttered with the rightness and the sadness of it all.

Weeks later, with the long days stretching before you, you remembered the job in the glass-glinting high-rise, and you recalled your yesterday-dreams. Suddenly, the train commute didn't seem so long, the city not quite so far, that old life not nearly so distant, and you yearned again for the shuffle of paper and the tap of keyboards, and the whirl and twirl of industry.

So, one evening when your daughter was asleep, one evening under a waxing moon when there were just the two of you—you with your tea and your book, and him with his whisky and his podcast—you leaned back and told your lover of your dreams. It was what you wanted, you told him. You weren't asking for rainbow prisms, after all, just everyday tread-quiet things. Important things. Important to you.

The curtains fluttering, you clung to his wrist and hushed, expectant, while he cleared his throat.

No.

His refusal hung weightless in the air, and you stilled, stunned, your mind spinning. For an instant, your breath stopped—the shapeshifter had returned, its cruel shadow stealing across your lover's face. A gibbous monster, it hissed and spat and slurred and sloshed, its censure filling the air like shards of cut crystal.

Useless. Lazy. Selfish. Slut.

The creature clutched at your hair, yanking you close, its breath rank in your face.

My parents will look after our daughter after school, you whispered, but your lover was gone, replaced by a monstrous usurper with red-rimmed eyes that swirled with darkness.

I said no.

Your heart fluttered, fearful. You shrivelled, shrank, made yourself small. All your protests died away, and in that moment, you felt the heaviness of it all. You wanted to laugh. You'd been floating through life on a dream.

That night, you slept barely at all.

Waxing crescent

When the moon dipped and the sun rose, your lover returned, full of promises of wondrous new beginnings. In the kitchen, he wrapped his strong arms around you and held you close. Please, he said in that familiar intoxicating way. He whispered in your ear, a lullaby of lasting love, of soap bubbles and dandelion seeds.

We need you here, he said. It was what you wanted, too, really. Of course it was. A career was all very well, but you shared a daughter, a gift from the heavens, and she was the most important thing, the only thing.

Beautiful, beautiful whisperings.

Your mind whirled and twirled and swirled in confusion, but your daughter descended, swept up in her own rainbow prisms and demanding your attention. So, putting aside yesterday's dreams, you served her cereal and plaited her dark hair. With her school bag bumping against your thigh, you pressed your hand gently in the small of her back and guided her out of the house and into the street.

When she was safe behind the iron-clang gates, you went to the library, then shopped at the mall, and afterwards you sat on the beach, your toes in the warm sand, while you breathed in the salt air. Still later, you took your daughter to the pet store and bought a rabbit, white like the moon, which she named Jade in the manner of children.

At home, that afternoon, you played in the backyard with the moon rabbit, the goddess's own companion bounding between you and your daughter in the overlong grass. When it grew tired, you carried the rabbit in your arms, so tiny, it was almost weightless. You and your daughter caressed and coddled and kissed and cuddled that little treasure. And though night was approaching, it seemed to you that the darkness had faded. It was a new beginning, you decided. The monster had left, and all was well.

Moonbeams spilled across the coverlet when you tucked your daughter into bed and kissed her on the cheek. You pulled the curtains closed against the gentle light. There were always misunderstandings. After all, you could not have the east without the west, ying without yang, the sun without the moon. But things would be different now. Yes, now was the time for new beginnings. He'd promised.

But that night, you slept barely at all.

Full moon

Your lover came home less and less. On the rare days when he would find his way home to you, he was barely a husk, and his visits were fleeting. More and more, the shapeshifter took his place at the table, bloodshot eyes watching you, ever swirling that blood-dark liquid in the cut crystal glass.

And later, the shapeshifter would join you in your bed.

Wary, you made yourself smaller and smaller, until you were almost invisible. Over time, the dark smudges beneath your eyes deepened, and you grew thin. Threads of silver grew in your hair. While your daughter spent her days laughing and playing with her friends behind the iron-clang school gates, you cooked meals and did laundry and walked the house, up and down and up and down, alone in your tread-quiet nightmare. Because you'd made a contract, hadn't you? Sealed it with the gift of your body.

Now you were trapped, like the moon rabbit in its cage.

The shapeshifter came home early. No longer needed, it said, and you trembled at what that meant. It paced the house, sipping its lifeblood from a cut crystal glass and gathering the darkness around it.

There was still your job a train-commute away in the glass-glint high-rise in the city, you said, your voice barely louder than a whisper. You could go back. . .

The monster whipped its head up and snarled at you, drool dripping from the side of its mouth. It staggered closer, grabbing your wrist, and pressed its face into yours, so you couldn't help but breathe in its foul breath.

I said no.

You nodded, cringed, and twisting free, you backed away, fleeing into the garden to cuddle the rabbit, while inside, the monster gnashed and roared and spat and thrashed. It was still raging when you left to pick up your daughter from outside the iron-clang gates.

Much later, you crept back home, the two of you—where else could you go?—slipping through the hedge into the backyard. You stilled, stunned, your breath stopped. White tufts. The rabbit, the moon goddess's companion, lay in the long grass in a mulch of bloodied fur. You spied a severed ear. A mangled foot.

Your daughter gasped, so you swept her into your arms and held her close.

But a knife tolled, a blade tapped against glass, demanding your attention. Behind the windows, in the kitchen, the shapeshifter prowled, pacing back and forth, back and forth. Your skin burned as it raised its glass.

It's your fault, the monster said, that night when you lay at its side in your nuptial bed. *Always your fault.* It pressed its hands around your throat, while you lay there, shrunken and small—and trapped. At that moment, the full moon shone through the curtains to reveal the shapeshifter in all its hideous cruelty.

You did not sleep. How could you sleep?

You didn't dare to cry.

In the morning, when the sun rose, it was a wonder that your heart still fluttered.

Waning gibbous

You met your mother at the edge of the schoolyard, a scarf wrapped around your throat, and, in hushed tones, you told her of the murdered rabbit.

It's just a rabbit, your mother said, stern-faced.

It was a pet, you whispered.

Deep creases formed at the corners of her eyes and she pulled you to one side. Remember your contract. Remember your daughter, a gift from the heavens. She's the most important thing—the only thing.

You almost laughed at that. As if you had forgotten. It was only you who were forgotten. You were weightless, worthless, invisible.

Of course your mother saw only your husband's husk with his drifting soul waning like the moon. Hovering at the edge of your lives, she'd never glimpsed the monster's shifting visage or its claws clutching at your throat. Instead, the creature had wooed her with a mask of humility and grace. Your lover was gone, leaving only a shadow. How could she know?

Too ashamed to show her the battleground of your body with its legacy of bruises, you went home.

Where have you been? the shapeshifter demanded.

Your pulse fluttered. You pressed your hands to the scarf at your throat. I went to the school, the library, the mall, you trilled, your voice full of exaggerated bravado.

It narrowed its eyes. Pressed the cut crystal glass to your throat. Tell anyone, and I'll kill you, it promised. And you wondered, how it had come to this?

Last quarter

For days, you lived on edge, floating in a nightmare, mindful of the monster. Silent and tread-quiet, you cooked meals and did laundry. You took your daughter to school. Hovered at the edge of the playground until she disappeared inside. Careful not to put a foot wrong.

Tell anyone, and I'll kill you.

By now the monster could not be placated with shots of blood from the cut crystal glass. It wanted yours. You do not remember what you did, but you must have deserved it. It waited until there were just the two of you, then it turned on the music, so the neighbours would not hear, and it hurled you across the kitchen. Tiny, almost weightless, you smashed and crumpled against the edge of the table. The monster revelled. It kicked and cut and clawed and struck until you drew your legs up to your chest.

Rainbow prisms danced behind your eyes.

Still, it raged. It puréed your face. Burst a rib. Ripped clumps from your hair until blood-dark liquid trickled tread-quiet into the boards.

At last, the music stopped—oh God, it's stopped—and through swollen splintered eyes, you watched, dazed, as the creature contorted, shifting its features until it resembled your husband.

Don't move, it said.

You didn't move. Couldn't move. You barely breathed.

It was a privilege to stay at home.

You floated, imagining yourself safe behind iron gates, emerging only when the door clanged. The monster was back. It clutched your daughter by the arm, yanking her towards the stairs. Heat rose in your throat when you saw your baby's red-rimmed eyes, and your heart was cut crystal. *She* was most important thing.

Later, when night had fallen, you pulled the shadows around you and crawled into the garden, where you lay trampled in the long grass. Hushed. *Still.*

Above you, drifting across the dark skies in her swirling silver gown, Chang'e the moon goddess reached out and touched you with her gentle light, with a gift from the heavens, a dream of yesterday, and you tensed, remembering. How could you have forgotten? You were the granddaughter of the moon goddess, that brave warrior princess who chose not to live with a tyrant, who escaped to live her own life beyond the stars. Coughing, you scrambled to your knees and raised your fist to the sky. The goddess's blood ran in your veins; this was the last time you would give quarter.

Fierce, you would take your power back.

Waning crescent

Now you'd decided, your power returned. The goddess's blood hummed in your veins. It was intoxicating. The tasks didn't seem so impossible, the waning crescent of the moon not quite so distant.

The monster didn't notice you. Of course it didn't. You were weightless, invisible.

Where are you going? it demanded.

To the library, to return my book, you said.

At the library, you tapped at keyboards and concocted battle plans for the day when you would sever your contract with the monster and reclaim your body. While you were shuffling papers, you stopped, suddenly yearning for the lover who had whirled and twirled you on the dance floor so long ago. Your heart fluttered and you felt a trickle of regret; if only you could save him, too. But he was a ghost. Nothing more than a yesterday-dream, replaced by a monster.

On the last day, you entered the iron-clang gates and told the teachers. You spoke softly of your daughter, who was the most important thing, but not the only thing. They looked at you, full of wonder, then they clasped your hands and promised to help.

You couldn't help blushing when they said it was the right thing to do.

That night, you lay awake, waiting for the moon to rise. This time, you didn't draw the curtains. When the monster slumbered, slack-jawed, you crept from your bed. Your hands fluttered over the coverlet, gathering up the scattered silver moonbeams. Then, tread-quiet, thread-quiet, you crafted a cage to seal the monster in. For hours, your needle waxed and waned. East and west, up and down, your fingers aching at the immensity of the task. You didn't sleep. You couldn't sleep.

No time to sleep.

But, spurred on by your dreams of tomorrow, swept up in your fervour, you knocked over the cut crystal glass. You tensed, your heart in your throat, as the vessel smashed, draining blood-red liquid down the wall.

The monster woke. It rose from its bed, malice glass-glinting in its eyes. What do you think you're doing? it hissed.

Tiny, weightless, you slipped between the magic moon-spun threads and beyond its reach. Leaving, you said.

The demon laughed at that.

You lifted your chin and stood your ground. Leaving, you whispered.

The shapeshifter swelled and burst from its husk, exploding in a legacy of fury and hate. Grotesque, its cruel form twisted and contorted to fill the room. It was monstrous. Terrifying. You shuddered as it crouched and charged at the moon-web, slashing razored claws across the threads, and, for a moment, you remembered those claws clutched about your throat. You remembered fractured ribs and splintered lips. Recalled the rabbit's bloodied corpse and the disembodied tufts of white fur. Trembling, you backed away.

But, gossamer-thin, the moon goddess's threads were iron-strong. The monster surged and thrashed and writhed and grasped, it roared and spat and raged inside that cold palace; still the cage held.

Then, suddenly, the creature stopped, your lover's face flickering across its features. His voice floated on the air, whispering that familiar lullaby, promising you the moon and the stars. A soap-bubble dream, bursting as quickly as it formed, and your heart broke because it could never be, because nothing would ever change.

I'll kill you, the monster screamed.

You turned away. Let the creature prowl the empty house, impotent in its empty husband-husk. Let it roar and gnash and thunder. From now on, it could endure this soulless nightmare alone. Your body was a realm the monster would no longer conquer.

You were the goddess's own granddaughter; already, the moon was yours for the taking. Still later, you buried the remains of the rabbit, the goddess's faithful companion, in the backyard.

New moon

In the hush of the early morning, under the dark skies of a new moon, you left the house, just the two of you, the moon goddess's granddaughters, your black hair swaying and your bags bumping at your hips. You breathed in the dawn scent of autumn, apple shampoo, and long grass. Expectant, full of promise. Like dandelion seeds tossed to the wind, you would begin a new life together. It was just a train-commute away.

You took your daughter's hand and stepped into the street.

The sun would soon rise.

Note from the author

In older versions of the Asian moon goddess legend, Princess Chang'e drinks an elixir of immortality to escape her husband, a former hero turned tyrant. The goddess's pet hare delays her husband's pursuit, allowing her to escape to the moon, where she endures beyond his reach. With my prose-poem "The Moon Goddess's Granddaughter," I hoped to capture the essence of this poignant tale, which, for me, embodies the experience of abuse survivors, especially Asian women encumbered by expectations of submissiveness and face, for whom escape is a rare recourse and any revenge is likely to be quiet and without violence.

— Lee Murray

The Kindly Sea

Dana Cameron

The hairs on the back of Lucy's neck stood up, even before she turned around. When she saw him, he smiled, and she wanted to get out of there. Her coat was on, she'd said her goodbyes, and the door was *right* there. He couldn't already have—

"What have you done, you stupid, stupid bitch?" No one watching them from a distance would have observed the stark difference between his warm smile and his bitter tone.

"You're not supposed to be here," she blurted. Electric adrenaline shot through her system. Somewhere at the party, laughter erupted.

"I wasn't invited, and I have important work to do. You went and fucked things up. So, I had to drag myself all the way out here to deal with you spreading shit about me. A formal complaint? How could you?"

Lucy thought of the carefully rehearsed language she'd prepared for the next time she saw him. She got as far as taking a deep breath, when she felt his hands clamp on her shoulders, fingers digging deep.

This couldn't be happening, she thought, as he slammed her head into the wall.

"You had to go around spreading shit? You led me on, and now—"

Stunned, all she could do was shake her throbbing head, tears blinding her.

"Who needs another drink?" A voice came from the living room, nearing the kitchen.

As quick as thought, he unhanded her. Lucy's feet were moving before she realized what she was doing.

Lucy flung open the kitchen door, sobbing, running for her life. Someone, probably B, closed the door quickly, quietly behind her.

The snaking coastline played tricks on her. Every time she thought she would be farther away, she found herself even closer to the house. She just wanted to get far from him, be alone, and scream out her emotions to the uncaring sea, but all the paths led back closer to the house and the party going on there.

If that wasn't an apt metaphor for her shitty life, she didn't know what was.

She also saw that the local saying was right: *You can't get there from here.* Nothing was point A to B, nothing was a straight line.

Finally, she found an outcrop over a little cove, out of sight of the big house. The waves would be enough to cover her sobs. No one could see her.

Eyes blurred, the heel of her boot caught in a crack in the stone. Lucy went down, hard, on her left knee, her right leg splaying out across the granite, and she felt the shock of the impact and the deep abrasion. She leaned over and, groaning, straightened her left leg. The pain didn't fade, and she saw the shining black of her blood on the rock and her knee reflecting the moonlight.

It began to rain, hard.

She sat and rocked, and when she caught her breath, she screamed. And screamed again. "I did everything right! I did *everything*. And still—"

And still what? She caught herself. *It didn't matter, was what.*

Lucy got up. She'd walk up to the road, call a rideshare, and go home. She'd figure out what to do in the morning.

She tried putting weight on her left leg. Her knee buckled, and her foot slid. She was sliding off the wet granite outcropping, knowing she had to stop herself or fall. There was nothing to grasp, nothing to hang on to. She scrabbled, nails scraping at the surface, sand and pebbles acted as ball bearings—

She hit the air.

On the way down, time slowed. Anger at the injustice of it grew, then slammed into her as she broke the icy surface of the bay—

***

It wasn't nearly as dark beneath the waves as Lucy expected. She was no longer angry or afraid, just. . .tired.

She saw the lights: glittering, neon jewels suspended in a sinuous and glassy body. Kindly, alien eyes regarded her and sucker-covered arms waved gently, hovering in the water. Lucy realized that the Sea had taken the form of this creature to speak with her.

The Sea asked Lucy, "How did this come to pass?"

Lucy thought of the steady, sly progression. The chummy nudges on the shoulder, eventually turning to little squeezes of encouragement. The odd hug of excitement. Nothing overt or obvious, just enough to normalize his proximity. As she reached for a book, his hand grazed the side of her breast. He apologized, horrified and embarrassed.

At their first official meeting, she arrived at his office to hear the sound of urination; he'd left the door to the bathroom off his office open. He said nothing about it. The next week, she arrived five minutes later and found the same situation. She considered saying something but was stopped by her need for a job, one that could only come after he'd signed off on her dissertation. Only a few more weeks, maybe two months, and she'd be well away from him. She could do that. He was of another generation, friendly and awkward, after all. . . She might have been misinterpreting it all.

The next meeting, however, he slid his hand over her breast, looking her straight in the eyes. She left hastily, lodged a formal complaint.

Later, she went to the party to try and reclaim some of her day. Her self.

"I wasn't even supposed to be here," she explained to the Sea. "My dissertation lead was killed in an accident before she could give me her notes. The university decided I needed one more senior scholar in addition to my other readers. And he was it."

A thought struck her, filling her with dread. "I didn't try. . . I mean, it was an accident. I didn't jump to. . . Am I dead?"

"No, you are not dead," the Sea answered, "and you did not try to destroy yourself. We would not have allowed that. But you are at a turning point, and we, who are everywhere, observe."

The words should have worried her, but Lucy was too entranced by the elegance of the Sea, too reassured by its empathetic manner.

"What do you want?"

Lucy felt the ancient intelligence of the Sea and knew this question somehow mattered. It was not to be answered frivolously. She thought of the doubt she'd felt, the humiliation of being frozen in a moment, the way her adult self had abandoned her to panic in her encounters with him. The feeling of violation and the self-recrimination for not having stopped it. After a long heartbeat, then two, she answered. "I want him to feel what I've felt. To know what it feels like."

"It is done." The Sea handed her a small shell, a token of their promise.

Lucy took it without thinking. "Like that? How will I know—"

"You are the author of this wish. You will see it work." With a gesture that was either farewell or a dismissal, the Sea turned and scuttled along the sandy bottom, its translucent arms and bulbous mantle vanishing instantly into the black.

"Thank you." Knowing that she no longer had any use for breath, Lucy took a last deep breath, filling her lungs with water, and saw no more.

***

When she woke the next morning, Lucy's leg was throbbing. Her head ached and the world wheeled around as she stood up. Her hand cramped, and she saw that she clutched the shell she remembered from her dream the night before.

Using her phone, she reconstructed what had actually happened. She'd slipped and fallen, then summoned a rideshare service. The receipt said she'd arrived home about twenty minutes after she'd escaped *him* at the party.

She should have someone check her for a concussion when she got her knee—which was swollen and crusted with blood—examined. The fall, after his battering her, had resulted in memory loss and that crazy dream. She tucked the shell into her pocket; although she'd probably picked it up on her way back to the road, she liked the idea of the reassuring Sea and those understanding eyes.

Escaping the campus health services wasn't easy; she didn't want to stay overnight, just wanted to hide away at home. After promising to rest and keep off her leg, they gave her a cane and painkillers hardly worth the name.

Exhausted by the effort of going across campus, the idea of adding this incident to her complaint against Dr. B was so repugnant, Lucy returned home. She satisfied herself by calling to make an appointment to follow up with this new complaint the next day.

One apocalypse at a time, she thought, and giggled, a little madly.

She picked up dinner on the way home and ate dutifully, without tasting it. She went to bed early to avoid the temptation of working— screen time was forbidden. She dozed, began to dream, and the deeper her sleep, the more clearly she observed. . .

Dr. B felt a vague sense of unease, of not belonging and waiting to be caught. The longer he stayed in this place, the worse he felt, but there was nowhere else to go, no matter how far he walked. The plain was gray and barren, and the

49

sky ocher, a dry wind blowing but moving nothing. At last, he found a band of travelers heading in the same direction, and they agreed to share their food with him. He knew, just knew, if he could travel with them, he'd survive, and more. But every time he tried to speak with their leader, the man turned away. Every time he reached for a plate of food, someone snatched it from him. A distraction, and his own plate was whisked away from him, with an admonishment for not being grateful for their gift. His hunger grew into a yawning void as the other travelers vanished, with mocking laughter, leaving him despite his pleas for company or assistance or direction. "You're not even trying. You're overexaggerating. You know better than this."

As he walked, he could feel his body rotting, although, at first, he thought it was sunburn sloughing off his skin. The smell of rancid meat grew and he could not find a place on his hand that the skin was not coming off. Stomach crawling, he realized that it was happening on his arms, his neck, his face—all over. The shedding skin left sores and the worsening smell drew tiny mice. One bit him, and it was no more than a sharp, stabbing nuisance, but then the others, emboldened, swarmed him, and he screamed as their teeth seemed to grow, and tore larger and larger pieces, until he was crawling on the stumps of defleshed bones.

As he died, one of the mice eating his way through his eye—he no longer had hands to shoo them away or a spine to roll over on them—with tattered lips he muttered, "Abandoned. Forsaken. Desperate."

***

Lucy awoke the next morning, her head remarkably steadier and her sense of purpose strengthened. Crazy dreams aside, she'd slept well and it had done her a world of good.

Picking up another bottle of acetaminophen at the pharmacy, she ran into a colleague, another graduate student, Ellen. Looking around, she pulled Lucy aside. "You know Dr. B is talking about you, right? And not in a good way."

"No, but it wasn't hard to imagine he might. What did he say about what happened at the party?"

"That you're hysterical. That you're making up lies, spreading them around about him. That you're trouble, you called him up and threatened to kill yourself if he didn't—"

"Oh, for fuck's sake. What a load of shit." Lucy told Ellen what had really happened. "I filed the first report, then he showed up to 'sort me out.' That's when he did this." She showed Ellen the lump on the back of her head. "I'm adding that to my formal complaint today."

Ellen was quiet a long time. "I'd heard stories about. . .others. All very vague, all explained away."

"Well, apparently, they're true. Do I seem hysterical to you? Have I ever acted irrationally?"

Ellen shook her head.

"Well, there you are. I'm going to stay clear of him for the meantime, until I know what my next step is."

"Let me know. . .if you need anything."

Lucy added the incident at the party to her report and returned home. She didn't feel well enough to read, but she began a mental checklist of the remaining tasks to finish her dissertation. She'd found one new advisor; she could find another, no matter what Dr. B hinted.

And if I can't, she thought, *I'll work in a supermarket for the next forty years. That will at least make a dent in the interest I owe.* For the first time, this didn't feel like the terrible end she'd occasionally used to motivate herself.

That night, Lucy dreamed of Dr. B again. She was aware of being a spectator this time, but she didn't have any of the dread in seeing him that she would when she was awake.

She felt his disgust as he chewed a meal and winced, realizing that one of his teeth had chipped. Saw him move his tongue around to spit it out, and then feel through the mouthful of food to make sure he'd gotten all of it.

Swallow again, and then feel a grating against his gum—another small piece, just a fragment of the first, he thought. Annoyed, he spat it out. He reached a finger in to check the gap, and knocked a larger tooth out. He gagged on the bony grit and spat out a mouthful into his hand, yellowed and nicotine-stained, glistening. He cast them away and began to run away but had to stop when another mouthful of splintered teeth threatened to choke off his breath. The more fragments he removed, the more his mouth refilled with new ones. An overpowering sense of despair gripped him as he found his mouth empty of teeth. He saw a future of slurping pap, his rugged looks reduced to sunken cheeks and sucking, unsupported lips. He'd almost taken that in, accepted it, when his mouth filled again with broken bone, and with an antiquarian's eye, saw that it was a fragment of mandible, his jaw disintegrating. As his skull collapsed, he could no longer spit out the other bones that were fleeing his body: toes no longer able to balance him, vertebrae incapable of supporting the rest of his frame, fingers uselessly trying to hold himself together.

When he collapsed, Lucy squatted on the ground and gazed into his eyes, not yet turned to jelly by the collapse of his skull.

"How do you feel?" she asked. It was curiosity she felt, not power or revulsion.

Powerless, came the unspoken reply. Defenseless. Vulnerable. . .please.

She stood, dusted her hands, and nodded.

"Not yet."

***

The next day, the department administrator emailed her to cancel her regular meeting with Dr. B. A foreign sense of contentment enveloped Lucy, grateful to have the extra hours reclaimed for her day, free from having to think about him. She felt good enough to work and to start listing potential candidates to direct the rest of her dissertation. She went to bed with a sense of optimism that was unfamiliar and certainly, for her situation, unusual.

The children were just. . .there. He recognized them, from long ago, though he couldn't have given them names. They were only kids, most of them, but some in their early teens. They began to make demands, becoming more physically aggressive by the moment. Some swarmed over him, some came in sneaky, single assaults, round, sticky faces with goblin teeth, pleading for things he could not give, screaming curses at him.

When he tried to shoo them off, they fell to the ground with operatic screams of abuse and unfairness more familiar in professional soccer players. Lucy watched from a distance as their parents materialized and chastised him for being so rough, before they vanished like mist, black marks going into books and fines levied. When he tried to summon up his thoughts and arguments, trying to reason with the children, they snuggled up to him, pretending to comply, but bit into his shoulders, fingers, face. Little fingers and mouths everywhere, poking, prying, pinching, and no way to keep them off him. Reason wouldn't work—he hadn't done anything to deserve this, he didn't know what grudge they might have, he didn't know them—but they came all the same, and more and more of them. He tried arguing, pleading, and logic; appeals to reason and to civility and law, but none of it worked: all of his learning and experience mattered nothing in the face of their onslaught. He screamed, then, out of rage and fear and helplessness, but one of the little goblins produced a taser and pressed it into his neck, burning a hole in his flesh and rendering him mute and immobile. He raged against his inability to extricate himself from their trap but couldn't move. Couldn't act, couldn't resist, couldn't scream for help.

Again, only his eyes remained. He looked to Lucy for help, for somehow, he knew she had the power to disperse his tormentors.

"How do you feel?" she asked.

Voiceless. Powerless. Violated. Ashamed. Exposed. Please, it's. . . Please. It won't stop.

"No," she said. "It will always be waiting to haunt you."

***

"What the hell have you been saying to Dr. B?"

Dr. Walden, a senior colleague in her department, called Lucy, insisting that she meet with him the next day.

She was surprisingly calm, given that this probably meant the end of her career in academia. "I haven't seen him, haven't spoken to him for days."

"He says you're torturing him. If you guys have had some kind of lovers' quarrel, you should just—"

She burst out laughing.

Walden looked startled and confused. "I'm just saying, if you have—"

"No. We're not lovers. We never have been, and frankly, I'd be happy if I never had to see him again. You know I tried to file a complaint against him? For. . .harassment?" Emboldened, she said it out loud. "For sexual harassment? And when he found out, he slammed my head against a wall."

Another look of shock; Lucy realized that he believed her. "I heard something about. . .a misunderstanding," he said slowly. "Why didn't you say something?"

She looked at him in disgust. "Given what you just told me, why would you have listened?"

He shrugged, nodded.

She spoke slowly, as if to a child. "No, I'm not torturing him. I didn't plan to work with B; I never wanted to be *near* him. He can take a flying fuck at a rolling donut. The only reason I'm still here is that I need my piece of paper. I have a mountain of student debt and I can't afford the reputation of being a troublemaker."

Walden opened his mouth to say something fast, and comfortable, and easy, but the look in her eye told him not to. "Okay. Let me. . . Let me think about this."

Another bark of a laugh; she was surprised at how comfortable she felt contradicting him, speaking up. "Sure. You *think* about it. But if anyone else asks about me torturing B, you tell them what I told you."

She left before he could demand any more of her. She'd officially reported Dr. B twice now; she was terrified. She owed so much money, and now. . .

At the same time, it was done. It was out in the world, and there was nothing she could do about it now. One way or the other, it was over. A negative certainty is still a certainty and, in some ways, still a comfort.

Lucy was everywhere. Omnipresent, omniscient. And she wasn't alone; a circle of women ringed Dr. B.

One struck a fragment of rusting barbed wire into his shoulder. It was dull, but it pierced skin and muscle readily, deeply. He reached back for it and pulled it out, with relief that it came, but also a spurt of blood and wrenching pain. The next woman whooped and clapped her hands: bramble prickers suddenly stabbed his arms. As he tried to pull each one out, it came, reluctantly and painfully, leaving long tears from where it pierced and where the brambles dug in like anchoring spikes. Another woman stuck feathers into his cheeks, and their barbs pulled against the muscles in his face. Every time he managed to remove one of the fragments from his body, it would come out only at great expense. Sometimes, it came out cleanly, sometimes, pieces broke off and he had to root around in his skin and muscle, trying to pull it out. If he was too slow, the fragments would fester and bleed. If he was too quick to remove them, the tears in his flesh couldn't heal. Fishhooks, pieces of broken bones, old wire brushes, more twigs and prickly roots. All of them left some part behind, and he grew desperate, trying to clean them from his body, and finding more and more polluted cuts. His hands were in shreds now, and his fingernails peeled off. He tried to protect them, but his hands twisted and crabbed. The infected wounds filled with worms, writhing and swelling, and he tried, with his useless hands, to squeeze them out. We all felt his excruciating pain, and humiliation, to be seen so broken and weak, and unable to do anything about it.

Defenseless. Helpless. His thoughts were scattered and panicked.

It was almost enough for Lucy, but the Sea appeared. "You are not the only one. And you are not done yet."

In the first dream, Lucy had only been aware of B's dream, and in the second, she could speak to him, judge him. Now Lucy could actively participate in B's punishment, simultaneously feeling his agony and enjoying the sensation of the knitting needle sliding through his ear, fucking with his brain. She could sense the satisfaction of the other women as they worked. Some split his bones and sucked the marrow. Some flensed the flesh from a long bone, delighting when there was always, always, a little bit left to remove again. Some simply danced. They had reclaimed themselves.

They told their stories to her: years of groping, harassment, rape by B. Threats of retaliation, should the women speak up. Stolen data, claimed as his own. The occasional broken bone that was always probably an accident.

Lucy tried to apologize to the women. "I'm sorry. I don't really belong here—he only touched me a couple of times, hit me once—you had it so much worse. I don't mean to intrude."

"Enough," the oldest of them said. "We don't keep score, who was more or less hurt by him. He would have robbed you of your career, your means of support, your dignity. He would have continued, had you not stopped him, with you, and others, after you. You allowed us to come back for him. So, no more of that. We all deserve this moment."

They began to strip away the parts that he'd taken from them. Flesh, brains, hardened hearts and deadened souls sprang back to life in their rightful owners. They grew stronger and stronger, brighter and more alive as he cried out, diminishing: gory wounds blossomed, then desiccated; the light went out of his eyes, his mind, his heart, leaving a void in a human husk; his body shrank, withered, and collapsed. Finally, there was nothing left but ashes and the fillings from his teeth. One of the women hiked up her skirt and squatted over him, a stream of urine further dispersing the ash. The others applauded.

Lucy felt herself at peace for the first time in months.

The scene vanished, and Lucy found herself on the cliff. The Sea appeared.

"Thank you."

"You have been successful. A great many others will also have peace now. One day, you will take my place and guide others to revenge and repair." The Sea nodded—*or was it a trick of the waves?*

***

Lucy woke in her own bed.

Dr. Walden called her. "You heard the news? About Dr. B?"

"No." She wasn't sure she wanted to.

"They fished him out of the ocean today. Dead."

"What?"

"He's been acting so strangely lately. The cops are calling it a suicide." He took a deep breath. "When you told me. . .what you told me, about him—I looked into it. You weren't the only one he's done this to. Not by a long shot. Yesterday, I brought the news to the dean, and B was told that he'd be on unpaid leave while the complaints were investigated. You might imagine Dr. B didn't take that easily. They had to call security to drag him out."

Walden paused. "The body. . . Well, the rocks and the fish. . . They had to identify him by his dental records."

Lucy recalled the ash and metal fillings of her dream.

"I thought you should know," he said.

She had too many thoughts: another search for another advisor, the delay in finding a job, the mounting interest on her loans. Her pleasure at knowing just how painful he'd found the beginning of his end. His end itself. She shook her head.

It was as if Walden read her mind. "I'm prepared to sign off on your thesis. I've read it and spoken with your other advisors."

She smothered a snarl; he was buying her off.

Again, as if he could hear her thoughts, Walden said, "It's what you deserve. He kept you hanging for far too long. And since now I'll be the director. . .there's a line opening up to replace me for this year. I'll need a temporary replacement until a permanent is found. You're my choice; I hope you'll apply for the permanent one as well, but even if you don't want the permanent place, or if for some reason you don't get it, this will be a nice bullet on your professional CV."

Lucy forced herself to answer calmly. "Thank you, Dr. Walden. I shall give it my serious consideration."

***

Three months later, Lucy sat in her office. On the other side of her desk was a young woman who'd come to her for advice.

"He's never done it before. Promised it would never happen again." The student's face was stained with tears and she had a fresh bandage on her cheek. "I don't know what I could have done to make him—"

"Don't," Lucy said. "You did nothing. This is on him. Believe me. It's not you."

"I can't go back to him, can I?" the young woman said. "I'm staying with friends now, but—"

"No *but*s. You stay with them. You call the numbers I gave you if he so much as looks at you funny. And take this."

She reached into a drawer and pulled out a small seashell on a gold chain. A twin to the one she wore around her own neck.

"I can't. . . Why?"

Lucy shrugged. "I have a lot of them, given to me by a friend, when I needed it most. Take it and remember: You aren't alone. We hear you. We will always be here for you."

The student's face cleared, and something in her seemed to change as she clasped the chain around her neck. She said her thanks as Lucy regarded her with kindly, alien eyes.

Note from the Author

How would you give the Devil his due? The times I've imagined it, mere physical punishment never seemed like enough of a response to violence against women; it's too easy, over too soon. If I had a wish, it would be for the perpetrator to experience what it feels like to be so targeted—and then to live with the physical pain, the self-doubt and self-recrimination, the nightmares, and the lifelong need to constantly be on guard, even in the most innocuous of situations. It's a hell of a thing to understand that half the world's population experiences this violence.

— Dana Cameron

Just Us League

Angela Yuriko Smith

Contrary to the name, the Gladd Shop wasn't.

It had been a happy place at one time. Mr. Gladd did his best to live up to his name, but eventually, age caught up to the sweet old man and his son stepped in to run things. Unfortunately, Matt Gladd was everything his father wasn't.

Matt hired pretty young cashiers and then fired them when they wouldn't date him. He consumed whatever he wanted from the shelves, literally eating away profits. The back office was littered in wrappers, empty cans and overflowing ashtrays. The smell traveled through the entire store.

Where once people came from the surrounding neighborhoods to shop Gladd, now they went out of their way to avoid it. Matt didn't care. He had grown up with the shop as his playground, and that hadn't changed.

His best friend was Will Bangor, an equally loathsome character and his second-in-command. The third part of the management trio was Jack, a young kid saving up to go to business school. If it weren't for Jack, the Gladd Shop would have been ruined years before. He kept things going, if not well, then the best he could.

The break room in the back housed a fifies-era dining room table that wobbled and a small set of salvaged lockers. The walls were dingy beige cinderblock flecked with decades of grime. Rumor had it the old table had witnessed a number of disgusting things, the most recent of which involved a fourteen-year-old bagger with shiny hair that smelled like cinnamon. . . and Matt and Will.

Her English wasn't great and her parents spoke it even worse, so the whole thing just seemed to evaporate. It had been Gertie, Gladd Shop's matron of maintenance, that had held the crying girl. Gertie believed her, but that was no help. People listen to old female janitors even less than they listen to pretty Hispanic girls with broken English.

Like using nasty mop water, Gertie often thought when she cleaned the breakroom. *It can dry up and look okay but the filth is still there, leaving a stink.* It was under the chipped old table that Gertie first discovered the curious business card. Lying face up on an oily stain, it read:

Feeling oppressed? Let us help. The Just Us League specializes in discreetly disposing of tyrannical leadership and bullies. We guarantee our work. As a not-for-profit agency, we do not require deposits nor will you ever receive a bill. To utilize our services, simply write the name of the offender in the space provided. We promise it will remain between Just Us.

Gertie picked it up, read it three times and flipped it over. On the back, there was a line to write on, and underneath in small block type was *NAME YOUR TYRANT*, with an empty line waiting for a name.

Obviously, this was a joke, but she couldn't help but daydream for a minute. As a socially awkward, middle-aged woman, her life was a long line of tyrants, starting from her heavy-handed father to now. The years unwound as she watched her life collapse like a spent party balloon. If only it was as easy as the card said. It was like the working-class equivalent of a magic lamp.

The swinging doors slamming open around the corner startled her. She shoved the card in her pocket as Matt came in with a six-pack. She was pinned against the lockers by his gaze.

"Is this what I pay you for? To stand down here looking dumb?"

Gertie couldn't answer. She just shook her head.

"You're lucky I keep you on. Anyone else would fire your fat ass."

Gertie bit her lip and nodded again. She knew from experience the best thing to do with words was bite them back until they tasted like blood. Her heart was trying to break its way free from her ribcage, but whether it wanted to attack or flee, she never knew.

Matt stared at her and then raised his eyebrows. "Well, move it, dumbass! Someone pissed all over the toilet. I've been looking for you for over an hour."

Gertie jumped. "Oh. . . sorry. I was checking the break room. . ." Her voice scrambled to hide as she passed by him toward the exit. Her shoulder brushed the opposite wall as she gave him a wide berth. He swiveled to watch her pass.

"Oh, Gertie. . ."

She stopped to listen, barely turning. Her body was one big flinch waiting to spring away.

"I think it might be my piss all over the toilet." He laughed and opened the fridge.

Gertie let the flinch loose and it carried her away through the swinging doors.

At the bathroom, she pulled her cart up, went in and locked the door. It was a mess, all right, and she didn't doubt that Matt had done this. He frequently left puddles of urine for her to clean up. He thought it was funny. She wanted to punch him in his vacant, spoiled face. If only that card wasn't a joke.

She pulled it out of her pocket and read it again. *If only. . .*

There was a pen or two on her cart. She reached out, found it hiding under the pile of rags and closed the door again. She locked it. She placed the card on the sink edge and wrote on the back of the card. *Manager Matt Gladd.*

If only. . . she thought. If there really was such a thing as a Just Us League. He would deserve anything they could do to him. *Him and all the rest like him.* She imagined a group of superheroines dressed like ninjas in black with gold tiaras. But it was just a stupid joke, like her stupid life. She stuffed the card and pen in her pocket and started mopping up pee. She forgot about the card as survival returned center stage.

She was halfway through her first cup of coffee the next morning when she remembered the card. She pulled her jeans out of the laundry bin and searched the pockets. There it was, crumpled in the denim. She smoothed it out on her kitchen table, took a sip of coffee and then set the cup down so fast, it spilled. She picked the card up with both hands and flipped it over and back several times. The name she wrote was gone. The empty line where it read *NAME YOUR TYRANT* was blank, the paper clean and smudge free.

"There must have been two cards. . ."

Gertie was digging through her dirty jeans again when her phone rang. It was Will, Matt's assistant and cohort. He was babbling, stumbling over his own words. Gertie had never heard him so upset.

"Look, I don't have time to explain it. Just don't come in today. Someone will call you if the police need you."

Gertie felt panic start up in her belly like a motor, stirring the blood around her heart until it wanted to explode.

"The police. . . Why would they talk to me. . ." The card lay on the table next to her forgotten cup.

"It's none of your business. . ." His voice trembled. "Your job is to shut up and clean up, not ask questions. I've got a hell of a mess on my hands right now, and I'll let you know when I need your mop. Now Matt's. . . gone. And the fucking idiots didn't even take anything." He choked up. "I don't have time to explain it. Just listen for once and don't come in, got it?" The line disconnected.

Gertie sat down with a long, trembling exhale to take it all in. *Just Us League? Impossible. And yet. . .* Normally, Gertie would have been relieved to have a day off, but there was no way she was going to be able to stay locked up in her apartment with so many unanswered questions. She was told not to come to work, but that didn't mean she couldn't go and just walk past. Carefully, she picked up the business card and slid it in her wallet.

The Gladd Shop looked normal except for the police cars filling the small parking lot and the officer posted just inside the door. She could see him leaning against the doorframe. Something had definitely happened, and it had happened to Matt. And it may have happened because of her. She had to see.

With a rare boldness, she walked across the street and pulled the door open. The officer whipped around and stepped in front of the door so she couldn't open it wider. He blocked her view, but in the glimpse she got, everything looked normal.

"Um, I work here," she said.

"Oh, not today. There's been an incident. Your manager should have called to tell you to stay home."

"He did call. . ." Gertie's brain whirred. "It was hard to understand him, but I'm pretty sure he asked me to come in for. . . a cleanup? He was pretty confused. I'm the janitor."

The officer looked her up and down. This short, thick woman with iron-grey curls could have been his mom. "It's pretty bad back there. You won't be back there, cleaning that mess. There's special crews for that. Forensics isn't done, anyway."

Genuine frustration blossomed in the back of her eyes, causing tears to well up. "Please, I can't afford to lose this job. Can I just check in with him?"

The officer sighed. "Sure, okay. But save yourself some grief and don't go to the office. I think he's giving a statement in the break room."

Gertie nodded and dabbed at her eyes. "Thank you. . . I just need to let him know I showed up."

He nodded and stepped back, opening the door for her. "Just go straight to the break room, okay? They probably want your statement anyways."

Gertie slipped through and headed toward the break room until she was out of sight in the shelves, and then doubled back to look in the office. She wouldn't believe any of this was real until she saw it herself. She came out of the shelves and went down the hallway toward the office and storerooms and became a believer.

The office door was open. There was a man inside, bent over, picking something off the floor with tweezers. He wore plastic booties over his shoes and blue latex gloves. Whatever he picked up, he dropped into a baggie and sealed it. It looked like some hair stuck to something. Gertie felt nauseous.

Around him was chaos. The shelf was overturned, littering the floor with owner's manuals and paperwork. The desk chair was upside down on the desk, one of the wheeled legs jammed through the old-school computer monitor. Glass from the large candy jar was everywhere and peppermint candy was ground into the floor. A sticky spray of what looked like blood spattered the wall, desk and floor. Gertie thought she could see teeth in the crushed candy.

A shiver of fear shot through her. Matt was a jerk but had this gone too far? The man in the booties stood up and saw her watching. "You can't be here, ma'am." He started toward her and she backed up.

"I didn't believe it. . ." Gertie started crying.

The guy came out, passed her and shouted at the end of the hall. "Hey, can I get an escort? I've got a wrong turn over here."

Gertie covered her face with her hands. She felt like laughing but not because it was funny. The laughter inside her came from the absurd notion that stupid old Gertie wrote a name on a card and then this happened to the owner of the name. It was impossible, coincidental and real. Crazy people in movies always laughed. Gertie felt pretty crazy.

She collapsed against the wall and slid to a sitting position on the floor giggling and sobbing simultaneously. A few officers came out of nowhere to help her up and escort her outside to a police car. She struggled a moment when she thought they were trying to put her in the back seat like a criminal, but then an officer was holding her face, calming her down.

"I'm sorry you saw that," he said. His words bounced against her without sinking in. She nodded anyway. "We're going to take you home so you can calm down, okay? It'll be all right." She nodded again and he led her to the passenger seat, where she watched out the window, seeing nothing.

Her thoughts were still turned inward, whirling as they led her down her hallway like a child and coaxed her into finding her keys. Gently, a woman officer led her inside, sat her down and made her a cup of tea. Gertie had stopped cry-laughing, and her mind slowed to rest on the Just Us League. Was it true? Did it work? Was this her fault?

Beneath that was a smaller, quiet feeling she couldn't admit to. It was gladness. It whispered that Matt had gotten what he deserved. It told her justice had been served.

When the officer left, she carefully opened her wallet and took the card out. She felt cool and calm inside. There was something else she couldn't define. It made her grind her teeth slightly. Her breath was shallow and fast, and though she sat still, her heart was racing. She felt. . . powerful.

She pulled a pen out her purse and took a deep breath. She had to know if this was real or a coincidence. *Imagine if it was real. . .* No one would ever treat her like shit again. She pressed her lips together, laid the card on the table and carefully wrote *Manager Will Bangor* on the empty space. Then she stared at it for quite some time and then went to bed.

She hadn't expected to sleep, but then her alarm was suddenly screaming at her, sending her nerves racing like lightning bolts through her flesh. Trembling, she went through the motions to shower, make coffee and get dressed. Finally, she looked at the card where she had left it the night before. Once again, the line above *TYRANT* was blank and clean. Her heart yammered in her ears. She had to know. She found the number she was looking for on the paper taped next to the phone, picked up the receiver and dialed.

Ringing. . . ringing. . . ringing. . . and then *"Hey, this is Will Bangor's phone. Did you miss me? I guess you did. If you leave your number, I'll call you back. If you are one of my girl fans, I'll call you right back. . . . beep.."* Gertie didn't leave a message.

Instead, she shrugged her jacket on, made sure her keys and bus pass were in her purse and carefully picked up the Just Us card. She slipped it in her bra. It didn't feel right to toss it in her wallet like a receipt. She wanted it touching her, sending its magic and power into her skin. Then, carefully locking the door behind her, she went to work.

She arrived to find more police cars jammed in the parking lot, a fire truck, and an ambulance blocking part of the street in front of the shop. The Gladd Shop certainly didn't look normal now. Uniforms were rushing back and forth through the glass door. Radios blared instructions. She joined a small group of gawkers across the street. The words *I'm sorry* were scrawled on the window in blue chalk marker, sold in aisle five.

"What happened?" she asked.

"I think some guy committed suicide," a man said. "You could see him hanging in the shop window there. They just took him down a few minutes ago."

Inside, Gertie was all cool ice. Outside, the card burned against her skin like a firebrand. It was true: the Just Us League was real and she was responsible for the deaths of two men. She didn't feel sorry. She felt uneasy. They both sucked. Most the men she had ever known sucked. . . but did they deserve this? It didn't matter now; it was done.

Across the street a figure she recognized came out of the door. Jack, the assistant to the assistant manager, was leaning against an officer and wiping his damp face. She'd never known him to be cruel. Often, he'd come behind Matt and Will as damage control. More than once, he'd "forgotten" to ring up Gertie's groceries after she'd clocked out. The card in her bra felt like a threat and she had the urge to hide it away back in her wallet. Jack's eyes fell on her across the street.

"Gertie!" He waved at her and started toward her.

Outed, she could do nothing else but come toward him. They met in the middle of the street, police cars throwing out red and blue lights in a frenetic race on the pavement around them.

He bit his lip. "I am so sorry. I don't know what to tell you. I'm not saying it was right, what happened to Matt and Will, but you reap what you sow. And they did a lot of sowing." Behind him, an officer was taping sheets of brown butcher paper across the outside of the window. Another officer was stringing yellow tape across the storefront. Other officers were ducking to go under it. "It is what it is. . ." He swallowed hard, his Adam's apple bobbing like a cork on the ocean. He cleared his throat.

"Look, I know your landlord isn't going to stop charging rent because this disaster happened, but no one is going to be working here anytime soon, if ever again. I've been doing payroll for the last year, so I reckon I'll keep doing it for a while longer until all this is figured out. I'll be mailing out paychecks the same as always until this is settled. Old man Gladd isn't going to know or care, and I don't even know if there's anyone to keep the shop going now. Anyways. . ." His face crinkled up. ". . . just don't worry about paychecks for a while, Gertie. Use this time to find something better. You deserve it."

Gertie nodded. The card burned against her skin. He hugged her. Gertie hugged back. Then he let her go. "I gotta go take care of this mess. You have my number. Call if you need anything." His face was like milk, shining in the mad lights. He gave her a brief smile, a warm flash of sun, and turned away. Gertie walked away too, thinking.

For the first time in her life, she felt free. She wasn't worried about making rent for at least a week or two. She'd be able to keep food in the fridge while she found something new. She didn't have to dread waking up each morning, knowing she had to face humiliation. This was a fresh start. She could use this time to find something better. She could make better choices.

She decided to walk home instead of taking the bus. She needed time to think and plan. For once, she wasn't in a hurry. Three blocks down, she saw a thin woman twice Gertie's age sitting on a sidewalk, back to a low wall. As Gertie got closer, she saw the sign asking for money. The woman's head hung down, her hair covered part of her face in grimy cords. Above the wall Gertie could see a man lying out under a tree on the grass, resting his head on a backpack, one eye half-open, watching the woman.

Gertie stopped, rummaged in her purse and pulled out her wallet. She had a $10 in there. She pulled the Just Us card from her bra and held it. It still felt dangerous to her. It was dangerous, but not to her. And it was no longer for her. She wrapped the $10 around it and approached the woman, dropping the folded bill into the waiting cup. Above them, she felt the man watching.

"We gotta stick together," Gertie said. "Sometimes, it's up to us to change things for the better. Just Us."

The older woman nodded. "Thank you. God bless," she said. Her voice lacked life.

Gertie walked past to the end of the street and looked back before she turned the corner. The old woman was holding a white card, reading it. She looked around until she saw Gertie, who only smiled. *You can do this,* she thought. The old woman slipped the card into her shirt, where it vanished, and looked away.

Gertie rounded the corner and moved on.

Note from the Author

Writing "Just Us League" was a cathartic experience. I had a real Manager Matt and I was the female custodian. Like Gertie, I had a history with abusive relationships and felt I had to put up with it. I found my way free with an unofficial Just Us League consisting of lawyers, advocates and social workers. They were not the tiara-wearing, ninja-clad group of superheroines Gertie envisioned, but they didn't need to be. To end violence against women, we just need to be there for each other. Just us. . . and we can be our own league.

– Angela Yuriko Smith

American Murder

Peter Tieryas

I.

My grandmother told me that our neighbor used to be a Chinese gangster and lost his left eye in a bar fight. I knew him as an arthritic old man who pissed on his flowers every morning and took his poodle for a walk just before the sun went down. He used to be a soldier and fought for the US in the Vietnam War. But when he came back to the States, he found he had nothing left except poverty and radiation poisoning. He joined local gangs to make a living for himself and took part in death matches for money, pushing the martial arts to the extreme. The victor got booze and some money to hold him over till the next fight. The loser got dumped in a lagoon, where worms made a feast of his corpse. Allegedly, my neighbor killed more than twenty-two people during his run, and Grandma said the games ran until the police shut them down. Decades later, we'd evolved. Not into the gladiatorial contests of old or hokey neon-lit death matches with futuristic undertones. Instead, *American Murder*, the most popular show in America.

"What's that supposed to be?" Bridget asked the man across from her, who I was recording as part of the camera crew.

I'd gotten this gig because I used to work in the coroner's office, taking photographs of corpses. When the show offered quadruple my pay, I jumped at the opportunity. Now known as the "four horsemen," we had become celebrities in our own right. Audience members and fans alike wanted to know the secret eyes behind the most popular show in America. I was Saul Blainesford, the "Asian" guy with the non-Asian last name.

"Do you watch much online streaming?" Tom Dirkson asked Bridget.

Tom was the male host for the show—dashing with perfectly combed hair and a smile reeking of ambition and insouciant insecurity. You would never guess he'd been in jail twice for embezzling and identity theft.

"I don't have a TV or an internet connection, and I work three jobs, so I wouldn't have time to watch it even if I did," Bridget replied. "What's this all about? The lady who called me said there was a lot of money involved."

Bridget's hair was a tangled mess and her skin had bruised welts that had been scratched into rouge marshes. Her studio was a warzone of cigarette stubs, magazines, broken CD cases, unpaid bills stacked as high as a ziggurat. The space was tiny; a mattress on the ground, a small closet for a bathroom, shoeboxes storing her goods.

Our coordinators did a thorough job with their research to help select candidates. "You've been hospitalized eight times in the past two years," Tom stated. "Why is that?"

Bridget peered quickly in our direction, our four cameras pointing her way. I was one of the cameramen zooming in on her expression. On the side of my camera was the crimson logo, *American Murder*.

"What's that got to do with anything?"

"According to the police report, your husband, Jake Park, has been arrested five times for assault and released each time because you refused to press charges."

"We-we're getting a divorce."

Tom was handed a laptop by one of the production assistants. She was accompanied by three other PAs, one of the field producers, two attorneys, and three grips holding portable lights so we could get the best footage. Six aerial drones surrounded us to get all the angles; there used to be more, but external hack attempts had us change our policy to minimize the numbers.

Tom flipped the computer open and brought up the images of her husband, Jake. In the photos, he was having intimate contact with three different women.

"Why are you showing me this?" Bridget asked, distraught by the images.

"Were you aware your husband's been unfaithful to you?"

"Yes," she said, turning away, her eyes moist. "There's nothing I can do. Anytime-anytime I mention a divorce, he gets really upset. I moved out and am staying by myself. Ever since Jake lost his job, he's just been this way. I mean, he-he used to be so sweet. He'd send flowers to the office every day and-and we used to go to all these expensive restaurants and. . . And then. . . And then he lost his job and living expenses were too much and he got rough." She shook her head, remembering. "How can someone change so much? Two years, every night, he'd just. . ." She rubbed her forehead with her palm. Tom put his arm around her, rubbing her shoulder, doing his best to comfort her. "God, I hate him. . . I hate him. . . I wish he were dead. I wish he'd just disappear," she said, and bit her fist in frustration.

"What if you could make that happen?" Tom asked her.

"What do you mean?"

"What if you could defend yourself and stop him from ever hurting you again?"

"How?" Bridget wanted to know.

"By killing him."

"But I-I'd go to jail."

"Normally, you would, but what if I told you there was a way you could get away with it?"

She laughed uncomfortably. "Is this a joke?"

"This is *American Murder*, Bridget," Tom said with a bright smile and a tilt of his head to make sure we got his "handsome" side (he'd yell at us later if we didn't). "And we have government sponsorship for our program set up just so we can help people like you."

"Like me?"

"People in unfortunate circumstances that are in dire need."

"I don't understand."

"Of course. You know how in the recent past, prostitution and robbery were legalized and turned into entertainment?"

"I think I've heard about that."

"Murder is now the property of the government, trademarked, copywritten, and taxable," Tom replied. "*American Murder* is a reality show about heroes. Heroes like you who've been victimized. It's about ordinary people standing up for justice and doing what's right." He sounded like a car salesmen, except in this case, a car salesmen that cared. "If you agree to murder your husband live on our show, you'll be absolved of *all* responsibility. We have our team of lawyers here and our local representative from the police department. You can ask them any questions you want."

"Is there. . ." A shy glance followed, first at Tom, then to the cameras. "Is there payment?"

"The final payment is determined by voters watching the show, but the minimum pay is a million dollars," Tom said without blinking.

She startled, but the glint in her eyes was unmistakable.

The show was on.

II.

Because of the volatility of the human mind and its pretensions on morality and guilt, we filmed at a rapid pace. Once a person made a decision to take part in the show, they were expected to murder their target that very day.

We pulled into a nicely sized house in the suburbs that looked almost like every one next to it. Bridget had chosen a kitchen knife as her weapon of choice.

"I can't pick a gun?" she asked.

"Sorry, Bridget, guns aren't allowed," Tom said.

"Why not?"

"Production decided early on not to allow them."

The unspoken reason was that they made murder too easy, translating into lower ratings. People wanted to see their blood and guts.

The editors had already put together a biopic on her life, her sweet childhood rife with dreams and aspirations, to make her seem more human, more vulnerable.

"I used to teach Sunday school because I grew up Baptist and I'm from a really religious family. I really wanted to be a teacher because I love kids, but Jake didn't like me going to school. He wanted me to get to work right away to help pay bills, so I worked as a hostess at the Naipul. Have you heard of it? It used to be real fancy and they paid well," she explained as part of her testimonial. "Then when the last viral outbreak happened and all the restaurants closed, the Naipul shut down. There weren't any more stimulus checks this time, and we were stuck home all the time. That's when things changed. . ."

As we approached the steps to their house, we came to a halt. I moved to get a better angle to make the residence look more ominous. Special adaptors on all our cameras let viewers watch from VR goggles, and the drones helped enhance the immersive feeling. Bridget herself had a body camera on her and microphones attached so viewers could hear every utterance. We had tried cameras via contact lenses in the past, but eyeblinks, and tears, were too disorienting for viewers, and we ended up canning those.

"Is this it?" Tom asked.

Bridget nodded.

We walked up to the front door. She took out her keys and unlocked the door. We went through. The four of us in the camera crew spread out, following behind her. I wondered what kind of music the editor was superimposing on top of the footage.

The living room was dark but the bedroom light was on. Bridget hesitated.

"Are you okay?" Tom asked.

She shook her head. "I-I don't know what I'm doing. . . This. . . this is crazy. . . This isn't me."

"You can back out any time you want to," Tom assured her. "Just say the word and we cut."

She took a deep breath. "I'm sorry. I-I don't think I can do this."

"It's all right. Take a deep breath, we can just—"

"What's going on out there?" a male voice demanded.

Bridget nodded. "Jake."

Jake was unshaven and smelled of cigarettes. Somewhere underneath the swath of stubble was someone who had once been suave.

"Bridget. Wh-what are you doing? And why do you have a camera crew with you?" Then he noticed the logo on the side of the camera. "You really wanna. . ." He stared at us, befuddled and scared at the same time. "I-Is this about Terry?"

"Who's Terry?" Tom asked.

"My best friend," Jake replied. "She told me she wanted to leave me for him and has been making up stuff about what I've done to her."

"Don't lie!" Bridget shouted. "You've been hitting me since our honeymoon."

"Is this some joke? Is that"—then staring at us—"Is that what she told you? That it was *me?*"

"It is," Tom answered.

"I would never lay a finger on you."

"He's lying. Stop lying to them, Jake! They already know about you."

For a second, Tom looked at us and we looked back, confused.

Then Jake glowered at Bridget. "You-you're making shit up again. Did you-did you think you could"—then seeing her weapon—"Christ, are you serious? You-you really wanted to. . . Give me that."

"We're leaving, Jake," Bridget said.

"You're not going anywhere. Give me that knife right now."

"Why?"

"So I can show you how it's done."

"What?"

"Why'd you go to her?" he asked Tom. "Why didn't you ask me to sign up for *American Murder*? *She's* the one who deserves to be murdered. You know what she's done to me?"

"Shut up, Jake."

"Every day, nagging, Jake, go do this, Jake go do that, Jake, what do you think about my hair, Jake, what do you think about my dress, Jake, what should I do with my future, Jake, can I borrow some money? I'm broke, broke, I don't have a goddamn job, and she's worried about her manicure. And you know why she's worried about her manicure?"

"Shut up, Jake."

"'Cause of Terry. Oh, Terry, you're so dreamy with your cute blond hair and your tight muscles, the—"

"I never slept with him. We were just friends! He was protecting me from you!"

"That's why I find used condoms in the trash almost every other day while I'm looking for work?"

"I don't know who that was from."

"They just magically appeared in our garbage, right?"

"He's lying. Don't believe him! He always does this to make it sound like it's my fault. It's all an act, he's so cruel, he-he—"

"I'm cruel?" he cut in. Then turned to us. "You know how sick she is in the head? She wants me to beat her up because it gets her off since little Bridget used to get beaten up by her dad, so it reminds her of when she was a little kid. Daddy, oh, daddy."

"Stop it, Jake! Stop twisting everything around!"

"You love it. You told me you loved it." He guffawed ruthlessly and it was chilling, even if it seemed a touch melodramatic. Was he playing for the cameras? I signaled one of the drones to cast a stronger light from the side of his face to accentuate the shadows and make him appear more villainous.

Bridget's eyes became cold.

"She steals, she lies, she—"

Bridget suddenly rushed him and stabbed him in the stomach. Jake was too surprised to react.

"I told you to shut up," Bridget said.

The knife turned into a barrage of crimson and veins, flesh simmering in the flash of a blade. I zoomed the camera in at the point of contact. There was blood everywhere, Jake laughing the whole time as he lunged wildly at her, smashing a few punches into her face. She didn't flinch, didn't hesitate, instead stabbing and stabbing all the while screaming, "Shut up, shut up, shut UP!"

But Jake wouldn't shut up. Not until he died.

And even when he finally became quiet, Bridget kept on slashing and cutting.

"Why won't you shut up?" she demanded. "WHY?"

Jake was silent, limbs splayed out awkwardly in a collage of sundered humanity. It wasn't him she was hearing. Instead, the screaming voice accusing her from within.

She wasn't the only one.

Five years ago, I got into a huge car accident. My mom was in the backseat. The other vehicle had smashed her legs in half, only her upper torso intact. She was bleeding to death and a fire had broken out in the rear. I was pinned to my seat, unable to move. Mom was saying something and I was trying to reach out to her. Outside, I remembered people watching, not doing a thing to help. They pointed and gasped. Then they flipped out their camera phones and snapped pictures.

"Mom, hold on. Hold on," I begged.

She shook her head and reached out her hand. I couldn't reach back. The fire burned closer and closer. As the metal got hotter, she began screaming.

I realized it was the last time I'd see her alive. I didn't know what else I could do, so I took out my phone and recorded my last moments with her. It was the only way I could think of to save the memory of her.

Later, after I was healthy enough to return to my "normal life," I quit my minimum-wage office job, then got work with the coroners, losing myself in the imagery of corpses. It was my hope at normalizing, or maybe shielding myself from, death by oversaturating my life with it. And the rest, as they say, was reality TV's version of an edited history, embellished and sliced into commercial-friendly pieces for histrionic purposes and higher ratings.

III.

"That-that wasn't me," Bridget said defensively at the office.

She'd been cleaned up, hair done, makeup over her like a *Top Model* redo, the only trace of the murder being a black eye.

"What do you mean?"

"I don't murder people. You guys-you guys tricked me into this. . . I-I don't even kill spiders; I skip around silverfish. I've never hurt anyone in my entire life. Never! This horrible thing. . . You guys preyed on me and exploited my situation. You knew I was behind on bills and my rent. . . You took advantage of me. . . You tricked me into this. I'm not a murderer! I'm not!"

"Of course not, and people understand that. No one judges you for what you've done," Tom said in his gentle voice as the cameras were still rolling. That's why he was there: to present an image to calm and soothe. "You did what you had to. You defended yourself. The polls are already open and people love you. They want you to come back next week."

"This is bullshit. I'm so gonna sue all of you! You guys are going down," she said, standing up. "You can't play this kind of game with people. You can't! It's unholy; it's morally wrong."

"I know you're troubled by everything, but I want you to sit down for a second," Tom interrupted her.

"What?"

"Sit down and take this." He had a phone in his hand.

"What is it?"

"It's your bank," Tom replied.

"What's this gotta do with anything?" Bridget asked.

Behind us, I could see our producer signaling that we were eight minutes behind schedule.

"Bridget, please, just take the phone," Tom snapped in a rare spark of irritation.

Bridget glared at him and snatched the phone.

The operator was speaking in a pleasant voice. "I'm pleased to inform you that your current balance is five million dollars."

There was a subtle shift in Bridget's face. The anger melted and turned into confusion. Hints of excitement and relief crept in as her expression brightened. She hung up the phone, shifted her hair left. Her brows squinted; she sucked her cheeks in and looked up at the camera.

She was beaming.

As We Stand and Pray

Jason Sanford

They say you can't go home again.

That's a lie. You can always return to the places you once lived. But they may no longer be your true home. And sometimes you'll be killed for going back.

Still, there I was, pulling into a rundown truck stop in the West Virginia mountains. The truck stop hadn't changed in the last five years, and I didn't mean that in a nostalgic, folksy "great to be home" kinda way. It was a little before midnight on Saturday and an eerie fog of diesel exhaust hovered over the ground, illuminated by the scattered lights the truck stop kept in working order. Dozens of trucks were parked up and down the massive gravel parking lot behind the diesel pumps, store and restaurant.

I parked my car alongside an expensive red SUV and stepped outside. The kids in the SUV were eager to burst free from what looked like a long drive. But their mother froze as she opened her door and looked around.

Maybe it was the vampires and succubi walking around the parked semis that scared her. Or the horned deer god arguing with an irritated and frightened truck driver over the fee for dropping him off. Or the skunk ape swatting away a will-o'-the-wisp that kept floating around her head.

"Keep driving," I told her. "There's a safer place ten miles down the interstate."

The mother started to ask what a young woman like myself was doing here if it wasn't safe. But then the crow on my shoulder cawed loudly. The mother stared at my black clothes, at the crow, at my eyes that sparkled like the entire damn Milky Way. She dropped her keys and picked them with shaking hands, telling her kids to get back in the car.

The SUV drove off as the kids whined. One little girl pointed at me and asked excitedly, "Is she a witch?"

I didn't hear her mother's answer, but I wished I was a witch. A witch wouldn't be as afraid as I was right now.

Still, it was good to be around my people again. As monsters climbed off the trucks they'd hitched rides from, they started walking up the dirt road to the village. I fell in beside a vampire in shimmering couture clothing and expensive high-heel leather boots, who hissed as she mistook me for human prey.

I pointed at my eyes.

"Stars in the eyes don't make you a monster, hon," she said with a flip of her hair. Vampires were always divas, but at least she didn't attack.

"There's more to me than just the eyes," I said.

"Yes, the crow on the shoulder. What's his name?"

"Infinity Eyes."

"Ah," the vampire said with a smirk. "I'm sure that name sounds vastly better if you speak crow."

It actually did, but I refused to take the vampire's bait by saying that.

As I walked up the hill to the village, the scene before me was so beautiful, I almost stumbled. A full moon hung behind the white steeple of the village's wooden church. The smells of baked bread and hot stew and fresh beer and campfires floated down to me from the houses and tents.

Then the recorded bells in the church steeple began to chime. As a kid, I'd thought they were real bells and that tiny elves rang them to announce each hour. I still half-believed it.

I'd always loved this place. And I'd been forced to flee because of what Brother Walker did.

Tears slid down my face.

"Here, hon," the vampire said, holding out a silk hankie. "As a side note, monsters shouldn't be caught crying in public."

"Thanks." I wiped my eyes as we approached the checkpoint.

We maintained the checkpoint to keep humans from wandering into the village. The truck stop was the main way we kept humans away — the monsters who ran it always freaked people out so they never stayed long. And a witch had long ago cast a spell so any human who left the truck stop would soon forget they'd seen any of us there.

But the stone wall surrounding our village was the main protection. Thanks to a number of spells over the years, no monster or human could scale it. The only way in or out of the village was by the main gate.

I'd worked the gate countless times myself, but a vampire I didn't recognize now stood guard there. I'd expected someone who knew me to be there and had worried that they'd kill me before I could explain why I'd come home.

Was it good or bad the guard wouldn't know me?

"Okay, you're fine," he told the couture vampire as he waved her through. "But you, human girl, hold up."

His fangs grew a little longer and he hitched up his skintight black jeans, which were covered in metal studs and leather belts and buckles. He wore a T-shirt with the words *People Are Strange* on it, except he'd marked out the word people and written in "I."

I Are Strange. Infinity Eyes yanked my hair to stop me from correcting the grammar on the vampire's shirt. He always knew when my mouth was about to get me in trouble.

"She claims to be a monster," the couture vampire said.

"I am. Grew up here. Name's Sefi."

The punk-rock vampire didn't seem impressed. And the couture vampire was still hanging around, perhaps wondering if she'd get a meal out of me in the end.

I sighed. I'd had to prove myself all my life. I wasn't an obviously dangerous monster like the werewolves and vampires and goblins, but come on. My parents had dumped me at that damn truck stop when I was only five. In my charitable moments, I wanted to believe they knew this was a place where monsters lived, but I'm pretty sure they just feared their little girl would reveal all their darkest secrets to the world.

I remember sitting on the bench outside the truck stop restaurant for hours as a small mob of crows comforted me by standing guard or offering me bits of food. Occasionally, a truck driver or passerby asked where my parents were. But the moment I'd look at them, my eyes would rip into their soul. They'd suddenly realize that I knew every secret they'd carefully hidden deep inside their soul.

Everyone who asked if I was okay ran away and left me, just like my parents.

Until Brother Walker arrived. When I looked at him, I didn't see into his soul. Instead, he was a blank wall as he leaned over and smiled. He took my hand and walked me to the monster village and handed me off to a grandmotherly werewolf, who ran the village's orphanage.

At the time, I thought Brother Walker was an angel. But I've since learned that people I can't see into are dangerous. That they've taught themselves the ability to completely hide who they are from the world.

The punk vampire, he wasn't dangerous at all. He was beautiful like all vampires and could have easily been a model showing off a new line of punk clothes on a catwalk. But even though he could easily kill me and drink my blood, I didn't fear him.

My eyes sparkled in the darkness. Infinity Eyes cawed softly, which was how he laughed.

"You call yourself Sid," I said, peering into the vampire's soul, "even though you actually hate the Sex Pistols. But you love that punk look, what with full-on goth being a little too much for you. And, oh. . ."

I stopped. He knew what I'd found—Sid was a vampire who hated killing people for their blood.

"But maybe I'll keep the rest between us," I said.

Sid shivered as he looked at the couture vampire beside me. I knew he didn't want me sharing his hatred of killing with his fellow vampires. There were few sins in the vampire world, but yeah, not being willing to kill humans was one of them.

"Fuck me," Sid said. "You're a monster, all right. Go on in."

I started to walk on when someone yelled, "Oh hell no!" as she ran straight at me from the village, her ears pointed to the side, her nose wrinkled and an angry fanged snarl on her face.

The one monster you never want mad at you is a werewolf. I'd hoped to sneak in and not have this encounter until church tomorrow, where I knew she'd behave because there'd be so many other monsters around.

"Hi, Kana," I said nervously.

Sid laughed. "Oh, yeah, you're totally a monster," he said. "A dead monster!"

***

Kana paced up and down inside her old RV like an angry wolf. Which she was.

"I can't believe you," she screamed. "Five years. No messages, no calls. And you just expect to come back here like it don't matter that Brother Walker's going to order some ghoul to kill you the moment he sees you?"

I sat on the sofa seat before the RV's tiny Formica table. The RV was a faded Winnebago with a big green W painted on the outside. This

87

wasn't some yuppie, fixed-up, vintage RV; this was run down, a half-century-older-than-the-age-of-both-of-us RV.

I kept my eyes down, staring at the yellow table. Not because I was subservient to Kana but because I hated the tangle of emotions I was feeling.

Kana took a deep breath and calmed down. I watched her beautiful wolf ears perk up as she stared back at me. I used to love nibbling on those ears when we made love, their silky fur always making me feel both happy and content.

"You okay?" she asked.

"I just missed you," I said.

She ran her fingers through my hair as she sat down on the sofa chair on the other side of the small table.

"I missed you too. But you can't stay here. Sid didn't know who you were, but everyone else will. Someone will kill you."

"Sid doesn't seem like the killing type," I said.

"You looked inside him, didn't you?" she said excitedly, as if it'd been years since she'd had a best friend to confide in. "Okay, keep it a secret, but he's, like, the world's worst vampire. Hates to hurt anything. I have to give him blood from deer I hunt down or he'd starve."

I laughed, so happy to be near Kana again. Not being around her was yet another way Brother Walker had punished me for standing up to his abuse.

"Look, you'll hide out here until the sun comes up. Most of the village is nocturnal, so as soon as people are sleeping, you sneak back to the truck stop and go on your way."

I grabbed Kana's hand and squeezed it. "This time, I won't leave without you."

Kana whined, then growled, releasing my hand as she stood up and again paced the RV. "If I don't stay, Brother Walker will tell the vampires to hunt you down," she said.

Which returned us to why Kana had stayed when I'd been forced to flee to the human world. Brother Walker did that to hurt both of us.

I looked around the RV. While clean inside, on the outside it looked like something you'd find in a junkyard, with the wheels dry-rotted and flat and rusted holes in the metal siding. There were plenty of nice homes and trailers in the village. If Kana was living in a place like this, it was because Brother Walker gave her no alternative.

Infinity Eyes sat on top of the fridge, watching me and Kana. I'd told him all about Kana, and he'd long wanted to meet her. Wolves and crows usually got along and sometimes even helped lead each other to food, but he still kept his distance. Infinity Eyes didn't trust anyone until they earned his trust.

"I'm not going to get killed," I said. "Today's solstice. I saw the revival tent set up outside the church."

"So?"

"So, all monsters are welcome for the revival. All sins forgiven. Anyone asks, I've come to seek forgiveness during the revival."

"You're going to confess to Brother Walker? You did nothing wrong."

"'Course I'm not going to confess. But I've got a plan."

Kana looked like she wanted to howl. "Then they'll kill you once the revival is over. Hell, they'll probably serve you up during the potluck afterwards."

"They won't kill me. I'm a monster."

Kana smiled that irritating smile of hers, the one where she tries to be nice by not disagreeing with you. While I knew she loved me, she also didn't consider me a true monster. Not a human, to be sure, but also not a scary monster like her and everyone else here.

"I'm going to the revival to confront Brother Walker," I said.

"Okay, fine. I'll fight beside you, then. But you know we can't win. There are too many of them."

"I'm not going to fight that way," I said.

I pointed at Infinity Eyes.

"The crow?" Kana asked. "How's a crow going to help?"

When Kana didn't understand, I gently reached out with my eyes, taking care to ask permission before reaching into her mind. She nodded and I connected with her.

A moment later, I pulled out. Kana stared again at Infinity Eyes.

"For this to work, you'll have to meet Brother Walker," Kana said. "I mean before the revival. Can you do that?"

She was right. I didn't want to see Brother Walker any more than I had to, but I couldn't let him discover me before everyone gathered for the church service in the revival tent. My plan only had a chance if there were plenty of other monsters around.

"I'll go see him," I said. "Tell him I was wrong to accuse him. That I want to live here again and I'll do anything to make that happen."

Kana squeezed my hand. "I'll go with you."

I hugged Kana and kissed her on the cheek.

Kana and I talked and cuddled on the RV's main sofa for the rest of the night. I didn't have to tell her how afraid I was, because she could smell my fear. But even if Brother Walker had me killed, I refused to be apart from her any longer.

When dawn began to break, Kana stood up and closed all the blinds.

"Aw," I said, "I hoped we could watch the sun come up, then get a little sleep. You know, together."

Kana laughed. "Fine, you can share my bed. But we can't do anything else."

"Why not?"

Kana had always been very private about physical displays of affection, but with the blinds down, it's not like anyone would see us. Before she could explain, the door opened and Sid walked into the RV. He looked disappointed at seeing me still alive.

"Damn," he said. "I thought Kana would have killed you already. I haven't had any blood all night."

"Don't tell me," I said.

Kana rolled her eyes. "Yeah, Sid's my roommate."

***

I woke well before noon. Kana and I had slept on the pullout sofa in the back of the RV while Sid slept in the loft over the driver's seat. Evidently, that was Sid's usual daytime hiding spot. He'd even wrapped the loft in aluminum foil and blankets to prevent any sunshine from sneaking in.

Kana was still sleeping, so instead of waking her, I slipped out the door. As she'd said, most of the village was nocturnal, so I shouldn't have any trouble walking into the church. And while I loved Kana wanting to be with me when I talked to Brother Walker, if he tried to touch me again, she might lose control and attack him. Which would mess up all my plans.

As I walked across the meadow where Kana's RV was parked, I heard a familiar cawing. Infinity Eyes flew down and landed on my shoulder. He wanted something, but instead of asking, he grabbed a beakful of my hair and ripped it from my scalp and flew off.

I cursed. I watched Infinity Eyes fly to the edge of the meadow, where a large number of crows were gathered on the ground. I hated the term *a murder of crows* because who really says that in real-life except to show off that you know obscure collective nouns? But in this case, *murder* was a good term; the hundreds of crows there bobbed their heads and stepped clockwise in sync, as if weaving some disturbing avian spell.

My eyes are powerful, always have been, so even at this distance, I could easily see Infinity Eyes land in the middle of the spinning circle of crows. He walked confidently and held my hair out to one of the crows, who took a single strand. Infinity Eyes walked around the circle, giving my hair to other crows, until it was all gone.

And then, at an unheard signal, the entire group of crows flew into the sky and disappeared behind the nearby trees.

No wonder people found crows eerie. And while I wasn't even part crow—not even a werecrow, as Kana used to jokingly call me when we were kids—I'd always felt most comfortable among them.

Was this why most people had always treated me as an outsider, even in a village of monsters?

I walked toward the wooden church, passing the trailers and small homes of the monsters who lived here year-round, along with tents set up for all the visitors. Down the hill lay the truck stop, and farther on, several garages and assorted other companies. Monsters owned the truck stop and the other businesses there, providing work for those who lived in the village full-time.

According to what everyone said about Brother Walker, when he was a teenager growing up in these mountains, he discovered an injured mothman. Instead of killing the monster or revealing it to others, Brother Walker nursed it back to health. Mothmen were massive, standing nearly ten feet tall, so Brother Walker built a small shelter over the creature and returned every day for two months with food and water until the monster healed.

Each time Brother Walker saw the mothman, he also preached the Gospel. And when the mothman could finally fly, Brother Walker led the monster to a creek and baptized him.

The place where he nursed that mothman back to health? The same spot where this village would spring up. The mothman built the church there and started this village. And he invited Brother Walker to preach to our people.

Even though all that took place fifty years ago, Brother Walker was still a legend among our kind. One of the few humans who'd ever tried to help monsters. He even preached the gospel to us, convinced that we were as human as anyone else who walked God's green world.

Monsters loved him. I totally understood this feeling, because I also worshipped him after he rescued me.

At least, I worshipped him until he showed me his true self.

I walked up the steps to the church and tapped the white-painted wood for luck before opening the front door. I passed the pews I'd sat on for so many years. Passed the altar I'd prayed before.

I knocked on Brother Walker's office door. "Enter," he yelled.

He sat at his desk, working on his sermon for tonight's revival. I remembered helping him with his sermons in this very office when I was a teenager. And how one summer day, when I was only fifteen, he closed this office door and kissed me. Then he pushed me to the floor and. . .

I took a deep breath, trying not to again remember that awful day.

Brother Walker hadn't changed in the last five years. Even though he was now over seventy, he was still a tall man and towered over the desk. The rolled-up sleeves of his plaid shirt showed off large muscles.

"Hello, Sefi," he said. "Interesting that you're here. Sid was on guard last night, right? Guess you can't trust a vampire who hates killing."

I tried to say something, but the words gagged in my mind. It took all my willpower to keep myself standing in the doorway. To keep from fleeing this evil man.

"Did you want something?" he asked impatiently. "If you're thinking about getting back at me, all I have to do is ring the bells and every monster around will rush to help me. Not that I need help dealing with someone like you."

I glanced at the remote control for the church bells, which sat on his desk next to the draft of his sermon. The first time he'd let me activate the bells had been one of the best days of my life, even better than when he rescued me or baptized me.

"It's revival," I whispered, angry that I again felt like a scared kid before him.

"What?"

"Today's the church revival. You always preached that any monster could come here on this day and seek forgiveness."

Brother Walker stood up and stepped around the desk. I gripped the doorjamb tight, trying not to run back out the front door of the church. He noticed this and laughed softly.

"Yeah," he said, "that's true. But are you really seeking forgiveness? I think this is just you trying to trick me."

He stepped closer. I felt so afraid that my eyes reached out to him before I could stop myself. But as before, I felt only a blank wall within him. The wall was a little fuzzier than I remembered, as if I'd grown stronger. I could almost see into all his secrets, but it still wasn't enough.

Even after all he'd done and all these years, my powers couldn't reach into him like everyone else.

"You told some cruel lies about me," he said. "Told people I'd done things. . ."

"They weren't lies," I snapped, desperate to remain calm.

"Maybe. But I'll still give you a chance to redeem yourself. You be at that tent when we start the revival. If you confess that everything you accused me of was a lie, I won't have you killed."

I nodded.

Brother Walker turned back to his desk. "I have a sermon to finish. Get out."

I walked slowly out of the church, forcing myself to not give him the pleasure of seeing me flee. But once I was outside, I ran as fast as I could.

***

Kana was ticked at me going to see Brother Walker without her. She and I sat in folding lounge chairs in the RV's shade as the late-afternoon sun eased down behind us. Sid sat on the metal steps by the RV's door, sipping a blood smoothie in a massive thirty-two-ounce insulated travel mug. Infinity Eyes perched on the ground near Sid, watching him drink the blood as if trying to convince the vampire to give him a taste.

"So, your powers still don't work on him?" Kana asked.

I shook my head. "I got closer to reaching into him than five years ago, but it's a no-go. And being around him still messed with my mind. Makes it hard to break through his mental defenses."

"Then how can you do it during the revival?"

"Infinity Eyes will help me."

All three of us looked at the crow, who ruffled his black feathers as if shrugging his shoulders.

"How about we kill him right now?" Kana said, standing up as she growled. She was such the wolf sometimes, ready to charge, fangs bared, at whatever needed fixing.

"Sit down, wolf-brain," Sid said. "There are hundreds of monsters here for the revival. You try to kill him and they'll kill us."

"Us?" I asked.

Sid took a big swallow of his drink. Evidently, Kana froze blood from deer she killed, which Sid later blended into smoothies. The smell was awful, which was probably why Infinity Eyes wanted a taste. While I loved crows, their tastes in food were way more extreme than mine.

"Yeah, I said 'us,'" Sid muttered. "Kana's my friend. She likes you, so that default means you're also a friend."

I snorted, not sure friendships transferred like that.

"No, I'm serious," Sid said. "The vampire who turned me always said the lives of monsters were shit, so the least you could do is make a few friends along the way. Kana's my friend. And maybe you'll be my friend too."

"Sid, that's actually kinda sweet," Kana said. "One day, I'll have to meet this vampire who turned you."

"Can't. I staked her through the heart. I mean, shit, it's damn evil to turn people into vampires in the first place."

Kana and I laughed.

"What I'm trying to say," Sid continued, "is most of the monsters here don't give a shit about Brother Walker's church or this revival and his preaching. But they like that his church helped create a place where they can come and see their friends. Everyone needs friends. For some of us, that's the only family we'll ever have."

Sid set his mug down for a moment and asked about my plan to take down Brother Walker. But before I could say anything, Infinity Eyes grabbed the lip of Sid's travel mug with his beak and dragged the drink out of the shade and into the sunshine.

"Hey," Sid yelled. "Get that bird to give me back my smoothie."

Infinity Eyes bobbed his head, as if daring Sid to take it. Sid paced to the edge of the RV's shadow but didn't go into the sunlight.

Infinity Eyes dipped his beak in the blood smoothie and drank deeply before cawing. As if by magic, dozens and then hundreds of crows landed around him. They all stared at Sid while Infinity Eyes continued to drink the smoothie.

"Okay, that's creepy," Kana said.

I laughed and walked out into the crows, who stepped aside just like they'd done earlier today for Infinity Eyes. A number of them still held strands of my hair.

I sat down next to Infinity Eyes and picked the mug up, which had tipped on its side. I held it as my friend drank more of the smoothie. I'd been stupid to go see Brother Walker by myself. Sid had been right about friends being the only family some of us had. Crows were just like people, picking their family and making friends, all of them supporting each other. Infinity Eyes had taught me that long ago, but I'd been so focused on Brother Walker since returning there, I'd forgotten.

And it wasn't just the crows. I'd also found my family years ago in Kana and had wrongly let Brother Walker separate us. I'd never let that happen again.

I smiled at Kana and Sid. I wasn't alone. I didn't have to fight Brother Walker by myself.

Infinity Eyes cawed, setting off the other crows into their own cries before they all took wing and flew around me in a spiral before taking off to the nearby trees.

I handed Sid back his mug, which had dirt and feathers in it from Infinity Eyes. Sid shrugged and drank what was left.

"Tonight," I said, hugging Kana.

***

As the three of us walked to the revival tent that night, we passed every type of monster imaginable. I saw elves and goblins, werewolves and haints, skunk apes and will-o'-the-wisps, witches and warlocks. Old, forgotten gods and demons from around the world stood talking with creatures who at first glance looked human but out of the corner of your eye resembled bears and deer and mountain lions.

And all of them were talking and hugging, excited at seeing friends old and new.

Sid was right about monsters and religion. No one was there for Brother Walker's revival service. They were there for each other. And this fellowship was what I'd loved most about growing up there. Even though I'd always felt like an outsider, I'd still missed this so much.

Infinity Eyes perched on my shoulder and offered appraising glances at everyone we passed. Brother Walker must have spread the word that I was back, because even those who recognized me didn't attack. A few growled or hissed, but that was it.

At midnight, the church bells rang and everyone filed into the massive revival tent and sat down among the rows of folding chairs.

Kana, Sid and I sat in the back row, what Brother Walker had always called the sinner's row. We wanted a quick route out of the tent in case things didn't go our way.

I saw a number of monsters I'd known growing up there, but none of them looked at me. And even monsters I didn't know ignored me, as if they'd been warned I'd displeased their beloved Brother Walker. Only the couture vampire I'd meet coming into the village acknowledged me, throwing a haughty wave before she sat down at the front of the tent. Otherwise, it was like I didn't exist.

Kana held my hand. Infinity Eyes tugged my hair once to reassure me before flying up and perching on one of the tent posts.

There's a rhythm to religious services, known only to those who have spent years in a church. And I knew this church. I knew it as well as a crow knows the winds and sky.

When Brother Walker entered, I felt the crowd breathe deep out of respect. When an aged elf stepped to the podium by the altar and thanked everyone for coming, I tasted the same words I'd heard at services and revivals across the years. And when we all stood and sang, the same songs I'd heard all my life flowed in and around me.

But I felt oddly detached from the service, as if I was a crow watching some puzzling human ritual. Because I'd seen how all these fancy words and prayers and rituals didn't mean anything if you tried to reveal the truth about someone everyone there loved.

And then Brother Walker stood at the podium and gave his sermon. He spoke on lies. He spoke on deceit. He spoke on the devil slipping in among us, looking like a friend. He looked everywhere except at me even though his words were aimed at no one else. Every monster in the revival judged me in their mind. Every monster found me lacking.

Every monster, that is, except for Kana and Sid.

But I didn't care what all these fools believed. Instead, I glared back at them. I reached out with my eyes and truly saw the monsters around me.

As I looked, I also saw Infinity Eyes. I felt the other crows arriving, landing silently in the darkness outside the tent. A few joined Infinity Eyes inside, where they also stared at me and Kana and Sid and everyone else. The crows watched and judged this service of monsters. They saw what was in people's hearts and they weren't impressed.

I was so lost in the ebb and flow around me that I almost missed when Brother Walker's sermon began to end. Kana elbowed me in the arm.

"Get ready," she whispered.

I nodded. Brother Walked always ended his sermons by inviting anyone who wished to be saved, or to confess their sins, to come down while the congregation stood up and prayed. Infinity Eyes looked at me and nodded.

It was time.

"So, if you have sins to confess tonight, won't you come down and be saved, as we stand and pray?" Brother Walker intoned.

As everyone stood and the ancient elf from earlier led the revival in a prayer, I eased down the row toward the front. Where before the monsters ignored me, now they glared dangerously. Brother Walker had indeed told them I'd be confessing. If I tried to back out, they'd kill me.

Instead of fleeing, I walked to the front row and sat down next to Brother Walker.

He embraced me and pulled me close, as if we were to have a private confessional. He whispered that I didn't need to say anything. That we'd sit like this for a minute, then he'd stand up and announce that I'd confessed my many sins.

But as he whispered, he noticed the smirk on my face. He saw that I wasn't afraid of being next to him or having him touch me, unlike how I'd been only hours earlier in his office. And how I wasn't even looking at him.

"What are you staring at?" he asked.

Brother Walker raised his head and followed my gaze to the altar, where Infinity Eyes stared back at him. Three more crows landed on the altar and also stared at Brother Walker, then more landed on the podium and elsewhere in the tent and also stared at him.

Hundreds of brown eyes burning into him.

The monsters around us tittered, not sure how to react. A couple of birds always flew in during revivals, but they'd never seen anything like this.

As more crows flew in, Brother Walker shoved me away from him. "What the fuck are you doing?" he said.

I turned from Infinity Eyes and looked at Brother Walker with my star-filled eyes. I saw the white wall behind which he'd always kept his secrets. But as Infinity Eyes and the other crows also stared at Brother Walker, the wall began to crack. His hands shook and he stood up, attempting to run.

The wall shattered before he could go anywhere.

I saw all his secrets. All the evil he'd done in this world. Not only how he'd sexually assaulted me but also how he'd done the same to other young monsters over the decades, young people who'd looked up to him and believed in him.

I saw it all as Brother Walker collapsed before the altar, still trying to escape. I pulled in the power of all the crows surrounding us. Pulled in the support of all my friends, from Infinity Eyes to Kana to even Sid.

With all that support, I reached into Brother's Walker's horribly hidden world and shared what I saw with every monster in the revival.

The monsters screamed as I slammed them with visions of the evil Brother Walker had done in his life, of him assaulting young monsters whose only sin had been to love him. A witch behind me fell to her knees, massive tears flowing down her face as she beat her forehead against the back of a folding chair. A skunk ape at the end of the tent pulled at the hair on his body, ripping it out over and over, unable to stop.

Several minutes passed as I shared what Brother Walker had done to each and every young monster he'd hurt. While the audience cried and screamed and begged for all of this to end, my eyes kept them spellbound and unable to leave the tent. A few monsters tried to push back against the truths I shared. I heard them whisper that Brother Walker had also done good in the world.

I screamed at this and revealed even more of the harm Brother Walker had done. How he even molested a twelve-year-old werewolf who'd come to him for solace after both of her parented were hunted down and killed by humans. The werewolf later killed herself because of what Brother Walker did to her.

The monsters in the audience howled as the pain Brother Walker had caused to their own kind washed in and out of their minds.

No excuses, the crows cawed as one. *No excuses!*

I shoved all of this down the throat of every monster in the revival for a few more minutes. Then I stopped and stepped up to the podium.

The revival tent before me was a mess, with chairs overturned and monsters standing and sitting and flat on their backs, all of them crying and cursing and shaking and hugging each other for comfort. As I looked at them, the monsters looked back with fear. Infinity Eyes flapped over and landed on my shoulder.

Beside the altar, Brother Walker had recovered somewhat and was crawling toward the exit.

"That's the end of my sermon," I announced. "Shall we stand and pray?"

The couture vampire yelled, "Hell yes!" as she strode up to Brother Walker and yanked him to his feet before biting his shoulder in a massive explosion of blood. A young mothman joined in by clawing one of Brother Walker's legs as a werewolf bit the other.

I smiled as Brother Walker screamed. And he kept screaming as the monsters piled on him and ripped him into nothing but blood and meat and shattered bones.

The crows cawed loudly, causing every monster to look back at me. I stepped forward and the crowd parted before me, every monster either in awe of me or completely scared of my power.

When I reached the back row, Kana hugged me.

"I was wrong," she said. "You are one hell of a badass monster."

***

The next day, Sid slept in a dark house with the other vampires so Kana and I could have some private time in the RV. When Kana asked if he was worried the vampires would harass him for not being a killer, he laughed.

"They know they mess with me," he said, "they'll have to answer to my best friend Sefi."

I laughed. I still wasn't certain that Sid and I were truly friends yet, but I liked the direction things were going.

When night came, Kana and I waited at the gate from the village, saying goodbye to everyone and telling them to come back next year.

"You're going to do a revival next year?" the couture vampire asked as she was leaving.

"Hell no," Kana said. "But how about a big party?"

The vampire nodded. "I might return for that."

Infinity Eyes and several crows perched on the stone wall, daring any of the departing monsters to mess with either them or me. Most of the monsters were afraid to speak with me as they left, but a few gave their thanks for revealing who Brother Walker had been and said they'd consider coming back next year.

"Not many," I said.

"It'll be enough," Kana said. "Even if this village was rotten for so long, with Brother Walker gone, maybe we can turn this place into a true home for our people."

I hugged Kana and gently nipped one of her ears with my teeth.

"Doesn't matter how things started," I said. "Only matters what we're going to do from now on."

Infinity Eyes and the other crows cawed loudly and flew into the sky, circling the village as Kana and I kissed.

Note from the Author

I grew up in a conservative church in the rural American South. This upbringing gave me a painful education in how religion can be used to both ignore and excuse violence against women, especially when the ones doing these evils are thought by others to be fine, upstanding, God-fearing men. As the crows say in my story, "No excuses!" Religion should never be a cover for violence against women and girls or used to suppress their rights. And never forget that the true monsters in our world are frequently hidden behind a friendly, self-righteous smile.

– Jason Sanford

Finding Water to Catch Fire

Linda D. Addison

Fanya came to as she sank in the cold river. She was strapped in her wheelchair and couldn't think clearly enough to unlatch the seat belt. Then two voices started talking in her head.

They always say it's an accident.

Mami Wata, how many have died as accidents in your water?

Many more than I like to remember, Atabey, said Mami Wata.

This one carries powerful Taíno ancestors in her, Atabey said.

And African, Mami Wata added. *She may be exactly who we need to help restore some balance.*

Perhaps, if she can find her strength, Atabey said.

The two women's voices faded as Fanya lost consciousness again, water filling her lungs.

***

Fanya coughed violently. The stinging sensation of water being drawn out of her lungs made her shake her head, which brought waves of pain. Her right hand went to the side of her head. She slowly opened her eyes. A full moon lit the river in front of her. She was on the grassy section of the Three Rivers waterfront park. She looked at her hand and saw blood.

Water ran like an army of ants, down from her hair, clothes, over her wheelchair into the ground. What is going on? She must be dead. Was this heaven or hell?

"Neither, although that has been debated by many," a woman's deep voice whispered in Fanya's ear.

Fanya slowly turned to her right. A tall, dark-skinned woman wearing a white gown stood next to her with intricate loops of braids on her head. Dots of gold created curved patterns on her forehead and cheeks. The woman smiled, a gold nose ring reflected in the moonlight. She was the most beautiful woman Fanya had ever seen.

"Who. . .who are you?" Fanya asked slowly.

"I have been called Mami Wata." The woman reached to touch Fanya's head.

Fanya flinched, expecting pain, but the woman's fingers were a cool, gentle breeze against the wound. The throbbing in her head stopped. Mami Wata lowered her hand, which was covered in blood for a second before the red fluid soaked into her skin. Mami Wata closed her eyes, lowered her head. When she lifted it, Fanya saw a flash of gold light in the woman's eyes.

"As you said, Atabey, there are strong African ancestors in her, at least one priestess." Mami Wata looked to Fanya's left.

"And Taino," another woman said, her voice soft as a child's.

Fanya turned. A young woman stepped out of the shadow of a nearby tree into the moonlight. Atabey wore a sleeveless blue-and-green jumpsuit, covered in patterns that reminded Fanya of a map. An intricate tattoo laced along her arms and neck like some kind of sea creature with long tentacles that glowed against her mocha skin. Her long dark hair hung in curly waves around her face and shoulders. Red, brown, and gold leaves were caught in her hair, as if she had rolled in a pile of fall foliage, but it was early spring.

Fanya rolled the wheelchair's push rims to back away from the women. "I don't know what's happening here. I must be seeing things. I-I hit my head." She stopped moving. "I fell and hit my head."

"Do you remember how you fell?" Mami Wata asked, her eyes

holding Fanya's attention as sure as if she held her hands.

Fanya pushed the wheel locks on, suddenly feeling sick to her stomach. Atabey stepped next to Mami Wata; with the moonlight to their backs Fanya couldn't see the details of their faces, but the eyes of both glowed with a soft light.

"To see truth, you must release denial, Fanya." Atabey held out her fist. As she slowly opened her hand, Fanya threw up in the grass over the side of her wheelchair.

She wiped her mouth with the back of her hand. "I was with Peter," she said, gasping. "We were arguing."

"Again," Mami Wata said.

Fanya nodded. "He hit me. . .again," she said. "He promised he wouldn't after the last time, but he loses control when he's angry."

"Yes," Atabey said, kneeling next to Fanya. When Atabey put her hand over Fanya's, her stomach convulsed, but there was nothing left to vomit.

"He knocked me over and I-I hit my head on a table." Fanya touched the side of her healed head. "I don't remember anything else, just being in the river, and then here with you two."

"How do you suppose you ended up in the river?" Mami Wata put her fists on her hips. Something slithered in her hair.

"It had to be an accident. Peter wouldn't purposely throw me in the water. He must have thought I was dead and panicked. He—"

"—loves you." Atabey spat the words out like poison.

Fanya opened her mouth, then slumped back against her seat.

"His love comes with bruises, cutting words, and apologies," Atabey said, tightening her grip on Fanya's hand.

"Ending with your death," Mami Wata said, folding her arms across her chest. A milk-colored snake slid out of her hair and wrapped itself loosely around her neck.

Fanya pulled her hand from Atabey's grip. "My death?" she asked, looking around. Fanya saw moving cars on the distant Thirty-First Street Bridge but no one else in the park, no boats on the Allegheny River. She put her hands over her eyes. "You two aren't real. I must be dreaming." When Fanya opened her eyes again, they were still standing in front of her.

"The water in your blood called to the water spirits of the Earth, Fanya." Mami Wata put her left arm around Atabey's shoulder. "Here, on this land of much denial, so many lives have been taken in the name of love for things and people."

"We offer you a gift," Atabey said. "We can teach you what you have forgotten, the power of your ancestors."

"Or we can return you to your death," Mami Wata added, slowly lifting her right arm as Atabey lifted her left.

Muddy water pooled at Fanya's feet, crept up her legs, crawled around the bottom of her wheelchair, soaking up through her sweatpants, the edges of her jacket. There was no feeling of wetness until it reached her waist, where the nerve damage ended from her spina bifida. She couldn't move her arms to maneuver away from them. The memory of drowning came to her like a lightning bolt.

"Wait-wait-please," Fanya yelled. The cold water stopped at her chest.

"Yes?" Atabey asked.

"I don't know if I believe this, but I don't want to drown again." She shook her head. "Please."

"Then you accept our gift?" Atabey asked.

"Yes," Fanya said, taking a deep breath.

Both women lowered their arms. The water flowed off Fanya, back into the ground, until she was dry and able to move her upper body again.

"Where things end is where they begin," Atabey said, walking past Fanya, away from the river, toward the city.

Fanya turned the wheelchair more easily than she expected. It moved as if she was on a polished floor. She looked down and saw no indentation of her wheels in the grass. Mami Wata walked past her, trailing the scent of the sea. Fanya spun the push rims forward once and her wheelchair glided up the hill, past both women, to the paved path. She barely had to touch the right rim to stop; a gentle forward move of the left turned her to face the women or whatever they were, as they reached the path. Fanya felt like she had been flying.

"You're beautiful when you smile," Atabey said to Fanya.

"I don't know about that," Fanya replied, "but I've never felt so strong before. Usually, I would be out of breath coming up a hill like that. I don't feel tired at all. This must be a dream."

Mami Wata pulled a beautiful hand mirror from the fold of her dress and handed it to her. "There's unlimited strength in you, and beauty."

Fanya shook her head and laid the mirror face-down on her lap. The back of the mirror was gold, covered in a pattern of inlaid turquoise, pearls, and diamonds that resembled a series of waves topped with foam. "I don't like to look in mirrors."

Mami Wata caressed Fanya's cheek. "If this is a dream, what is there to fear?"

Fanya turned the mirror over with her left hand and saw the sky reflected in it. Morning light softened the night with light blue streaks. She slowly turned it toward her face. Instead of the uneven complexion, dull hair, sad eyes, and lackluster skin the color of weak tea, she saw a beautiful young woman.

She barely recognized her reflection, the thick swirl of hair that reflected the rising sunlight, full lips glowing like red earth, and eyes bright as starlight. "This must be a magic mirror. I've never looked like this."

"Perhaps you weren't looking with your heart," Atabey said. "Maybe you've been seeing yourself through the lens of others' expectations."

"Maybe." Fanya tried to give the mirror back to Mami Wata.

"Keep it, as a birthday gift from me," she said, waving her hand. "I have many more. Now let's go."

Both women started walking on the path to the left.

Fanya put the mirror in the side pocket of her wheelchair. "Where are we going? My apartment is in the other direction." She pointed right.

"We're going somewhere else first," Atabey replied, without turning around.

Fanya started to speak but decided to follow them since they didn't seem to be influenced by her opinion, especially since it took little to no effort to maneuver the wheelchair.

By the time they reached the main street the sun was up. A few people passed them, entering the park to jog. Delivery trucks and a few cars were on the road. As the city woke, Fanya expected the dream to end and she would wake in the hospital or even in her own bed, the nightmare over, but no sign of reality made the two women fade. Fanya was used to being invisible in her wheelchair, or people being overly polite, but no one glanced at the two regal women.

As they moved through the streets to a neighborhood she rarely visited, Fanya asked, "Mami Wata, can others see you?"

She glanced over her shoulder and smiled. "If we want them to."

They turned the corner and stopped in front of a motel.

"Let's wait in the shade," Atabey said, pointing to an island of trees and bushes on the edge of the parking lot.

"What are we waiting for?" Fanya asked, easily bumping over the low curb to the trees.

"Do you recognize any of these cars?" Mami Wata stroked the snake draped over her shoulders.

Fanya looked over the ten or fifteen parked cars. She was about to ask why, when she noticed a car near them that was the same model as

Peter's. One look at the license told her it was his. "Why would Peter be here?"

"That's a question you should ask him." Mami Wata pointed to the second-floor balcony.

A room door opened and a tall, brown-skinned man stepped out, his arms around a woman clearly naked under a semi-sheer, red robe. He stopped in the doorway to kiss her, taking his time while he pressed her against the door frame. The woman finally pushed him away, laughed, and shut the door.

"I can't believe he's with another woman after-after. . ." Fanya couldn't finish. Her nails bit into her palms. This man, whom she thought so good-looking, whose attention she believed herself so lucky to have, didn't seem at all bothered after dumping her body in the river last night.

"After thinking he killed you," Atabey said calmly.

As he walked to his car, Fanya rolled out of the shade to him. She reached the passenger door at the same time he unlocked the car. He didn't notice her until he sat behind the steering wheel and she yanked the opposite door open.

"Oh my God, Fanya?" He pushed himself against the closed door. "I thought—"

"You thought I was dead?" Fanya quickly slid into the seat next to him, folded her chair with one hand, and threw it over the front seat into the back. It felt light as paper to her.

"How did you do that?" Peter asked.

Fanya shrugged, putting on the seat belt. "We need to talk. Let's take a drive."

"Um, sure." Peter's hands shook as he lit a cigarette. "I can explain everything, Fanya. I-I—"

"Drive to Almono," she said, her voice hard.

"Where?" he asked.

111

"The old steel mill site on Hazelwood's riverfront." Fanya looked straight ahead.

"Can't we go to your place and talk?"

"Almono. Now." She pounded the dashboard with her fist.

"What the hell!" Peter turned the key in the ignition. "I've never seen you act like this."

"Drive," she said, without looking at him. "We'll talk when we get there."

As they took off, Fanya looked behind in the back seat. The two women were sitting next to her folded wheelchair. Mami Wata nodded at her. She didn't know if it was their power or her anger, but she felt energy charging through her body. They drove the ten minutes to the riverfront in silence. Apparently, Peter couldn't see the two women, because he didn't say anything when using the mirror to check traffic behind them.

They turned off the main street onto an unpaved road to the old steel mill. There was a locked chain link fence at the entrance with a sign proclaiming it the new construction site of Almono Riverfront Park.

"We can't go in," Peter said, but before he could put his foot on the brake, Fanya pushed down on his right knee with both hands, forcing him to accelerate. The car crashed through the fence, hit some barrels, and swerved to the right down a road toward the water. It slammed into a concrete barrier at the river's edge.

Peter unhooked his seat belt and rolled out of the car to the ground. Fanya opened the passenger door. Her wheelchair was waiting outside the car. She pulled herself in and easily rolled over the rough ground to Peter.

"You crazy bitch! I think I broke my ankle."

Anger flamed through Fanya's mind. "At least you didn't die," she growled, rolling closer to him. She felt the two women behind her, even though he couldn't see them.

"I-I- That was an accident." He pushed himself up against the concrete barrier.

She moved closer. Her footrest hit his injured leg. He cried out in pain.

"I'm sorry, Fanya," he rasped. "I thought you were dead."

"You didn't check very hard before throwing me in the river. Do you know what it feels like to drown?"

Water surged up from the broken ground under Peter. He tried to scoot away but couldn't move fast enough. A column of water flowed around him, encasing him in an invisible container until he was floating in front of Fanya. He flailed his arms but couldn't break out. Unable to hold his breath any longer, a stream of bubbles left his mouth. He jerked back and forth as the water filled his lungs.

Then he was still.

The water fell away. His body crumpled to the ground.

"Did I do that?" Fanya whispered.

Mami Wata stood to her right, Atabey to her left.

"Yes," Atabey said, putting her hand on Fanya's shoulder.

She stared at Peter's body. "I didn't plan to kill him."

"There are worse things than death," said Mami Wata.

"But I'm not dead." Fanya looked up at her. "You two brought me back to life."

Peter's body jerked. Fanya rolled her wheelchair backward in surprise. A sound like underwater laughter came from him.

Both women took a step back. "I would say you've found your power, just in time," Atabey said.

Peter stood as if pulled by ropes. His arms hung to his side and he floated about an inch off the ground. When he opened his eyes, they were completely black. His head flopped back and hissing steam poured into the air from his mouth. The scent of decayed meat flew at the women.

Fanya coughed, covering her nose. "What's going on?"

Again laughter came from Peter as a screeching mad sound, followed by a voice that fluctuated between a man's and a woman's. "Oh, little girl, did they tell you they saved your life?"

"Take care; Fanya, do not believe what comes from this shadow." Mami Wata gently squeezed her shoulder. "It only knows lies."

"But you two are the givers of light and truth," it said, lowering Peter's body to the ground to stand. His ankle made an unpleasant crunching sound. "Did you tell this child the truth about the gift you gave her? That you made her a spirit ghost like yourselves, so you could use her against me?"

"We didn't lie to her. There wasn't time to explain everything," Atabey said. "Unlike the promises you make to those you want to possess."

It took an unsteady step toward them. "Possession is three-fourths of the law."

"You're not in complete possession yet, shapeless one," Mami Wata responded.

The three women moved back two steps.

"Peter?" Fanya asked.

That horrible laugh came out of Peter's mouth again. "Peter's busy right now," it said, shuffling a half-step closer.

"Enough! Stay where you are, destroyer of life." Mami Wata and Atabey lifted their hands at the same time. A ring of dirt with white crystals bubbled from the ground in a circle around them. "Stay in the ring, Fanya. You'll be safe here."

"Again, a lie," it said, shambling to the edge of the ring. It lifted an arm, pointed one finger, but when the fingertip started to cross the air boundary of the ring, its skin blackened. The smell of burnt flesh hung in the air. "This earth-and-salt protection will not last."

"It will last long enough," Atabey said.

It stumbled back a half-step. "Why do you entice me with this game piece? Do you care so much for a broken man who hurts others?"

"Am I a ghost, like this thing says?" Fanya turned her wheelchair to face Mami Wata. "Why would you want to save Peter?"

"There's more at stake than one human soul," Mami Wata explained. "You have been a spirit priestess in past lives. We gave you the choice to again take up the mantle of Light."

"Now the fable begins," it said laughing.

"We can't take too much time now," Atabey added. "Each second is in its favor. Like you, every human's life force reaches back through their ancestors and forward into potential lives. Your life and his life and the lives of all you know are intertwined, like a spider web."

Mami Wata held Fanya's hand. "When this shadow energy consumes a human's soul, it puts a crack in the infinite web of existence. We three can stop it."

"Yes, you see," it snickered. "They need you. The only reason they brought you here was to help them fight a useless battle. For each piece they gain, I have hundreds more lined up. Why involve yourself with the one who killed you?"

Fanya stared at Peter's body. The skin of his face, ears, neck, and hands was turning into charred flesh; tar-like fluid began leaking from his eyes, ears, and nose.

"You ended him," it said through Peter's mouth. "Why not let me have him?"

"Why me?" she asked Atabey.

"Because we need a triad," Atabey answered. "You come from a strong line of spirit warriors, Fanya. You and Peter were connected in a past life. This isn't just about one life. We can't make you fight with us, but what does your heart say?"

She looked at Peter again. Black, oily fluid dripped from the corners of his eyes. Most of his brown skin was cracked and burnt.

"Are you the devil?" Fanya asked.

"Oh, please," it said, plucking fingernails off one of Peter's hands. "That name doesn't fit me any more than the names you call these two." It threw a fingernail at Fanya. It sailed through the safe circle, landed on Fanya's lap, and began to burn a hole through her sweatpants. She quickly brushed it off and yelped at the burn it left on her hand. Half of the earth-salt circle had dissolved.

"I will fight with you," Fanya said to the women.

"You will lose," it said, and rushed at them in Peter's body.

Mami Wata and Atabey rose into the air. Fanya turned her wheelchair quickly to the left, entangling Peter's ankles in the footrests, causing him to fall. Before he could grab Fanya, the other two women swooped down, each grabbing an arm and rising with her.

"It's in a weakened state until it has completely absorbed Peter's spirit," Mami Wata explained.

"What should I do?" Fanya yelled.

"Let your energy follow ours," Atabey said. "We need to get it over to the river."

Mami Wata and Atabey linked arms with Fanya so that all three faced outward, making a triangle with their backs. Fanya felt her back become wet as a column of water filled the space inside the triangle.

The thing inside Peter roared with frustration as it untangled his body from the wheelchair. It rose in the air, dragging the wheelchair; Peter's right foot was still tangled in the footrest. It pointed at the ankle, splitting Peter's foot in half, allowing the chair to drop. Peter's body continued to rise until it was at the same level as the women, floating opposite Fanya.

"Leave these disillusioned ghosts and come with me," it said. Small flames danced on Peter's head. "With me you'll be normal, able to walk. Or stay with them and die again."

"I've always been normal," Fanya said. "And I've been dead." There was a surge of electricity from her back. An arc of lightning bloomed in the air from the center of the women's triangle and stabbed down into Peter's body.

His arms and legs convulsed so hard, Fanya thought they would snap off. She felt a huge drop in their mutual energy after the strike.

"You can't destroy me," it said through blistered lips. "Especially not with fire." Lines of flames flew from its eyes and whipped at them. They spun away to the river but not before the fire cut their arms, chest, and faces, setting their clothes on fire. Fanya screamed.

Once they were over the river, water rose to put out the flames, heal their wounds, and take the pain away. A stream rose to connect to the column of water at their backs, increasing their energy again.

"It's not you we're trying to destroy," Mami Wata said.

Atabey looked up. Sudden storm clouds gathered overhead, darkening the sky.

"What new game are you playing?" it asked. "I welcome your storm."

"So be it," Atabey said.

Another lightning strike reached up from the women's triangle to the sky. A deafening boom preceded an impossibly large lightning bolt, drilling from the sky into the top of Peter's head. Half of his body was engulfed in flames already; when the lightning connected, his entire body glowed red with fire and electricity.

Fanya watched in horror. The thing screeched while Peter's clothes, skin, muscles, and organs burned away, until there was nothing left but his skeleton. The lightning continued until his bones exploded in a cloud of dust, and a shadow shaped like a sword flew into the sky.

A sphere of water captured the fine powder of Peter's bones and followed the women as they floated back to land. They returned to where Fanya's wheelchair sat, upright and washed clean. Mami Wata and Atabey set Fanya into her seat.

They stood before her with the sphere of water that contained all that was left of Peter.

"One last thing," Mami Wata said. She put her hand under the sphere, as did Atabey, and nodded to Fanya to do the same. The water and bone dust soaked into their hands.

For a brief moment, Fanya saw all the ancestors that had led to Peter's life, and a flash of her own ancestors. She sobbed at the realization of their possible loss to the evil that tried to absorb Peter's life force. The two women held her while she wept. Finally, Fanya asked, "What do we do now?"

"There are others who need our help," Atabey said.

"But for now, you should take time to absorb this," Mami Wata advised. "And do some training with us."

"Could he have made it so I could walk?" Fanya asked as they left the park.

Atabey stopped and put her hand over Fanya's heart. "Is that what you want in this life incarnation?"

Fanya shook her head and smiled, remembering previous lives, in other bodies of different shapes, sizes, and sex. "No, this body will do just fine. It has so far."

Note from the Author

I wrote this to explore how the African goddess Mami Wata and American Indian goddess Atabey support a woman as she comes to terms with the fatal abuse in her relationship. Too often society teaches that mistreatment is justified by a twisted sense of love. This story shows the evolution from victim to empowered through seeing the truth of her own strength. Fanya is also in a wheelchair, which is an aspect of the character, not the reason for her being abused.

— Linda D. Addison

Escape from Pleasant Point
An Evelyn Northe-Stewart Origin Story

Leanna Renee Hieber

1900 – Manhattan, by way of 1855 Manhattan

Do I begin this tale at the point where my enemy ran screaming down a ravine or do I begin at the beginning?

I suppose, in the interest of a narrative where such a dire result is cheered as a victory, one must first appreciate the struggle that precipitated it.

Here in this new era of the new world, *1900*... Can we even imagine such a number as this? Yet in order to tell this tale, I must recall the 1850s. A time when the world was much different, vastly more unfair and unjust. When I was a young woman. A time I would just as well have blocked out.

Dearest Granddaughter, you've pressed me for this tale for so long and I confess, I do not want to tell it. But seeing as though it might prove useful to a future case involving involuntary committal—or to support your aim of helpful ghostly narratives—perhaps it is my duty to tell you. Take these words, you and the spirits, and turn them into something that brings light to darkness.

The day my parents finally had enough of my "mad" connection to spirits, clairvoyance, premonitions and other visionary notions was the day my world turned helpless and hopeless, and damn it all if my worst days weren't yet ahead of me.

My parents were hard workers, factory workers, my father having fallen from money to desperation through a series of financial errors. In the 1840s, New York City was booming with labor and so much of it was rough and hard on the body, for my mother in the textile mill and my father in the ironworks.

I was raised in an atmosphere where only work and puritanical devotion to an angry God mattered. My aunt, bless her, was a respite of kindness and an empathetic mysticism, but I was not with her often, as she was far upstate. My awareness of spirits and the Sensitivities that moved me, of the way I intuited things about the world around me before hearing any of the details, were all out of place in a home where the only storytelling was a biblical parable and the only praise came if I kept quiet and did my chores early.

My best friends, my only friends, were specters. I couldn't often see the spirits, but I always felt them: a cool presence at my side, an eerie whisper on the breeze, and the unmistakable way they asked me to help them. This was done mostly by just acknowledging them. By asking them about their hearts and, in doing so, allowing the weight of what tethered them to the living to be levied and set free. I didn't know why presences were drawn to me like moths to a flame, but something about my soul's light drew them. Late into the evening, I would speak to them in whispers when I wouldn't be overheard, when I wouldn't be reprimanded or swatted for "talking to myself."

When I was around the age of ten, I wondered if was indeed mad; if the voices I occasionally heard or the sights I saw, the temperature that changed, were my own invention. I expressed this fear to one of my favorite ghosts, a young woman named Lina who had perished of scarlet fever on the site of our tenement building years prior. Lina responded to my fear with a soft murmur that caught on the breeze and landed on my ear, a proposition: "Test us."

Through the next week, the three or so presences most often drawn to me proved their truth to me in different ways by moving objects, by reporting something I could not have known that was proven true. I knew after these simple experiments that I was a part of something inexplicable but very real.

I cannot blame my family for being unimaginative. What I will decry is not being allowed my *own* imagination. What they deemed at first a "fancy" grew in their minds, like a disease, into something they feared with every fiber of their being. As my abilities became hard to hide, and as the occasional poltergeist action would be witnessed, the only thing that could be true was that I was courting the devil himself, that I was a witch or possessed. Corrupted.

That was the most painful thing, I think, that something I felt connected me to God could be thought so suspect. The spirits only wanted my understanding and care, and they cared for me in turn. That relationship has always been beautiful. Never evil.

When I turned sixteen, my powers became unmistakable and a new onslaught of presences was drawn into my orbit. My life, mind, energy and interactions became unmanageable without a mentor or training. I was told to pack some things, as we were "going on a trip." Something within me stirred, one of my preternatural instincts that said to pack as if I were never coming back. Terrified, I hoped this premonition was more dramatic than would pan out. I packed a few favorite books, a favorite dress, and the two simple pieces of heirloom jewelry I hadn't been asked to sell. Simple tactile belongings. My other most valuable treasures, the spirits that chose me as a haunt, went with me no matter where I roamed.

During the ride uptown, far uptown, past the limits of what really could be called the city, my destination queries remained unanswered. I stopped asking and remained silent as my father drove the borrowed hack and my mother refused to look at me.

As Manhattan narrowed in width and rose in elevation and the trees grew thicker and the road less trodden, we curved along the upper western part of the island, a dramatic landscape I would find beautiful if I weren't so unsettled.

The carriage stopped in front of a house that looked nice enough, a whitewashed wooden two-storied farmhouse with rugged countryside around it. A placard on the iron gate stated: PLEASANT POINT.

It did not feel pleasant.

There was commotion getting me and my bag down from the hack as I returned to pleading, begging someone to tell me why we had come there.

I don't remember exactly what was said to me—not that any words mattered, in the end. The ghosts who had bonded to me made quite a tumult on my behalf, swinging the gate, opening and slamming the doors of the hack, tearing at my bonnet and the clothes of two people quite ready to dispose of me.

"Evelyn Pierce?" called a woman in a white dress, something a nurse or a nun might wear. She was halfway up the jagged slate walk, having come out to inspect the commotion. "Come in, would you come have a chat with me over a cup of tea?"

I stormed ahead, not knowing what else to do. This woman knew my name. I was expected. A ghost tugged at the back of my hair, undoing pins, as if trying to drag me away. I wish I'd let them.

Looking ahead, a few forms were visible in the upper floor of the farmhouse; dimly backlit at curtained windows. Shadows listening.

"Please quiet down," I murmured to the spirits as I stepped ahead and into the walk. "For all of our safety."

When I looked behind me, my parents had retreated to the carriage and it was already speeding away. My bag-laden arms shook with shock and I felt very weak as I turned ahead to see the woman holding the door open for me. Her face was blank; the gamesome expression gone.

"I am Mrs. Stone, your nurse. Mr. Stone, my husband, your doctor. He will see you now in his study. Be a good girl and go on ahead."

The only word that mattered next was the one that had been already written on my intake form. A condemnation. A lie. I was not ill. Plenty of people in the world see spirits or have had an inexplicable ghostly encounter. And yet. . .

I soon found myself in a small study with an unfriendly-looking man, Mr. Stone, dressed in a white laboratory coat with an unsettling glint in his eye. He opened a file to a simple intake form on the desk between us. By my name, Evelyn Pierce, glared a word that to this day strikes at my heart, a wound that will never heal:

DELUSIONAL

Seething rage flooded my veins, my cheeks, the tips of my ears. The idea that this had been written ahead, arranged, that this form already damned me before I could even offer testimony—this was, and remains, unforgivable. I continue to fight for laws that decry such false pretense and institutional imprisonment without just cause.

Panicked, I ran from the room. I fled the house and careened down the crooked slate walk, stubbing my toes and not caring a whit, my eyes only on the gravel lane beyond. There were lights and smoke in the distance. We were uptown but not so far as to be without recourse; this wasn't the wilderness, this was still Manhattan. . .

The gate was locked as I threw myself against it, trying my weight against the resistant iron hinges. A sudden, sharp sting blossomed on my neck. My hand grazed where the sharp pain was focused and my fingertips found a long needle lodged there, as if it had been shot from some kind of gun or bow. My hand came away bloody and the world went dark.

I have no idea how long I was under the influence of sedatives. Confined to a bed, while I was not physically restrained, my body was numb.

In those first moments coming to after my escape attempt, the most terrifying things were the sounds I heard. Footsteps went down a hall, a low, detached, unkind voice I recognized as Mr. Stone was at the doorway of another inmate. He went into a room down the hall and I heard the clatter of what sounded like chains, scrambling back, and a muffled noise of desperation.

Terror seized me and the jolt gave me enough strength to regain my feet, stumble forward to close the door that was ajar but that I could not lock. I placed a rickety chair sat next to my bed under the doorknob and retreated to the shadowed corner of the dark room, curling up, my knees to my chest. The patterns in the wooden walls, the knots in the old wood were perhaps what I remembered most in those moments of cowering; how they shifted and danced in nightmarish, moonlit mockery of my state.

I didn't know what else to do there, curled in the corner of a tiny room with no furnishings other than a cot, that chair and my unopened carpet bag, but to make a pointed cry to the heavens.

I clenched my fists so hard, I broke the skin of my palm, blood bubbling up between my fingertips, flooding under my nails.

A small swath at the hem of my skirt had torn during the tumult of my arrival, and I ripped the piece of cloth free and clutched it. My hands refused to unclench, but the fabric at least offset the pain and captured the blood.

Weeping not just tears, I used whatever talents I had within me to cry out inwardly, shrieking with my spirit, for help. I could not see nor hear all the words of spirits as expertly as other Sensitives and Spiritualists do, but I did know they were listening. While I had been categorized as delusional, I never once doubted my abilities and the spirits never once doubted me.

A wash of icy air enveloped me and a distant murmur glanced off my ear, the voice I could most easily recognize as Lina—the dear spirit who spoke to me the most. "What can we do?"

"Help me," I murmured to the spirits hovering all around me, their cold chill making my breath clouds of vapor. "Help me and any here who I don't see but whose various sufferings I have no trouble imagining." I was not alone in this place, as had been indicated from the figures first glimpsed in the window, from the creaks of floorboards, the occasional voice or muffled sob; that chilling shift of rattling chain down the hall.

There were far more ghosts present in this place than just the usual few who liked to float in my wake. This place was terribly haunted and my desperation had brought them all forth, a glowing, hazy, eerily luminous cloud manifest before me.

In response to my plea, the cold air became a whirlwind, a spirit cyclone that expanded and then tore away out a dirty window. All went quiet as the room warmed and I could no longer feel any presences with me. Only the sounds of shifting floorboards down the hall. A sigh. An all-too-human sob, muffled into a pillow.

Had ghosts deserted me too? Left me to whatever fate had in store? I would not have answers to this in the immediate.

The next passage of time was impossible to quantify. Sedatives must have been mixed into the porridge we were given, into the water, perhaps the occasional cup of tea offered as a treat but instead was a trap. I have to assume other indignities occurred, to me, to all of us. We were bruised. I was aching. I couldn't be sure of my mind or what was terror at work while the nightmare of my compromised agency and autonomy continued to unfold. Not knowing exactly what was happening was a part of the torture. I assumed the worst and was likely correct. I may also have blocked things from my mind entirely. I do not dwell on it, as I refuse to let injustices define me.

The sharpest of my memories during the next interminable days were those moments when the residents of the Point were gathered together in a sparse parlor with a meager fire and floral wallpaper that was peeling at corners. We would be called down for that occasional treat of "tea." There we sat, drooping, four of us, the other women given the same sedatives as I had been given.

It was clear to me from the furnishings and the state of the other inmates that this was a place that was thought to be a respectable step above the grim, dark wards off on small islands beyond. Here was a depository where families who could afford something appearing better than a cement cell could send their "wayward" or inconvenient women, a fine-enough place that might help them sleep better at night. I hoped anyone who had sent a supposed loved one there didn't sleep well ever again.

I got to know the other women of the house as well as was possible or allowed.

During my time, there were four other "residents"—prisoners, really, but Virginia, the longest resident, a wiry, dark-haired, olive-skinned woman, spoke of others. There had been more but were now "only four." That the numbers had been "whittled away'" was terrifying and implied we were all in grave danger.

"What happened to them?" I asked Virginia in a whisper when Mrs. Stone wasn't paying attention. We were not supposed to speak or fraternize. Virginia shrugged. It wasn't that she was nonchalant; I could see from the nearly black circles under her eyes that she was bone-tired and soul-beaten. About to give out. Give up.

Mr. Stone arrived, sweeping in dressed in an ill-fitting frock coat and a too-tight cravat to ask us intrusive questions. I told the truth about my experiences with spirits. He did not like the answers.

"And this is why you have been deemed delusional, Evelyn."

I glared at him, recoiling from his use of my familiar name. I desired no closeness with this man who I knew in my heart would do nothing more than cause us harm and pain. My instincts about a person were not usually wrong. A blessing of my Sensitivities in some ways, but a curse if one can't easily flee from the danger one presents.

"I am Miss Pierce to you," I countered. "You have not earned the right of familiarity."

I would have loved for a spirit to move through him, right then, to lift everything in the room, but spirits didn't always do the most dramatic or the most helpful thing right in the moment. I could not predict nor entirely rely on them.

Something changed for the worse in Stone's face, and the woman whose full name I did not know, who I knew only as Virginia, came to my defense.

"What does it matter if she does see or talk to spirits, or doesn't, what does it matter, who does it hurt, why do you care?" Virginia cried. "Leave her alone. Leave us *alone*." She spat at him. Stone lunged and struck her across the cheek.

"No, please don't hurt her—" I cried, and was struck just the same as Stone whirled back to me. The hatred in those eyes, eyes that clearly didn't see us as human or as deserving of any sort of kindness or mercy, will haunt me forever. We were subjects to him. Subjugated.

Mrs. Stone calmly, as if she hadn't noticed the violence, walked over to Virginia with a small, clear tincture in a glass cup. Virginia glared at her captors. Mrs. Stone stared back at her emotionlessly. Virginia drank the tincture.

Stone seemed uninterested in either of us then and moved on to check on the woman I'd not yet spoken with, as she seemed never to be conscious enough to do so. An emaciated, mousy-haired woman sitting in the corner, propped up against the wall, head drooping.

"Astra, how are you feeling today?" he asked.

"Tired," she said quietly. "Why did you restrain me again?" she asked mournfully.

"Because you had another seizure. For your own good."

He patted her head and she lowered it, leaning against the wall with a hopeless expression.

"That's a good girl," Stone said in a revulsive tone.

I was presented the same small tincture in a glass cup, brought by Mrs. Stone.

"To keep you calm," she said quietly. "You'll find it helps you adjust."

She stared at me, waiting for me to drink. Holding the solution in my mouth, I allowed a little to be swallowed to register movement as if I'd taken the whole thing. She nodded and walked out of the parlor.

I turned my head and dribbled the rest of the fluid into the scrap of fabric I'd been clutching so that I wouldn't dig my nails into my palm to the point of bleeding anymore. My hope was that I would be sharper than they assumed. To be able to react in the moment for my own safety.

"Hello," I said quietly to the woman next to me whose downcast gaze was staring at the floral embroidery on my dress. One of only two sets of clothing I owned, I feared it would soon wear down like these other faded flowers around this dreadful parlor.

"Susan doesn't speak," Virginia explained. "Accident, so it was said when she was dropped off by a man, perhaps her husband, who knows. She suddenly became inconvenient, like all of us. Disposable." The woman spat the words.

"That's enough." The matron clucked her tongue, the sound of our talking having brought her back to the parlor threshold.

"Enough indeed," Virginia muttered. "We've all had enough."

"How can you bear it? As a woman yourself?" I asked the matron. "I'm not mad and I doubt any of these women are in any way so broken that we cannot make our own way. We are victims of *circumstance*, not—"

"No one who *is* mad *thinks* they're mad. And it's true, not everyone here is mad. Some are here because they were a drain on their families," she said, nodding toward Susan. "We're here to make sure no one is left for dead," she said with forced, insincere cheer.

I knew then that I had no ally in her and that she would not stand against Mr. Stone's abuses. Those who think in such a way as she, who have contorted assault, undermining and lying into something they deem to be aid cannot be of help to those of us seeking value in ourselves or in the hope of an equitable world.

"You're too uppity and it's unbecoming of a young lady," she said with clipped words. "You need more medicine."

She brought me another round and I did my trick with the trace of a swallow, waiting until she huffed back out of the room before I turned to deposit the rest into my scrap of fabric.

I noticed Virginia watching me closely, nodding, indicating she would adopt the same practice. It was as if the idea of growing stronger made her so. I could see and feel the shift in her. It wasn't that I could read minds, exactly, but I did have a keen sense of them, and I would need the nuance of that talent in the coming days.

If there was supposed to be a "treatment'" regimen, that was news to us. It was just heaping beratement and, as has already been glimpsed, abuse. It should go without saying we were only allowed into the parlor, a washroom or our narrow, cell-like rooms. We could not inspect or explore any of the pantry or medicine stores nor any part of the rest of the building; doors in and out were iron-clad and with locks impossible to pick (Virginia assured me she'd tried them all many times) and wide bolts. Windows were sealed shut.

We made the bonds we could between each other, as best as was manageable without being shushed or under fear of reprisal or further sedation. I promised Susan if we got out that we'd learn sign language together. It was the first smile I'd seen out of her since my arrival.

But finally, a visitor brought clarity and a second chance for all of us.

I sat with weak, cold tea, rereading one of the five books I'd packed with me that I'd read countless times already—wishing I'd been able to bring a trunk full of Gothic adventures to commiserate with all the trapped women under thumbs of unimaginative men whose small-minded purpose seemed fulfilled in controlling them—when I heard a pleasant voice at the front door.

"Hello, Mrs. Stone? I'm here with my mother. We corresponded."

"Ah, yes, Mr. West, come in."

"Is Mr. Stone here?"

"No, he's at his chemist shop, a few shifts a week to keep up with the new advancements in medicine and pharmaceutical aids!"

"Of course. May I bring my mother into the parlor as you show me around the facility?"

"Happily, Mr. West."

A handsome, light-brown-haired man, clean-shaven and bright-eyed, entered the room wheeling an older woman in a fine dress into our parlor. Her face looked deadened, lifeless; however, the sense I had of her energy and her thoughts were anything but.

Mr. West bent over the woman, pressed his hands to her shoulders gently, and kissed the top of her head. I ached for such a kindness. As if he could feel that sentiment as if I'd reached out and grabbed him, his eyes pinned me directly, and the look that crossed his face was one that said everything. He was angry. His look at me was a promise. I felt like he understood something about me. It was a look that changed our lives.

He retreated and his expression of righteous anger was like a spark of fire on dry kindling: hope.

Had we just gained an advocate?

There was a silence.

Even Astra was awake, looking at the newcomer through dark, bleary eyes from her place by the window, hands trembling.

I could feel the temperature in the room plummet. The older

woman, likely in her mid to late forties, brought ghosts in her wake. All I could see was the hazy, glowing nimbus of them, but there were several flanking her wheelchair.

Mrs. West's drooping head snapped up suddenly, making everyone start, including the ghosts, whose cloudy forms flew back, startled.

"All right, girls," she began, in a matter-of-fact tone which spoke of years of taking charge. "Which one of you sent the message?"

We stared at her.

She stared back at each of us, searching our faces. We turned uneasily to one another.

"Come now, we've not much time," she continued briskly. "Which of you sent the spirits to me, asking for help? Miss Lina was *most* insistent that we respond, and we came as soon as we were able."

The chipped teacup I'd been holding clattered to its saucer and I raised a fluttering hand. I was too frightened to do or say anything else. Mrs. West snapped her falcon-sharp gaze, the exact inverse of how she'd been presented to the room, to me.

"Ah. Indeed. What's your name, child?"

"Evel. . . Evelyn," I stammered. "I'm Evelyn and Lina has haunted me since I was little."

"Well, I heard your cry," she said, tapping her temple as if she'd heard my inner screams in her mind. Perhaps she had. "Lina cares for you very much and she's *appalled* by the state of things here, for all of you." Mrs. West declared. "But ladies, you're going to have to play along. We have to indulge a game and set a trap. Then I promise you'll be out of this place and somewhere with better care and opportunity. Do you trust me?"

"Do we have a choice?" Virginia asked warily. "Trust isn't something we've found bodes well for us here."

"You do have a choice. You can test me and my son. You could alert the missus that I'm plotting and they could subdue me. Though doing so would delay our strategy significantly."

"*Our* strategy. . ." Virginia narrowed her weary, dark-circled eyes. "And what might that be?"

"To get out."

Susan rose to her feet.

"What do we do?" I asked eagerly.

I turned to see if Astra was in agreement, but her head was resting against the wall as she struggled to stay awake. She was the one I was frankly the most worried about. The red marks around her ankle told me everything, her condition making them treat her more like an animal than a human, and she was clearly the most heavily sedated of all of us. I hadn't gotten the chance to encourage her to share my tricks of rejecting the sedation. Mrs. West followed my gaze.

It was then that Mr. West and Mrs. Stone returned. Mrs. West's head immediately drooped again.

"Excellent, Mrs. Stone, thank you for being so forthcoming. I'm sure my mother will do as well as she is able, better here than on those dreary island wards; terrible, aren't they?"

"We are far superior to any of the wards you might find, for this. . . price. . . anywhere else in the region."

Virginia and I couldn't help but snort in unison. Mrs. Stone flashed a warning look at us, and Mr. West pretended he hadn't heard anything, moving to stand in the threshold of the parlor with Mrs. Stone following.

"Very good. I'll be checking back in."

"Oh, that won't be necessary. We actually recommend against—"

"I'll be checking back in and I won't be questioned," Mr. West repeated firmly.

Clearly, the Stones were used to the type of person who wanted to get rid of someone and pretend they no longer existed. Her fluster at his insistence otherwise felt like a victory, turning our situation around to her discomfort for once.

"All right. . ." Mr. West was on his way.

That evening, as our gruel was served in the parlor, Mr. Stone returned and greeted Mrs. West with more kindness than he ever had us, surely advised to do so by Mrs. Stone. The Wests likely had paid more money. After all, their clothing was finer than ours, and the son would be watching.

Mrs. West, having told us nothing about what was next, only looked blankly at Mr. Stone as he asked questions she did not answer, pinning him with a fixed stare that would have been disconcerting, did I not feel it was for our benefit.

That night, as I tossed in bed, feeling all my sensitivities open and raw, my gift of preternatural levels of empathy making me feel the sting of every bruise my fellow inmates suffered, every indignity, Lina appeared before me, the only spirit I could recognize every time, the strength of our bond having made her more material to my eye. Hers was a youthful face I could just barely make out in a mist.

"The spirits of this place are preparing for a confrontation. You need to prepare too, psychically, for what's to come."

"What do I need to do?" I murmured to the spirit.

"Be ready to gather up all the pain you have experienced and forge it into something you could wield like a knife. All the haunts of this dread house, with the help of our new friend, will turn pain back against the source. Soon it will be time to take up your weapon."

I didn't want to meditate on the indignities, but I did think about pressing pain, derision, insult, abuse, imprisonment and injustice in my hands, compacting terror into an invisible blade whose energy pulsed in my hand, hot and pointed.

Within two days, Mr. West returned and asked to inspect all of Mr. Stone's medicines. During this visit, Mrs. Stone was called away by an urgent telegram about an ill relative and there was consternation between the married couple. We could hear commotion behind the thick, locked doors.

"The moment the wife is out, he's going to return to the parlor and to us," Mrs. West instructed. "I will bid him come close, and when I do, if you would indeed like your freedom as seems quite evident, we strike."

"Physical strike?" Virginia asked eagerly. "It would be only fair."

"If you like. You'll see. Follow my lead, please."

"What about your son?"

"He will be documenting the back of the house for evidence in a case against this place."

When Mr. Stone, looking as though he wanted to hit something and here was a room full of targets, came into the parlor, Mrs. West turned her wheelchair into his path.

"Come here, Mr. Stone, let me take a look at you," she said, in a grandmotherly way. "Let us take a look at you," she repeated. Stone, puzzled, leaned down over her. "Spirits," she called.

Mrs. West slapped both her wrinkled hands over Mr. Stone's ears and her thumbs pressed hard onto each of his temples. Every spirit I had ever counted or felt in this place, the ten inherent to the building and the four that frequented me, all dove at him in one glowing, ice-cold torrent.

Mr. Stone shrieked in pain and surprise, wavering on his feet. Mrs. West's grasp remained a firm vise grip.

"You will feel what you have done to these women turn back upon yourself." Mrs. West said calmly, this larger, stronger man seemingly magnetized to her clutch. "You will, for a moment, walk in their bruised feet and feel the stings on their cheeks and every unspeakable act; you cannot escape your sins."

"*See*, now," she raised her voice to the spirits, who clawed at him with incorporeal hands, causing his eyes to roll back in his head as his mouth sagged in a wail.

"Girls, come, show him what the receiving end of injustice looks like. *Feels* like. Add in the pain that's been done to you and give it away. Do not hold on to it any longer. Press it to his forehead and release your burdens."

Virginia leapt forward and gripped the back of his head, while Mrs. West still held him by the temples; she pressed the heel of her palm against his forehead, grinding it roughly.

"For every time you've hit me," Virginia seethed, "may you feel the same, as a thunderclap."

There came another astonished cry and Stone's chest went concave.

Susan stepped forward; her expression in her silence held volumes, the anger in her eyes palpable. I had no idea what had befallen her to know what to empathize with, but she put her hand around his throat, and without even squeezing, he began to choke.

Astra was on her feet, surprisingly, the strongest I'd ever seen her. Clear-eyed and focused. I avoided looking at her ankles, where the bindings or shackles for when she seized rubbed her skin raw; I saw that sight often when I closed my eyes and I knew that agony propelled her forward.

All Astra did was place a fingertip to the center of Stone's forehead and press hard. The man began to weep. He fell to the floor and Mrs. West turned her body so that she was still holding on to him, her arms expertly strong from what must have been a long time in her wheelchair from an accident or change in physical circumstance she had yet to disclose.

I approached slowly. I did not want to think of all the cruelties. I thought only of the pain I had compressed with my palms, the focus of my energies into a thin blade.

"I do not feel called to redemptive violence but I do, very much, believe every violent and overpowering act should have repercussions," I said quietly. "Who is delusional now?"

I drove the psychic knife I'd been cultivating into the center of his forehead, as if splitting open his mind with our experiences, forcing him to live through what he'd put any of us through, from the mundane dismissive cruelties to the most vile of violations. As I had empathic gifts that were larger than the common human allotment, so might he then feel our wounds all the more deeply. Perhaps he did now see the spirits as they began to echo and return his mounting wail that had a new tone of terror to it.

"Yes, girls," Mrs. West said to the spirits who were swarming around her and Stone's crumpled body. "You who lost your lives here due to neglect and those directly by his hand or his deadly chemicals, it is your turn." The older woman released him as if she were expelling a demon, throwing him aside.

Scrambling back, pursued by spirits, Stone tore from the room, down the hall, flinging open the door, running into the back property.

We followed to the point where the back lot fell away to a ravine; beyond that, further still, lay sharper drops towards the Hudson River far beyond. He flung himself down, out of view. We could not tell how far.

It was such a whirlwind of events that led to this precarious edge where my life turned for the better, all of us waiting for a sound from below.

I could see and sense each of our bodies uncoiling from tension, the unraveling of thread not from a piece of fabric but from a human form disentangling, releasing its knots of pain. The body stores terrors in the muscles. One has to take care when releasing a clenched heart and a flinching soul.

Susan just stared ahead, her eyes fire.

I watched horror slough off Virginia like leeches falling off her olive-skinned forearms. Her hands were clasped white-knuckled in prayer— or to keep them from shaking. Astra was tucked on to Virginia's arm, leaning on her wiry form, but strength remained in Astra's bruised limbs.

Mrs. West presided with us, having maneuvered her wheelchair carefully out the door and along the uneven lot, in silence.

Finally, I broke the quiet with my query. "Is he. . ."

"No, he's not dead. . ." Mrs. West replied.

A raving shriek confirmed it, followed by a bright mass of luminous spirits and a cold wind that swept down the ravine. Spirits, diving and wailing, whooshed past my ears. It was their turn to give him a piece of their pain, and I will never forget those righteous banshee screams.

"He may not be dead but he now resides in a place of punishment righteously dealt," Mrs. West explained. "We'll let the spirits take care of him going forward, if he makes it back out of that ravine. There are plenty of ghosts in that house and they're hardly finished with him. They just needed us to crack open the psychic doors. We'll be taking our findings to the press. We'll keep your names out of it. But this place will be shut down, mark my words, and he, well, he won't be in a state to do anything to anyone."

"What about Mrs. Stone?" Virginia asked.

"My son Peter arranged the telegram that sent her off. When she returns, it will be up to her to discover and to do with her husband what she will, I suppose; I don't know, none of us will be here by then."

Mrs. West clapped her hands, expertly wheeling her chair around. I followed her towards the house. The other women stayed, standing watch.

The raving screams, the swarm of spirits, I will never forget the sounds or the sights. But I preferred to take my delight in not considering Mr. Stone anymore.

Mrs. West's strong forearms had wheeled herself with impressive speed, considering the uneven ground. I helped her chair up the front steps.

"You know, dear, my son and I, must tell you, we're not Wests at all. We're actually Northes. Peter and Sybil Northe. Until you girls were free,

I didn't want to risk our actual names, as we're known to much of the city. But I don't like lying to you. No more lies. My late husband was a lawyer and I was an unspoken partner in his firm. So, when I say that we're building a case, I know the law and I mean it. The law may not be on women's side as of yet, but we're building towards it, piece by piece."

I nodded, all the more heartened. "Thank you, Mrs. Northe. I don't know what we'd have done had you and your gifts, with the help of spirits, not heard my call."

In the parlor, the room seemed brighter. The flowers on the walls seemed less dreary. There was a pleasant scent. I realized it was rose-hip tea, steaming from a fine pot.

Mr. Peter Northe stood behind a tea tray I'd never seen—perhaps he'd brought it out from Stone's quarters. He was pouring cups of tea as I entered.

"How do you take your tea, Miss Pierce?" the young man asked brightly.

It was this kindness that opened my floodgates. I broke down into uncontrollable sobs, sinking to my knees.

Mr. Northe came over with a tea tray. "I did not mean to make you cry," he said.

"I know you didn't. But no one has asked me how I'd like my tea since my aunt—she was the only one who—"

"Understood you? Your gifts?" Mrs. Northe finished.

I nodded. "My last kindnesses."

"I would like to know how you take your tea. I would like to know anything about your preferences, really."

"Peter, don't be forward—" Mrs. Northe waved a hand at her son.

"No, it's. . . I. . . It's fine," I said, looking into Peter's eyes. "I am very grateful to you both. More than I can possibly say. And I like just a tiny bit of cream and sugar, just a drop."

Peter smiled and made the tea per my request, handing me a cup, there on the floor, and sitting down nearby. Mrs. Northe reached out to stroke my hair.

I sipped tea and closed my eyes, relishing the taste of something precious. "This scent of roses from this teacup reminds me of that beloved aunt's garden."

"Tell us about it. Sharing joy will heal the wounds of this place and you must heal."

"She and I would sit in her garden and dream up mystical offerings and sacred spaces. I wanted to build a chapel, Episcopalian in honor of her tradition, for weary travelers outside the city. Just before her death, she'd actually begun construction on a little chapel with her funds; I'd like to think it's still being built by her spirit."

"Did it not go forward?" Mrs. Northe asked.

"It was halted after her death, and nothing I could say could resurrect it; my parents hated the 'pomp and circumstance' of my aunt's traditions. I'd like to think she's watching over us. She was always quiet; I'd wanted her spirit to speak to me—"

"She is here, summoned by your care, and she promises to be closer at your side. Regret fills her for all that came to pass."

"You see—hear her?" I asked, getting to my feet with Mr. Northe's help, and I didn't realize I'd kept holding on to him after.

"I do," Mrs. Northe answered gently. "She's hanging back."

"Will you teach me?" I exclaimed. "Will you tutor me in your psychic talents, how to better see, hear the spirit world?"

"As best I can, dear girl, as best I can."

I turned to Peter excitedly, wanting to share my joy at the spirit of a relative found, at the idea of a mentor. We both stared at the place on my forearm where he'd grasped me and where I'd clasped him back, as if our touch were the most natural thing in the world. I wanted more of it. It was the right kind of touch. We all know that feeling. And can always tell the difference.

"What. . .is next?" I gulped, suddenly uneasy. "I can't. . . I can't go back; surely you know that."

"We wouldn't dream of it," Mrs. Northe stated. "We've a boarding-house. You're welcome to stay. We've connections to respectable work."

"Yes, thank you."

Now, dearest Eve, my namesake, my great treasure. From the moment I introduced Peter and his real name, knowing mine, you had to know something had turned for the better; why else would I become his wife? The breadth of our romance, our adventures in life (and in reconnaissance), committed to aiding those as we could, and admittedly too-short time together before his illness—all is a story for another day.

I included these additional moments in this narrative, my dear granddaughter, to bring us back around to kindness, to promote it, to live into it. Peter proved to me that there was another road for a man than the choices Mr. Stone made, a presence that had become so all-consuming for us, we lost track of a man's multitudes and possibilities. But Stone was one man. There are others like him, to be sure, but we must try to build a world where cruelties are not allowed to grow more powerful at anyone's expense. Would we could imprint all the woes onto every culprit to force them to see their errors. But I would like to think such a thunder-strike rumbles other hearts and minds, even in a cosmic way. May we be that cosmic rupture, together.

I promised the spirit world, that day, that I would listen for a call for help, into the future; to be the kind of saving grace Mrs. Sybil Northe proved to me. Little did I know, Eve, that it would be your father's call for help, trapped, bound against his will, that would lead me to seek out his imprisoned soul and everything that followed as your mother rescued him. May we all hear the call of someone helpless who needs us.

Don't ever ask about these circumstances again, Eve, my darling, gift of my life.

I have survived so that I might usher your mother and you, and the talents of our friends, into safe places where such gifts as ours could be cherished, nourished and utilized.

Let us talk only of what is to come, fighting our good fights, listening to the calls the external spirits and our own inner spirit asks of us. In spirit, in action.

Now and through every age.

Note from the Author

If you enjoyed the heroine of this tale, you're in luck, as she is the Spiritualist, psychically inclined and beautifully haunted matriarch of three of my Gothic gaslamp fantasy series. Evelyn Northe first appears in my Magic Most Foul trilogy, beginning with Darker Still. She continues through that trilogy, then plays a starring role in the Eterna Files trilogy and is the beloved "Gran" to Eve Whitby, the woman she is writing this account for, in the Spectral City series.

Evelyn came to my mind and heart as an adult. Her not wanting to tell this story to me, or to anyone, meant her youth and early days were entirely blocked to me until a moment during the Spectral City when a woman is about to be taken away to an institution against her will. Evelyn's reaction against that illuminated these events for me, in a glaring, terrible lightning strike into pitch darkness. I understood with solemn clarity why she fights so hard for women's agency and independence.

I am driven to write historical narratives because strong women aren't a new invention; fighting fiercely for one's own safety and sanctity is a tale as old as time. I involve spirits and Sensitives, as the history of Spiritualism is directly entwined with women's rights, suffrage and autonomy. We must never take for granted ground that has been gained, as we must continue to do all we can to fight for, strengthen and broaden all women's rights.

I hope readers who connect with Evelyn will join me and live into this woman's glory and mentorship; she is my Northe star, after all, and I have been guided by her light for most of my career.

— Leanna Renee Hieber

Daughter of Echidna

Nicholas Kaufmann

1.

In the car, Mom clenches her teeth, making the muscles of her jaw contract under the skin. Her grip is tight on the steering wheel. Kenna looks the other way, out the passenger-side window. Today is Sarah Lieberman's birthday, and although Kenna doesn't really want to go to her party, Mom insists on taking her there anyway.

"It's important to have friends," Mom says as Kenna keeps her eyes out the window. She can't look at Mom's angry, grinding jaw. She doesn't like how it makes her feel.

"Sarah and I haven't been friends since fourth grade," Kenna reminds her, as if Mom ought to know all the ins and outs of her life at school, even though whenever she asks how Kenna's day went, the answer is always the same: fine. She's in sixth grade now. That's two whole grades since she and Sarah used to insist on sitting next to each other in class, playing together during recess, having sleepovers. She doesn't remember how it ended, only that it did.

"She invited you to her birthday party, didn't she?" Mom asks. It's not a real question, so Kenna doesn't answer. "That means she's still your friend. She wants you there."

Kenna sits in silence, playing with one coppery red ringlet above her ear. What if Sarah only wants her at the party to pick on her? What if everyone there makes fun of her the whole time? She's not sure that's something Sarah would do, but then again, she's not sure it's not. A person can change a lot between fourth grade and sixth.

"It's important to have people you can talk to," Mom says. "I wish I did."

Kenna thinks she's going to add *when I was your age*, but she stops there. Does Mom not have any friends? Kenna thinks back, but she can't remember meeting any. Sometimes, Dad says Mom doesn't need anyone but him, which ought to sound romantic but doesn't.

Kenna looks at Mom, who looks more sad than angry now. In a way, that's better. Sad feels safer than angry. But Kenna knows she's not getting out of going to Sarah's party. Sometimes, it seems like Mom wants her out of the house as much as possible. Kenna was signed up for gymnastics, Little League, *and* drama workshop. It's too much. She told Mom that, but it didn't change anything. Frankly, she's surprised she even has time to go to Sarah's stupid birthday party.

Mom drops her off in front of the Lieberman house and tells her not to forget to give Sarah the birthday card they bought at the drug store. Kenna waves goodbye with the sparkly red birthday card envelope, as if to say *I know, stop babying me*. She presses the doorbell. Mom's car idles at the curb. She won't leave until Kenna's inside. It's a safety thing. It's also really embarrassing. Kenna hopes the other girls don't see. Finally, the door opens and Sarah's mom, Mrs. Lieberman, greets her warmly and ushers her inside, letting her know the others are in the kitchen. Kenna hears Mom drive away as the front door closes behind her and has a moment of low-grade panic. There's no escape now.

Mrs. Lieberman brings her into the kitchen, where Sarah and four other girls are sitting around the table. Kenna recognizes two of the girls from school. She doesn't know the other two and figures they must be from Sarah's temple. (That's what they call their church, isn't it? A temple?) There's a big cake in the middle of the table with Elsa and Anna from *Frozen* painted in icing and a sparkling candle on top in the shape of the number 11. Even though she doesn't want to be there,

Kenna's relieved she didn't miss the candle being blown out. That's the most important part of a birthday party.

"Hey, Sarah," she says awkwardly from the kitchen doorway.

Sarah squeals Kenna's name and comes over to give her a big hug, and just like that, it's like they're best friends again. Kenna sits at the table with the others, and Sarah blows out the candle. Mrs. Lieberman serves cake to everyone. Kenna gets half of Anna's face in her icing, which she finds hilarious, and everyone laughs along with her. Sarah opens the cards everyone brought, including Kenna's, though she almost forgot to hand hers over. (Later, when she tells Mom about the party, she'll leave that part out.) Then, when Sarah is ready to open her parents' presents, her dad, Mr. Lieberman, comes into the kitchen in a blue dress shirt, his sleeves rolled up along his hairy arms to his elbows, and a plain black skullcap on his head. He puts one arm around Mrs. Lieberman, and even though his touch is gentle, not rough, Kenna can't help but flinch right there at the table. Sarah's parents kiss. Kenna's parents would *never* kiss in front of other people. They don't even kiss in front of her.

The other girls laugh behind their hands, but it's not because of the kiss. It's because they saw Kenna flinch and now they think she's weird. Her face burns with humiliation. She was right. They're all making fun of her. That's the reason she was invited after all. They were just waiting for the right moment. She should never have come. She fumes silently and wills her tears to stay away while Sarah opens her presents.

Afterward, the children are ushered outside to play in the backyard. It's warm and sunny, and everyone's shadow is twice as big as they are. Kenna wishes she had a springtime birthday like Sarah, but hers is in February, the coldest, darkest month. No one wants to come to a birthday party in February. For this reason and so many others, Kenna believes her life is cursed.

The girls are supposed to stay in the backyard, but there's a new house being built in the empty lot next door that Sarah wants to explore, so of course they all have to. The other girls run off, squealing and laughing. Kenna hangs back. She's the odd one out.

The other girls run around a wooden beam that will one day be part of the new house, circling it like sharks. Kenna watches and kicks at the dirt. Her foot hits something that feels like a stone, but when she looks down, she sees it's got an odd shape. She digs it free of the earth.

It's a small statue of a woman's body. Her arms and head are missing, which reminds Kenna of some famous old museum statue. She rubs her thumb over it, brushing away the dirt and feeling the two small bumps of the headless woman's breasts, the subtle folds of the gown she's wearing. Where did it come from? Did one of the other girls drop it? Remembering how they laughed at her, she tucks the statue into her pocket. When the girls are called back inside, she doesn't tell anyone what she found.

Sarah's big furry collie is named Hamantaschen, which draws laughter from the girls from temple but not from Kenna, who doesn't get it and feels left out yet again. She spends the remaining half hour before Mom is scheduled to pick her up watching Sarah and the others try to get Hamantaschen to sit. They yell "Sit! Sit! Sit!" until the dog finally sits, bending to their will.

When Mom arrives to take her home, Kenna says goodbye to Sarah and the others, but they're too preoccupied with Hamantaschen to do more than mutter and wave. On the drive home, Mom is quieter than before. There's a red bruise like a ring around her wrist. Was it there before? Kenna can't tell. She's losing track of which bruises are new.

She doesn't tell Mom about the little stone statue in her pocket. It's hers, and she likes having a secret no one else knows about. A *good* secret for a change.

2.

It's after nine, which means lights out, but Kenna's up, hiding under her covers behind her closed bedroom door and reading by the beam of a flashlight. It's a book for school, but this time, it's interesting enough that she *wants* to read it. An encyclopedia of Greek mythology.

Her favorite Greek myth is Theseus and the Minotaur, but even though she's tempted to skip ahead to it, she promised herself she would read the book in order. Tonight's chapter is on Echidna, one of the oldest gods. She had the upper body of a beautiful woman and the lower body of a fearsome serpent. She was immortal, unable to grow old or die, and Kenna, completely enthralled by the idea, imagines Echidna is still around somewhere, sleeping under a bridge or hiding in a drain pipe.

Dad's raised voice comes from down the hall outside her bedroom. Kenna freezes. Mom's lowered voice warns Dad that he'll wake Kenna. She wishes she were asleep. She knows the sound of a fight when she hears it.

"I told you I didn't want her hanging around with those people," Dad yells. He won't keep his voice down, no matter how much Mom asks. He never does.

Kenna doesn't like the way he says *those people*, like there's something wrong with Sarah's family just because they're different. Even though she and Sarah are probably on the outs forever now, Kenna feels the urge to defend her, to tell Dad he's wrong. But she knows better than to *ever* tell Dad he's wrong.

She switches off the flashlight. She feels safer in the dark.

"It's important for her to have friends," Mom answers. She's angry too, and forgets to keep her voice down.

"She can have all the friends she wants, just not *them*! How many times do I have to tell you? They're not like us. You can't trust them."

"Who she makes friends with isn't up to you," Mom says.

A pit opens in Kenna's stomach. Mom has made a terrible mistake. She talked back to Dad. Kenna hears the hard, familiar sound of a hand smacking skin. However, this time, the shouts and screams are followed by a sound she hasn't heard before, something heavy thumping and rolling. It reminds her of the sound her rubber ball made when it bounced down the stairs.

She pushes the book and the flashlight out of the bed, hoping both of them land on the rug quietly enough not to be heard, and wraps herself in the covers. She knows better than to leave her bedroom now, or to even look like she's awake if Dad checks in on her. She won't close her eyes, though, not unless she hears him twisting the doorknob, then she'll pretend to be asleep until he leaves. She stares out into the darkness of her bedroom. The little statue she found in the dirt behind Sarah's house stands on the bedside table, where she put it when she got home. In the dark, it looks like a miniature cemetery monument.

Mom's pained cries come from the foot of the stairs, followed by Dad's footsteps stomping down to her. He tells her to stop being so dramatic, that she'll be fine, then makes a phone call. He tells whoever is on the other end to send an ambulance.

"My wife tripped and fell down the stairs," he says.

Kenna stares at the statue, concentrates on it, until there's nothing else, nothing but the armless, headless woman, until it's like Kenna's not in her bedroom anymore, not even in the same house, like she doesn't exist.

3.

Kenna hates the hospital. She's been there before and hates the antiseptic smell and the way something she can't see is always beeping. She hates the moans of misery and pain that come from the rooms she and Dad pass as they walk down the hallway toward Mom's room.

Dad stops in front of the men's bathroom. "Go ahead, Kenna. I'll be right behind you. I just need to pee." He hands over the bouquet of flowers he bought in the little shop downstairs. "Give these to Mom, okay? Make sure she knows they're from me."

He disappears into the bathroom. Kenna hopes he gets lost in there and never comes out.

She walks to Mom's room, and there she is, in bed with an IV drip in one arm and a brace on the other. Kenna pauses at the door, frightened at how banged-up she looks. One lip is cut, one eye bruised. Kenna grips the bouquet harder, crinkling the plastic wrapper. Mom's in the hospital because of her. She wouldn't be there, wouldn't even be hurt, if she didn't take Kenna to Sarah's party. A party Kenna didn't even want to be at. She wants to cry. She wants to beg for forgiveness. She feels like her body isn't big enough to contain what she's feeling and she's going to explode.

What if Mom never recovers? What if this time she never comes home?

A nurse passes behind her in the hallway. "In or out, dear," she says, and keeps walking.

Kenna finally steps into the room. She puts the flowers on the bedside table, next to a pill bottle full of little brown tablets. She picks it up, looks at the label. *Anzemet 100mg, take once daily, antinausea.* Kenna removes her backpack full of schoolbooks and puts it on the floor, trying not to be too loud. Mom's doped up on painkillers, but her sleepy eyes open like she can sense Kenna's presence. Those eyes used to be bright, sharp, even mischievous sometimes when she thought Kenna wouldn't notice, but now her eyes look dull and flat. The eyes of a barnyard animal unaware of what's happening to it.

"Hey, Mom," Kenna says. "How are you feeling?"

Mom smiles weakly. When she speaks, her voice is slow and slurred. "I'm okay, baby."

But she's not; it's so clear she's not. Kenna chokes back a sob. "This is all my fault."

Mom's eyes shift to her again. There's more of her in them this time, a glimmer of awareness. "Kenna, no. . ."

"If you hadn't. . .taken me. . .to Sarah's party," she says through her tears, sucking in gulps of air.

"No," Mom says again. "It's not your fault. It's mine."

Kenna wipes her eyes, feeling a sudden flush of anger at Mom. "Why would you say that? How is it *your* fault?"

Mom blinks slowly, surfing a wave of morphine. She drops deep, nearly into sleep.

"If you don't keep the viper happy, you'll find his fangs in your throat," Mom mumbles.

It's drugged-out gibberish, but it's also not. She's talking about Dad. She thinks appeasing him is the best way to avoid his wrath. Don't talk back and you won't wind up in the hospital. But she's wrong. Mom has tried again and again.

Kenna blinks, and finds herself in the small bathroom adjoining Mom's hospital room. She puts a hand on the wall's safety railing to steady herself. What is she doing in there? The toilet is empty. The sink is dry. Why did she come in there? *When* did she come in there? She turns to the door and sees her backpack leaning against it. Why would she bring her backpack into the bathroom?

She opens the bathroom door and peeks out into Mom's hospital room. Dad is there now, sitting on the edge of the bed and smiling down at Mom like he's not the one who put her here. How much time has passed? Why can't she remember? Kenna walks over to the side of the bed and puts down her backpack. No one gives her a funny look or asks what she was doing. No one seems to notice anything wrong at all.

"When can I take you out of here, baby?" Dad asks Mom.

Mom smiles and blinks sleepily. "Soon."

"Not soon enough," he says. He kisses her hand, the one that's not in a cast. "Did Kenna tell you the flowers are from me?"

Mom looks at the flowers on the bedside table. Kenna freezes, a deer in the woods hoping the hunter won't see her. She didn't tell Mom anything about the flowers. If Dad finds out she didn't relay his message, he'll be mad. Kenna will get a smack on the face for it when they get home. He only uses an open hand on the face, so it won't leave a mark people can see. Dad's doctor said he's not supposed to let himself get worked up because of his heart, but he does anyway. He gets worked up into an uncontrollable, violent anger, and then they get blamed for it.

"Yes, she told me," Mom says, and Kenna breathes again. "The flowers are beautiful. Thank you, my handsome man." Mom puts her good hand on Dad's cheek, keeping the viper happy.

4.

After visiting Mom, Dad drops Kenna off at school. She hops out of the car and doesn't say goodbye. She's too angry.

She missed first period, but she's in time for history class. The lesson is about the Trojan Horse. Even something that looks nice or pretty can have something dangerous hidden inside it, so you shouldn't judge things by what's on the outside. Kenna is only half-listening. The more she thinks about Mom blaming herself for being in the hospital, the angrier she gets. It's not Mom's fault. It's not Kenna's fault, either, really. It's Dad's fault.

At lunch, Sarah Lieberman invites Kenna to sit with her. Maybe she wants to smooth things over after what happened at her birthday party, but Kenna spends all of lunch quietly fuming, so nothing comes of it. Probably, their friendship is over forever now, but Kenna can't find it in herself to care. She has other things on her mind.

At her locker, she hoists her backpack over one shoulder. Something rattles inside it. She thinks of a rattlesnake and its tail. She thinks of a viper and its fangs.

Dad picks her up after school. She rides silently as they pick up a pizza for dinner. Back home, the symphony of silence continues, the only sounds coming from crinkly paper napkins and Dad's loud sips from his beer bottle at the dinner table. If Mom were there, she'd tell him he shouldn't drink because of his medication, but she's not, so he's making the most of it.

Kenna breaks the silence. "When is Mom coming home?"

"When the doctors let her," he answers.

He takes a bite of his pizza slice, the gooey cheese hanging off the crust like worms. Kenna puts her own slice down half-eaten. She's not hungry anymore.

"How did she fall down the stairs?" The words are out of her mouth before she can stop them. She feels very brave and very scared at the same time.

He looks up at her from his plate. His eyes are hot like lava, like laser beams. Why did she ask that? She's already shaking. She hides her hands under the table.

Dad takes another bite of pizza like a lion tearing the flesh off an antelope carcass. "Your mother fell down the stairs because she's clumsy and stupid," he says. "You'd be smart not to be like her."

Kenna gets the message. She doesn't ask any more questions.

When nine o'clock comes, it's lights out again, but she stays up reading her encyclopedia of Greek mythology. She can hear Dad watching TV in the living room downstairs, the clink of his second or third beer bottle as he puts it down after each swig. She tunes everything out so she can concentrate, holding the flashlight over the chapter about Echidna she started last night.

Echidna was married to Typhon, a fire-breathing monster so terrible and fearsome that even Zeus and the other gods were afraid of him. His legs were coils of deadly vipers, and he stood as tall as the sky, with huge wings that could blot out the sun. His head was surrounded by a mane of hundreds of snakeheads. Kenna can't imagine why Echidna would marry someone so awful. Even worse, they had children together, which Kenna knows means they *did it*. All their children were as terrible as Typhon, which was how Echidna came to be known as the Mother of Monsters. She gave birth to Cerberus and the Hydra, the Chimera and the Sphinx, and three daughters called the Gorgons.

A loud crash comes from the kitchen, followed by Dad exclaiming, "Ah, shit! Damn it!"

Kenna knows it's not safe to leave her room, but it sounded bad. She creeps out of her bedroom and down the stairs to see what happened. Her father is crouched on the kitchen floor over the pieces of a broken beer bottle. The pill bottle of his heart medication stands by the sink like a sentinel, watching with eyes of chalk-white tablets.

"Dad, are you okay?" she asks.

"I'm fine. Go back to bed," he says, picking up shards of glass and putting them in his palm. He flinches and sucks air between his teeth. Bright red drops of blood drip from his fingertip and splash on the kitchen floor.

"Your finger!" Kenna says, moving toward him.

He turns angrily to her and raises his other hand like he's going to smack her. "I said go back to bed, goddamn it!"

She runs up the stairs and back to her room. She pulls the covers up to her chin. And then, suddenly, she's back in the hallway outside the kitchen, only everything is dark now. The kitchen light is off and Dad's not there anymore. She hears him snoring upstairs. Kenna touches the wall to make sure it's real, feels the texture of the wallpaper under her fingertips. This isn't a dream. How did she get there? Was she sleepwalking?

She hurries back to her bedroom. The digital clock by her bed reads

1:30 AM. She gets under the covers and stares into the dark of her room. Bathed in light from the clock, the little statue on her bedside table looks different. It didn't have arms before, she's sure it didn't, but now it does. Slender, graceful arms, and hands with sharp talons for fingers.

5.

The next day, the hospital lets Mom come home. Kenna's already home from school when she's discharged, so when Dad drives to pick Mom up, Kenna waits alone, pacing the living room nervously. When the door finally opens and Dad helps Mom inside, Kenna runs to greet her. She still has the brace on her wrist, but the bruises on her face have faded.

"Mom, you're home!" Kenna says, giving her a big hug.

"Easy, baby, easy. I'm still sore." She wraps her good arm around her and squeezes her tight.

"Kenna, don't bother your mother," Dad says. "She's still healing up."

Because of you, she thinks angrily. Everyone believes the lie that Mom tripped and fell down the stairs, even the doctors at the hospital, but Kenna knows the truth. It was Dad. Either he hit her so hard she was knocked down the stairs, or he pushed her, threw her down the steps like he does with the garbage bags out front sometimes. Like she's garbage too.

"But you're okay now, aren't you, Mom?" Kenna asks.

"I'm fine, I'm fine," she says, but she turns away rather than look her daughter in the eye. "I should sit down. I'm still a little nauseous from the painkillers. They were supposed to give me something for that, but I think they forgot."

Kenna frowns. She's sure she saw a bottle of antinausea medicine in Mom's hospital room. Didn't she?

"It's time for me to take another painkiller, too," Mom says.

If she needs a painkiller, it means she's still in pain. Anger at Dad swells in Kenna's chest, but she pushes it down. She's getting good at pushing it down, even though she knows it's going to need to go somewhere eventually.

For the rest of that night and all the next day, her parents act like a normal family. No voices are raised, no one gets smacked, there's no screaming or crying or trips to the hospital. But this is the pattern every time. After a blowup, things get quiet again, sometimes for weeks, sometimes only for a day or two, before the next one. When she was little, Kenna used to hope during each quiet period that it was over for good, that Dad wouldn't hit either of them ever again, but she isn't a naïve little kid now. She's eleven, and she knows the quiet can't be trusted.

It breaks on the third day. Dad wants to have a beer with dinner. Mom tells him he shouldn't because of his medication. He waves off her concerns and pops the bottle top.

"Did you take your pills while I was gone?" she asks.

"Of course I did," he says. "Stop nagging me."

She stands up, pushing away from the table with her good arm. "Where are they? I'll go get them now. You're supposed to take them with food."

"Leave it alone," he says.

Kenna slumps low in her chair, ponders the benefits of becoming invisible. The fuse has been lit. Whether it's a long fuse or a short one depends on what happens next.

"Are they in the bathroom?" Mom asks. She starts out of the dining room.

"I said leave it alone!" Dad is on his feet, face red, eyes like a bull ready to charge. He points at Mom's empty chair at the table. "Just sit down!" She doesn't move, locks eyes with him. "Sit down! Sit *down*! Sit *down*!"

Kenna thinks of the girls at Sarah Lieberman's party trying to make Hamantaschen sit. And just like the dog, Mom gives in and returns to her seat. It's the safest course of action, but what Kenna feels isn't relief; it's shame. She's ashamed of her mother for sitting like a dog.

It occurs to her that this will never end. She and Mom will never be safe.

Dad gets up, storms up the stairs, then stomps back down with his pill bottle. He opens it, shakes a brown tablet into his hand, pops it in his mouth, and swallows it down with a swig of beer.

"There," he says. "Happy now? I took my fucking pill."

Kenna retreats to her bedroom after dinner and reads the encyclopedia of Greek mythology. Despite her promise to herself, she skips ahead from Echidna, the Mother of Monsters, to read about her three daughters, the Gorgons. The picture shows them as winged women with fearsome boar-like tusks, sharp brass talons on their hands and feet, and snakes for hair. The word *Gorgon* comes from the Greek word *Gorgos*, which means *grim and dreadful*, and that definitely matches the picture.

The eldest of the Gorgon sisters was Stheno, whose name meant strong and forceful, and who had red snakes on her head, which makes Kenna think of her own coppery hair. The second born was Euryale, whose name meant *far-roaming*, and whose snakes were muddy brown in color. The youngest of the three was Medusa, the only one Kenna has heard of before. Her name meant *to protect and rule over*, like a queen, and her snakes were green as emeralds. All three sisters could turn men to stone with just a look.

She closes the book and wonders what it would be like to turn someone to stone. The sounds of Mom and Dad arguing seep through her bedroom wall. She imagines herself staring at Dad so hard, he turns into a statue. Staring at him so hard, he dies. Then it would be only her and Mom. Then they would be safe.

She lies down to go to sleep, slides her hands under her pillow the way she always does. Her fingers touch something that shouldn't be there. It's small and hard, like plastic.

When Kenna opens her eyes, she's standing in her parents' bedroom at the side of the bed. Mom and Dad are lying back-to-back, curled away from each other. Kenna slaps a hand over her own mouth so she won't make a sound. How did she get there? Is she sleepwalking again? It hasn't happened since Mom came home. She thought it was over.

She tiptoes to the door. Dad stirs in bed behind her, and she freezes. If he finds her in their room in the middle of night, she'll get hit for sure. He mutters something. Her name? Something from his dream? She waits, still as a statue. When she hears him snoring again, she sneaks quickly out of their room and back into her own.

Her bright digital clock reads 1:30 AM, just like before.

The statue on the bedside table has grown stone wings from its back.

6.

The next day, Saturday, Kenna spends moping around her room and napping. She feels tired all the time now. Maybe it's from the sleepwalking. She writes a letter in her notebook to Sarah Lieberman, saying she still wants to be friends, but the memory of the girls at the party yelling at Hamantaschen to sit makes her angry again, so she rips it up and throws it away. Who is she kidding? No one wants to be friends with someone who's angry all the time. Dinner is a horror show. Her parents argue the whole time. Dad gets so red in the face, he looks like a cartoon devil. He threatens to hit Mom, who flinches just like Kenna did at the party. Kenna watches it all from a thousand miles away, from another planet. She eats quickly, then goes back to her room and continues reading about the Gorgons in her encyclopedia of Greek mythology.

(This is the last night she will read from the book. After tonight, it will be covered with blood, its pages stuck together, unreadable.)

The Gorgons were supposed to be monsters—they were the daughters of Echidna, the Mother of Monsters, after all—but Kenna's surprised to learn that all three sisters were actually sworn protectors of the Temple of the Oracle. The chapter goes on to explain that in ancient Greece, the face of a Gorgon was considered a symbol of protection. It appeared on shields and armor carried into battle. It appeared on women's shelters to let women know they would be safe there.

Kenna's confused. Why are the Gorgons considered monsters if they're actually protectors? Is it because of the way they look? Is it because they're protectors of women? The Gorgons don't strike Kenna as monsters at all. They strike her as heroes.

Lying on her back, she closes the book, clutches it to her chest, and closes her eyes. She's not sure how long she sleeps for, but she's woken by the sound of arguing coming from the kitchen downstairs. Dad is yelling, using words she hasn't heard him use in a long time: *cunt, bitch, harpy.* He's worked up now, and there's no stopping him. She wonders what he's so mad about. Did Mom say something? Did she talk back? It doesn't matter. She might not have said anything at all. Kenna pulls the pillow around her ears to drown out the noise. Something rattles and rolls out from under the pillow to land on the rug. She refuses to look, refuses to even open her eyes, but then she hears something crash downstairs. A plate? A glass?

She leaves her room and creeps downstairs to see what's happening. It's only when she reaches the bottom of the steps that she realizes she's still clutching the book to her chest. She doesn't want to let go of it now. It's the shield she will carry into battle. Gripping the book tighter, she makes her way to the kitchen and gets there just in time to see Dad shove Mom. Mom stumbles, her back slamming into the edge of the kitchen counter, and then she falls. Tears squeeze from her eyes as she sits on the floor and cradles the brace on her wrist.

Mom murmurs to herself between sobs. "I promised myself I wouldn't let this happen again."

"Oh, you promised yourself, did you?" Dad mocks her. "Stop your blubbering and get up off your ass. You're making a spectacle of yourself."

She glares up at him with hard, furious eyes. "You son of a bitch. . ."

He pulls back his arm like he's going to smack her. "What did you say?"

"Stay away from her!" Without thinking, Kenna runs into the kitchen. She pushes Dad away from Mom, putting her shoulder into it against his considerable weight. Her whole body feels like it's on fire.

"Kenna, no!" Mom yells.

Dad stumbles and catches his hip on the edge of the kitchen counter. He falls, splayed out like a scarecrow, face down on the linoleum. He turns over and stares up at her with eyes full of wild rage.

"Are you out of your damn mind?"

Kenna freezes, paralyzed and trembling with fear. She raised her voice to Dad. She fought back. She knows what's coming next.

Dad smacks her across the face. It's a hard blow, the hardest he's ever given her, and when she reels back, she tastes blood in her mouth. It spills from her lip to spatter across the book in her hands.

"Greg, that's enough!" Mom says, struggling to stand.

He hits Kenna again. Her mouth is full of blood. The book is covered in red. It drops to the floor with a heavy slap.

"That's *enough!*" Mom screams. "Stop it!"

"I'll say when it's enough!" Dad roars. His face is purple. Veins pop in his neck and temple. He pauses. His face scrunches up. "Fu—" He tries to swear, but he's out of breath. He drops to his knees and clutches his chest.

Kenna's on all fours, spitting blood on the kitchen floor. Did Dad knock one of her teeth loose? Mom rushes over to her, puts her arms around her.

"Oh, baby, are you all right?"

Kenna can't answer. There's too much blood in her mouth.

"My—my pills. Get my pills." Dad sounds desperate, a drowning man grasping for a life preserver that's just out of reach.

Mom lets go of Kenna. Straightens up.

"Don't," Kenna says, but Mom's already running up the steps two at a time to get Dad's medication.

Kenna drops from all fours to lie curled on her side. She swallows blood until her mouth is clear. Dad collapses on the floor in front of her. Face to face, they stare at each other in silence. She wills him to die. He reads it in her eyes.

He knows she killed him.

Kenna smiles a bloody-toothed grin.

Mom runs back into the kitchen with his pills, pops open the pill bottle, and shakes out a pile of brown tablets into her palm. "What are these?" she screams. "These aren't your pills! Greg, these aren't your pills!"

Kenna gets up. She picks up the blood-spattered book and carries it with her back upstairs to her room. She closes the door behind her.

On the floor, next to the bed, is the plastic pill bottle that rolled out from under her pillow. She picks it up. The label reads, *Anzemet 100mg, take once daily, antinausea.* Mom's pills from the hospital.

Kenna understands now. The forgotten memories come back to her. She takes the pill bottle off the bedside table in Mom's hospital room. She's in the kitchen after Dad has finished cleaning up the broken beer bottle and gone to bed, retrieving his pill bottle from where he left it by the sink, and switching the contents of the two bottles, knowing he's careless and would never notice the difference in color between his chalk-white heart pills and Mom's brown antinausea pills.

Kenna sees herself standing in her parents' bedroom in the dark, watching over Mom. Protecting her.

Mom's voice becomes hysterical downstairs. She calls for an

ambulance, but Kenna knows it won't arrive in time. Dad's gone too many days without taking the right pills. She looks at the clock. Once more, it's 1:30 AM. At last, she understands the significance of that time, why it kept repeating again and again.

It's the hour when her father dies.

Next to the clock, the little stone statue is complete. Arms, wings, and now a head. A woman's head with boar-like tusks and writhing snakes for hair.

Kenna smiles. She's not afraid. This is no monster.

In fact, she's beautiful.

Note from the Author

A few years ago, I had a scary, stalkerish encounter with a woman at the New York Public Library. Although nothing violent occurred, I spent the rest of the day looking over my shoulder, wondering if she was following me and if she had a weapon. When I shared this story with female friends, they all had the same response: this happens to them on an almost-daily basis. One friend actually had to find a police officer because she couldn't shake a man who tried to follow her home from the subway. I support stopping violence against women because I can't imagine feeling that fear and anxiety every day. No one should have to.

— Nicholas Kaufmann

The Devil's Pocket Change

Hillary Monahan

They found Susie after the spring floods burst the banks of the Saddleback River. She'd washed up two towns over, which is how the search parties missed her—the jurisdiction ended at the county line.

"We found remains in a fish ladder, Spike." Sheriff Anderson's voice rasped with thirty years of cigars. "By the old mill in Ellisville. Couple of fishermen last night. Can't say for sure til the coroner chimes in, but. . ."

Spike's tired eyes swung to his alarm clock. Half past five. He stifled a yawn into the back of his forearm and sat up, kicking the new sheets off of a bed he'd only recently reclaimed.

"I can come."

"Nope—" Sheriff Anderson started to talk, then stopped himself. There was a soft hiss of sound. Anderson did this thing with his mouth where his upper teeth overlapped his bottom lip. Spike could see it in his head, the weird way it made the old man's jaw jut. "Look, she's been in there awhile. You don't want to do this. Promise you, you don't. Let us take it from here, okay?"

Floaters and bloaters, Spike's brain said. *There's not enough left of her to ID.*

Ugh. Goddamn it, Susie. You and your crime documentaries.

Spike went quiet. Fuck if he knew what he was supposed to say. There wasn't exactly etiquette for *Your wife jumped off a bridge and we didn't find her for a few weeks. We think this moldering meat might be the woman you married.*

Anderson took it as a sign to let loose with the rehearsed platitudes. "You know how sorry I am," he said. "Can't imagine how you're doing. If you need anything, you know me and Carol are here for you."

"Yeah, thanks."

Hollow words from a hollow man.

He didn't feel anything, not pain or sadness. Not guilt. He was born of nothingness.

At least, that's what Susie said before she'd killed herself.

***

"She has sad eyes," Spike's mother said after meeting Susie for the first time. They were an odd gray-green, with heavy lids under heavier brows and early crows' feet flanking the sides. At the time, Spike had protested, telling his mother Susie's eyes were the most beautiful he'd ever seen.

Mom's reply, like most of her words, was efficient. "*Sad* and *beautiful* are not mutually exclusive things."

Sitting at Susie's funeral, looking at her portrait propped on top of her casket, he could finally see what she meant. It was more than the strange color or even how deep-set and large they were. It was the faint hint of blue beneath, and the V between as if worry had etched itself into her skin from a tender age.

Twenty-seven in body but a hundred million in her eyes. The photo taken on a *good* day, and she still managed to look like she'd seen things no one else could understand. The universe's mysteries. Or ghosts.

Or maybe she was just fucking crazy, like Chuck told me.

"Some girls got issues; this one's got volumes, man," Chuck said at Spike's bachelor party. "Not too late to chew your own leg off." Spike had told him to shut his mouth, that it wasn't too late to not be his best man, either, but in retrospect, how could Chuck see it when Spike couldn't? Even then, before it got so bad?

In the front pew, holding his mother's hand, the truth of it sat like stone in his gut. Because he hadn't wanted to, and in the earliest days, when he'd caught a glimpse of the darker side, where Susie's wild despair languished, he convinced himself if he loved her hard enough, she'd get better. She'd change because he wanted her to.

She just needed a hug. A coffee. A kitten. A vacation. More of him.

For a while, the self-sacrificing bullshit worked. Spike would give his everything and Susie would suck it up like a sponge. Eventually, with just the right combination of coddling, her carapace would crack and he'd catch a glimpse of the sun beneath that maudlin veneer. That was workable enough when the breakdowns happened every other month, but when they started coming every other week, and then weekly, it grew old.

Tears in the bathroom. Tears in the kitchen. Sleeping fourteen hours a day, then twenty. Single-sentence answers which became single-word answers and then no answers. The house was filthy unless he cleaned it. Hell, *she* was filthy, her mousy brown hair matted to her skull with weeks of built-up oil.

He'd begged her to get into the shower, offered to go with her and wash her. She'd just looked at him with those sad, sad eyes, whispered, "I'm sorry," and sobbed about how disgusting she was.

Their first wedding anniversary marked the first time his patience wore thin with her epic fits of sad. He'd made reservations at her favorite restaurant—an upscale Mexican place downtown, where they'd had their third date. Top-notch tequila on the shelf. The best carne asada this side of the Mississippi. He'd bought her a new dress from that online retailer she liked so much. It was teal with little cream-colored flowers over it. When he left that morning for work, she'd been fine. They'd eaten pancakes she'd made him to mark the occasion. Things were, for a pleasant change, looking positive. He even dared to look forward to seeing her after his shift.

When he came home, he could hear her sobbing in the shower. She hadn't started the water, hadn't even taken off her clothes. She just sat in the bathtub, crying. He asked her over and over again what was wrong, but all she could do was snivel and stammer.

"Tell me what you need!"

But she couldn't tell him anything. She couldn't do anything. Just cry.

And cry.

And cry.

Looking at her huddled, shivering form, stringy ropes of hair cascading down her back— he resented her. Like, truly resented her, with his whole heart. He'd flirted with it before when he was exhausted because she'd destroyed herself into yet another migraine, but that particular breakdown—the one that killed their anniversary dinner and saw him drunk by himself in front of the Xbox at midnight—put the first crack in the dam.

A dam that stood another three months before she eroded the last of his goodwill by crying nearly every night, wailing like a banshee. He stopped asking what was wrong then. He stopped listening when she talked about her new therapist or how her new medication didn't seem to be doing anything for her. When she went into the hospital for an inpatient stint, he didn't call to find out how she was doing, because he didn't care anymore.

And he never really learned to care again. He sat at his wife's funeral, staring at her picture, empty. Susie's relatives sniveled their sorrows two rows behind him, her mother nearly hysterical about the loss of "her baby," her sister Monica sobbing. He couldn't muster much of a shit at all.

***

The place Susie had carved out in his soul became a big, black void over the two years of their marriage. He'd grown comfortable with that void, embraced it. It made living with her tolerable. Knowing that all things reached their logical conclusion, including Susie's slow, miserable decline, helped him get by.

"Eventually, this will be over," he told himself.

He also told himself to prepare.

After a particularly bad day, he'd taken out a life insurance policy on her—one that cost a lot but was willing to take them on because she was consistent about treatment for her condition. He'd been playing *Call of Duty*, sitting on the couch, a half-eaten box of Chinese food on the coffee table in front of him. The remains of other meals were there, too: more evidence of cleaning she claimed she couldn't do which he'd take care of when he eventually got sick of the filth. She didn't come out of the bedroom anymore. He'd taken up roost on the couch. The one-bedroom apartment had seemed like such a good deal when they'd rented it, but as the months bore on, not so much. Funny how the chasm between them was miles wide, but the nine hundred square feet still managed to be claustrophobic as Hell.

He could hear her weeping into the late hours of the night. One. Two. Three o'clock. He had to work the next day. He screamed at her to shut up, and she muffled her cries into her pillow. The next morning, he made the call to Barker and Kline insurance.

And then he bought earplugs.

***

He dreamed *of* that night, when she left for the last time. The one where she drove herself to the Grab & Go, parked her Ford by the air pumps, and walked two miles to Marimer's Bridge. It wasn't something he'd talked about to anyone because he knew the condemnation that would go along with his honesty. It was, he knew, condemnation he ought to muster for himself, but he'd given up on that as much as he'd given up on her.

Cigarettes. Beer. Takeout and video games. His routine of self-isolation was as consistent as her misery.

Every fifteen minutes or so, she ghosted her way into the living room from the bedroom, a frail, malnourished whisper of a woman. He didn't look at her, not when she scooped up the cat from the chair in the corner, not when she put the cat in the carrier despite the cat's furious howls.

"Going to Monica's," she said, her voice raspy from disuse. He frankly couldn't remember the last time she'd spoken a word—to him, to the cat. To anyone, really.

He didn't answer.

"I'm giving her Louis. I think—" She sucked in a breath. "He'll do better there. She'll take him."

"Fuck. This dude is riding my ass," Spike swore, gesturing at the television.

She said his name, low and doleful. He reached for his cigarettes, lighting a fresh one before respawning in the game. "Whatever you wanna do. You never cleaned the cat box, anyway. Not living with shit stink all the time will be a nice change."

He'd never much cared for the cat, which had less to do with the quality of the cat itself and more to do with getting her a kitten representing another vain attempt at making Susie less of a misery to be around. He wasn't mean to it or anything, even let the thing sit on his chest sometimes when he was getting ready to sleep, but it wasn't his favorite thing. Anything of hers wasn't his favorite thing. Not anymore.

"Okay, yeah. I— Yeah," Susie said softly.

The next thing he heard was a snivel, the door closing, and the car engine roaring to life. He finished his game and stared across the living room, at the corner with the litter box. For reasons he wasn't completely clear on, he decided to clean it all up, dumping everything into a big garbage bag, along with the scratching post and the little basket of toys

Louis had been ignoring for years because he preferred Spike's socks.

. . . that acknowledgement gave him a moment of pause.

Okay, so, Louis was all right as far as cats went, and he did deserve someplace better. Monica, Susie's sister, was that better place. She didn't suffer from the mood disorder or manic depression or bipolar or whatever diagnosis Susie was on to that week. Best he could understand it, after a half dozen therapists and twice that number in medication trials, his wife defied classification beyond the ever-so-simple *Susie was a sad girl, had always been a sad girl, and always would be a sad girl.*

Spike didn't like sad girls.

He'd just finished sweeping up the last of the spilled litter when his wife came home from her sister's place minus one cat carrier. Those eyes he once thought he could drown in, those eyes that had drawn him in across a full sociology class freshman year of college, bulged, red veins spidering out across the whites. She'd lost so much weight over the past year, a papery sheaf of skin covered her skull with no fat to speak of. All those angles skewed the ratios on what had once been a quirky kind of beauty.

She licked her lips and glanced at the trash bag, then back at him. Her arms folded over the stomach of her sweatshirt, the orange dust stain there telegraphing she'd yet again partaken in her preferred meal of Cheetos for dinner.

"Do you ever just want to leave?" she said.

Maybe it was because he was only half paying attention that he didn't consider the implications of the question coming from her despite the fact that he asked himself the same thing a thousand times a day. And he had the answer, it was right there on the tip of the tongue, but he refused to give it to her. Petulant, probably, but she didn't need to know that he absolutely one hundred percent refused to be the bad guy. He couldn't stand the thought of it any more than he could stand the sight of her. He'd done his time, damn it. Ten years. Even if it meant his own misery, he'd stay.

"Why would I? My name's on the lease" was his curt answer.

"That's not what I meant and you know it." There was a pause. "I know you've given up on me. I don't blame you. You're so empty now, but it doesn't need to be that way."

For the first time in months, she smiled, albeit sadly.

Everything she did was "sadly."

"Actually, Susie, *you* gave up on you. I didn't have much choice other than to follow your lead." He threw himself onto the couch and reached for a cigarette and the game controller.

"You hate me that much?"

"Honestly? No." His eyes squinted against the puff of smoke billowing in front of his face. "I don't anything you. You're just here, like the mess. I've learned to ignore messes."

"I know. I get it. I can try one more time, though. For you. For us. With a new therapist. Maybe I can go back on the Lexapro. I got better on that for a little while. I just— We said *forever*, Spike, and I do love you. Forever. I know it's hard to believe, but it's true." She reached for him, those spindly fingers with their chewed, jagged nails creeping over his shoulder. A spider was crawling over his skin, feather-light and odious and teasing at the side of his neck. He jerked away from her, jumping to his feet. When she reached for him again, he slapped at her hand and shoved her away, until she stumbled back into the wall behind her, her head striking with a dull thud.

She crumpled to the floor a broken doll, her eyelids fluttering like moth wings.

"Spike, I'm sorry—" she groaned.

"For Christ's sake, Susie, shut up!" He put up a hand to ward her off, as if she *was* the one who'd escalated to violence, not him. "I don't want you touching me. Not today, not tomorrow, and definitely not forever. I'm sick of this. Sick of *you*. Just go away. Please. Go. Away."

He knew in retrospect those words were the end hours before her actual end. She'd been looking for the out. Not only had he given it, he'd implored her for it. He ought to have cared more about that, felt more, but like she said, he was empty. A walking, talking hollow man. When she picked herself up off the floor, a nigh-serene expression on her face, he asked no questions, nor did he voice objections when her fingers curled around her car keys and she reached for the door.

She peered at him, long and lingering with those ghost-seeing eyes. When he jerked his gaze away, unable to stomach her ghoulish visage one second more, she left the apartment for the last time.

***

It wasn't so much that he *wanted* his wife to die; it's just that he'd accepted she would a nebulous sooner rather than a nebulous later. When she didn't come home that night, he did the things he ought to do the next morning: called Monica, called her mother. When neither reported seeing her, again in Monica's case because she did indeed have the cat in her possession, he called the police and they told him to wait twenty-four hours before filing a missing persons report.

They asked him if they'd fought. He'd told them no, because they hadn't.

He knew on some level he could have pushed the issue, told them about her mental illness, told them how high-risk she was, but that wasn't a thing he talked about. Susie did; on the rare occasions she spoke, it was all she talked about, in fact, but Spike didn't feel comfortable airing that dirty laundry. Instead, he hung up the phone and passed out on the couch for another few hours. Susie's parents called him just after noon, asking if she'd come home, and when he told them no, her parents had gone looking for her, but where did you look for a person who never *went* anywhere?

She used to read a lot, but she didn't go to the library or the bookstore ever. She didn't even go to the kitchen most days. She'd done ballet for a time, and yoga, too, but she hadn't visited a studio in at least a year. She didn't even watch those stupid crime documentaries she used to love so much. Hell, her smart TV had broken three months before and she never bothered to tell him until a few weeks before her disappearance.

Monica was the one to demand he call the police back and reveal Susie's diagnoses. An officer came to the house at suppertime, more as a favor than anything else—they really wouldn't take a missing persons before twenty-four hours was up. It was a guy Spike had gone to high school with, Dick McCarthy, and despite the familiarity of their exchange, Spike wondered if Dick was trying to suss out foul play. He wouldn't find any. Spike had watched her kill herself slowly, tear by tear, but that wasn't murder.

It was torture.

For him.

At ten o'clock that night, they found her car. The Grab & Go had security footage of her arrival: she stepped out of the car, closed the door, and paused a second before reopening and tossing her keys inside. She walked away on foot in a mismatched pair of slippers. Eleven seconds of footage made it clear she had no intention of coming back, and so the community search parties started, headed by her parents. Spike went along, walking through woods, through swamps. He walked along riverbanks and highways, looking for a soiled sweatshirt, a sock, her hair elastic. A few times, he asked himself what he'd do if they found her body. Would he cry? Would he have to force himself to cry?

He feared his tremendous apathy would land him in an uncomfortable spot with the sheriff, but no one knew how bad it had gotten, save for Susie. To the world at large, Spike worshipped his wife. His stoicism was chalked up to trauma. Monica *maybe* suspected how unaffected he really was, but then, she was the only person who bothered with Susie toward the end. She'd leave messages, Susie wouldn't call back, so Monica would call him and he'd tell her the same thing he told her every time.

"I can't make her engage with the world, Susie. Encourage, sure, but not force. You know that."

Monica was well aware. After one too many barge-ins at the apartment where she forced Susie to see her, each time ending with Susie succumbing to panic attacks and Klonopin, Monica knew. She didn't like it, but she knew. Even if Monica suspected how distant he truly was, she never brought it up. Not then, not over the five-day course of searching, and not at Susie's funeral a month later.

It was almost too neat and tidy.

Everything was wrapping up so nicely.

***

There was catharsis in the cleaning.

Susie's clothes—the majority of which she'd stopped wearing a year before in favor of threadbare pajamas—were packed and donated to charity. The broken TV was moved out of the bedroom and onto the curb for the garbage. Spike hired cleaners to scrub the place from top to bottom, exorcising the dust and grime for the discount rate of a hundred and fifty bucks a day.

It took them a full week despite the smallness of the space, but he could justify it. He had a check coming, after all. Thirty grand for his troubles, once the coroner exonerated Spike of any wrongdoing. Not that anyone said they suspected him, of course, but people talked, and one thing Spike knew from those crime documentaries was the default mindset of "the spouse did it."

He didn't do *shit*. On that he'd swear.

New paint on the walls. The TV from the living room moved into the bedroom so he could justify the Porsche of flatscreens for gaming. The softest, squishiest couch he could find so he could play in comfort, in fabric, even, because he didn't have to worry about cat claws any longer. The books Susie could quote from memory donated, Spike replaced Plath and Dickinson with X-Men trade paperbacks. The one souvenir he kept, and he kept it on the new entertainment center, was the picture that had been propped on Susie's casket. Her at her best. Her with her beautiful, sad eyes, with clean, glossy hair and even white teeth. He had spent a couple years with her, after all. A memento was the least he could do.

Plus, he had to keep up appearances. The check wasn't in hand yet.

It was eleven weeks to the day of her leaving that the rains came again. They were the same heavy, unrelenting rains that had washed Susie out of her hiding space in the creek to land on that fish ladder in Ellisville. The constant *rat-a-tat* of the droplets hitting his windowpanes made Spike glad he was off for the long weekend. Monday was Memorial Day. He'd be going to a barbecue at Chuck's house and meeting Chuck's kid for the first time. They'd fallen out of touch after the wedding, but when Chuck found out about Susie, he'd reached out. The reconnection was nice. They'd been best friends once.

Spike fired up the Xbox and settled into the couch, a fresh pack of cigarettes and a cold beer on the table before him. There was a certain delight in putting the beer on a coaster so no ring could mar the gleaming wood. He'd just finished his first game of CoD when a clamor from the bedroom startled him enough his cigarette fell from his mouth. He cursed, grabbing for it before it could burn a hole in the carpet. His first instinct was to check for thunder. He craned his head to peer out the window, at skies as gray as the concrete below them. No lightning there or on the horizon. Controller tossed aside, he pushed himself to his feet, bracing for an unknown aggravation that could compromise his very good mood.

Two steps from the closed bedroom door, a smell stopped him cold. It was hard to describe it; fishy, yes, definitely, but sweet too. Sour and earthy, like a flooded basement, maybe. Or low tide. One time, when he was a teenager, a squirrel had gotten caught in their chimney and died. They'd lived with the odor for a week before figuring out they had rot in their home. This reminded him of that, only. . .

Wetter.

He looked up to see if the roof was leaking. No stain, no gray spot indicating compromised drywall. He checked the bathroom for a backed-up toilet and in the kitchen to see if the dishwasher had gone haywire, but everything was in order. No, the stench was definitely coming from his bedroom, and it definitely appeared following the loud crash that had startled him in the first place.

Irritation turned to confusion. Those two things ought not coincide, not with any logical explanation. He headed away from the sanctuary of his far-better-smelling kitchen and into the muddy, coppery cloud outside of his bedroom. He was reaching for the doorknob when he heard it.

Not it.

Her.

"Baby, the TV won't work. I want to watch my shows."

Susie's voice, only at the same time it wasn't her voice. Susie had a soft voice, a melodic voice even. She was shy, but she could sing when she thought no one was listening. He never told her he could hear her through the thin walls sometimes, that he spied on her for his own selfish benefit. This voice shared that same tone, the same quiet volume, but it was drawling and slow. It was Susie's voice but water-sodden, as if she gargled her words at him from the bottom of a lake.

Instead of barging into his bedroom, he scampered away from it. His heart thudded in his chest, heavy and thick, like it would pound its way out through his ribcage and splatter onto the floor.

Nah, this can't be. Susie's dead. They did the DNA. They confirmed it. She's in a box underground and she's the one who put herself there.

175

"Spiiiiiike."

His name was pulled like taffy, stretched far too long for a monosyllable. A wet smacking sound followed, and then another, and a third. Steps, he realized, each one bringing the entropic rankness nearer. His bare feet scuffed over the carpet as he retreated, not yet at a run because this couldn't be happening; he'd buried that bitch. He'd been there when they dropped the casket six feet into the ground, for Christ's sake.

Stress brain? Stress brain, yes. Sure. Just. . .it's been a lot. And you haven't grieved. Maybe you're upset. You're head's fucking with you, man.

Except grief didn't pull open a closed door, and grief certainly didn't have a form that stepped straight out of a nightmare, soiling the floor with river mud and slop. If it was his wife—and he couldn't imagine any other corpse having reason to manifest in his apartment—its was to the opposite of his last viewing of her. Then, she'd been all onion skin and knobby bones. This thing was bloated, enormous really, water distending gray-blue flesh with purple bruising until it looked like a series of overly filled balloons ready to pop. Black veins spidered out over the skin, and the facial features sagged, making her look more like a Dali painting than anything human.

"You're not real!" Spike's words ended on a shriek as he ran behind the couch, putting its hundred inches of overstuffed comfort between them. Still she approached, slowly, unevenly, each lumbering step accompanied by an obscene slurping sound. Her breasts, before so small and pert and a consuming part of his fantasies while they dated, were pendulous, not in the way heavy breasts ought to be but like the skin no longer had the strength to contain their bulbousness.

Like another few steps and one or both might fall off.

I'm imagining this. I wish. . .

Shit, why'd I throw all Susie's meds out? She had to have had something.

An exercise he used to do, in the early stages of Susie's decline, was to tell her to close her eyes and count to ten, breathing in through her nose and out through her mouth. It had something to do with increased nitric oxide being good for the overtaxed brain, but to follow his own advice, he'd have to take his eyes off of the ever-nearing *thing* that used to be his wife.

A thing he was loath to realize still somehow took breaths despite its decrepit state. The long, laborious draws of air rattled and sloshed inside the gelatinous torso, the exhalations ending on yellow, oily water spilling from the corners of her rubbery lips.

"What do you want? Stay away from me!" he shrieked.

Onward she stumbled, closing the gap between them, her left arm, near black and quivering, extending his way. The fingers tipping the hand were plump little sausages, like those cocktail weenies you served on toothpicks at parties, only they were the color of bread mold. There were no fingernails nor were there knuckles—the flesh was too swollen to allow for creasing. What there was, however, was a gleaming gold ring, far too tight, an unnatural edema building up to either side of it.

One of two things was going to happen. Either the finger itself would burst, or the ring would be absorbed inside, never to be seen again.

I can't. I can't. I can't.

His pulse raced. He thought he might throw up or pass out; he wasn't sure which. Rational thought had abandoned him, but then, this was about as irrational a situation as there could be. The dead didn't simply come back, and yet. . .

Something in the back of his brain still functioned—some small instinct to survive. He dashed across the apartment for the door, swiping his keys from the hook on the wall before running down the stairs. Behind him, she dribbled out his name, exaggerating it to obscene proportions, but he wouldn't stop. Couldn't stop. His hands shook as he thumbed his code into the car door and climbed inside. He'd kept

Susie's Ford, selling off his own truck because he'd make a tidy profit and she got better mileage. It didn't quite have the pick-me-up of a V8, but it was good enough, because he could drive away and she couldn't.

But where do I go?

The police station, maybe. Or a church. Shit, what did they do in the movies? Blow the zombie's head off? Salt the ghost's grave? Burn the remains? But those were movies. This wasn't a movie. This was Spike's real life, and his real-life wife who'd jumped to her death a few months before was back from the dead. Or, conversely, by some horrible twist of fate, maybe he was seeing shit. Going as crazy as Susie had been. Maybe he'd end up in some nuthouse for all time, drugged out of his goddamned mind.

I'll go to Mom's. She'll know what to do. Mom's the reasonable one. She can help.

He turned the car onto the main drag, cursing when the traffic light flickered from yellow to red. He wanted to *go, go, go*, not sit idly waiting for monsters that were likely his own making. His eyes cruised to the rearview mirror. He was a good half mile away from the apartment and there was, thankfully, nothing behind him. Just a street with some houses and trees. A hydrant. A kid playing basketball in his driveway.

Those therapy breaths he'd practiced with Susie so long ago could come lend a hand, then, as he sat waiting for red to go to green.

In through the nose, hold it, out through the mouth.

In through the nose, hold it, out through the mouth.

In through the nose, hold it. . .

Hauling corpse stench directly into the lungs was a terrible thing. His mouth filled with bile and he coughed a spray of it directly onto the windshield. He swallowed the remains, stomach acid burning its way down his throat. She'd simply appeared: one second, his sedan had no cadaver, the next, it did, as if all she had to do was want to be with him and he'd have to suffer her mountain of gore.

"Be dead! Be dead! Why won't you be dead!"

He screamed.

The corpse beside him turned her head, slowly peering at him. A beetle wormed its way out of the nest of stringy hair on her head to disappear into her ear, but she didn't seem to notice. All her attention, all her focus, was on Spike. And despite everything—the bridge, the leap, the weeks in the water, the funeral, the burial—she still had those eyes. Those sad, beautiful eyes, under sagging eyelids and a drooping, gray-tinged forehead.

"You said *forever*," she said with her waterlogged voice. A deep, shuddering breath expanded her lungs, forcing the skin of her shoulder to crack and another torrent of rank liquid to course over her unnatural curves. "And so did I."

Note from the Author

"The Devil's Pocket Change" is my attempt to show abuse's many forms; physical abuse is certainly an enormous part of it, but emotional abuse and neglect are also facets that contribute to the dehumanization of victims. Susie may start out as a depressed person, but even if she hadn't, a relationship devoid of genuine support can unmoor anyone. We need to help domestic violence victims not just with the injuries done to their bodies but their minds and hearts as well.

—Hillary Monahan

The Tawny Bitch

Nisi Shawl

My Dearest Friend,

This letter may never reach you, for how or where to send it is beyond me. I write you for the solace of holding you in my thoughts, as I would that I could hold you in my arms. So rudely was I torn from the happy groves of Winnywood Academy, I can only conjecture that you also have been sent to some similarly uncongenial spot. Oh, my dear, how I hope it is a better one, even in some small measure, than the imprisonment forced upon me here. I inhabit a high garret: bare of wall, low of ceiling, dirty-windowed. Through the bleary panes creeps a grey light; round their fast-barred frames whistles a restless wind. Some former inmate has tried to stop up the draughts with folded sheets of paper, and these provide the material platform on which stands my fanciful correspondence with you.

My pen is that which you awarded me, my prize for mastering the geometric truths of Euclid. Sentiment made me carry it always with me, next my heart. How glad I am! It is now doubly dear to me, doubly significant of our deep bond. As for the ink, I must apologize for its uneven quality, due entirely to its composition. In fact, I have rescued it from my chamber pot.

Yes, love, these words are set down, to put the matter quite plainly, in my own urine, a method imparted to me by my old African nurse, Yeyetunde. It has the advantage, in addition to its accessibility, of being illegible, almost invisible, till warmed above a flame. As I am allowed

181

no fire of any sort, I may not see to edit my words to you. I hope my grammar and construction may not shame me, nor you, as my preceptress in their finer points. But I believe I will soon cease to trouble myself about such things.

Whom do you suppose to have betrayed us? I am inclined to suspect Madame, as she was the only one, probably, who knew of our attachment. Certainly none of the other pupils was in a position to do so. Though Kitty was most definitely set against me on account of my race, and pretended not to understand the difference between mulattoes and quadroons such as myself, she had no real opportunity to do us harm.

It vexes me that I made no attempt to buy Madame's silence when I had plenty of gold at my disposal. She dropped the most enormous hints on the subject, which I see quite clearly now, in hindsight.

I must school myself not to fret about these matters, over which I have no control. There is enough with which to concern myself in my immediate surroundings. If I spend my days fussing and fidgeting, I will wear out my strength, both physical and mental. My first concern is to preserve all my faculties intact.

When I came to myself in this place, I did doubt my senses. I had lain down to rest on a bed of ease, confined, it is true, as a consequence of our discovery, but still with my own familiar toys and bibelots ranged round me. I awoke with dull eyes, a throbbing head and a fluttering heart, in these utterly cheerless surroundings.

Well, some evil drug, perhaps, subdued me to my captor's power. He has yet to reveal himself to me, and my two gaolers say not a word in answer to my inquiries, but I have no doubt as to who it is: my Cousin John. When informed of our behavior, he must have once more assented to be burdened with my maintenance. Certainly he could not have hoped to have kept me in school much longer, the backwardness ascribed to my race and colonial upbringing having by now vanished under your tender tutelage. I have thought much of these things during the two days I have spent here, there being little else to occupy my time, and I believe it must be so.

But now I have the comfort of writing. To hold intercourse with you, even through so attenuated a medium as this, will give me strength to endure whatever trials lie ahead.

I continue with the description of my prison. I believe I neglected to mention that the walls are washed a stark white: harsh, yet tainted, soiled with the careless print of unclean hands. The floor is a mere collection of loose boards. It is there that I shall hide this letter, and any other secrets my time in this place vouchsafes to me. Gloomy pillars rise at intervals to the rough rafters above, and a brick chimney, from which proceeds all the warmth afforded me. The windows, barred and begrimed, afford an ill view of the countryside.

That I am in the country I deduce from the silence surrounding me, unbroken save for the moaning wind and the monotonous nightly barking of a solitary dog. The glass is so befouled as to disguise all distinguishing visual characteristics of the neighborhood. I have just formed the project of cleaning it, when left on my own as now, that I may perhaps ascertain my whereabouts. There, you see how good you are for me, what a salutary effect so slight a contact with you even as this can have upon me? Then do not chide yourself for the predicament in which I now find myself, love. The danger may yet be won through, and the rewards have been so richly sweet as to defy description. No need; you know them. Back, then, to the present.

One door only serves my prison, and it is a heavy barrier, much bolted. It opens twice a day to a brutish pair, whom for a while I thought to be deaf-mutes, so little did they respond to my pleadings for release. But just this morning— Stay! I hear

***

183

I have been honored by such a visit, such attentions as would surely drive me to destroy myself were adequate means within my reach! No, I remember my promise to you, and there shall be no more attempts of that sort, whatever the goad, however easily the weapons were to come to my grasp. But oh, the insult of his touch! The vileness of the man, the ghastly glare as of his rotting soul, shining through the bloodshot eyes with which he raked me up and down, the moment he stepped in the room.

"Ho," said Cousin John (for it was he), "the little pickaninny loses what small comeliness she had. Martha, Orson, does she not receive good victuals? Remember, I pay all expenses, and shall have a thorough accounting made."

The shorter of my gaolers, a man (presumably Orson), replied that I consumed but a small portion of my meals. This is true, for who could be tempted by a nasty mess of cold beans and bloody sausages, or a bowl of lumpy gruel?

My cousin then turned back to me and said, "So, you would starve yourself, would you, my black beauty? Well, that's no good, for then your fortune will revert to that b_____ Royal Society, and though I am your guardian until you come of age, your father made no testamentary provision for me upon your death." These last words were almost murmured, and seemed to be addressed to himself. He sank into a silent revery, which lasted a few moments, then roused himself to his surroundings.

"Now Martha! Orson! You must bring up some refreshment, and the means with which to partake of it. And a chair or two would not be amiss." (For the lack of any furniture in my description of this room is not owing to your correspondent's negligence). "I dine with the young lady. What! Why stand you gawping there? Be off about your business!" Orson muttered something about the danger in which his master stood should I try to escape.

"Nonsense! This twig of a thing harm me?" And he laughed aloud at the idea, a heavy, bloated laugh. And indeed, he is much larger than me, and stronger, too, as he had occasion to prove at the conclusion of our interview.

For the moment, however, my cousin was all affability. He surveyed the sparseness of my accommodations and shook his head, saying, "Well, 'tis a sad comedown from Winnywood. But you have been a very naughty puss, and must learn to repent your errors before you can be allowed anything like the liberality with which you have been used to be treated. I must not throw away money on the cosseting of a spoiled, sulky, ungrateful schoolgirl."

Why should I be grateful? I thought to myself. The money is mine, though you seem inclined to forget this.

As though he had heard my unspoken words, my cousin showed himself somewhat abashed. He crimsoned, strode away, and hemmed and hawed for a moment before trying a new tack. The gist of this was that by my shameless behavior with you, I had ruined for myself all hope of any respectable alliance with a man. He veered from this presently by way of allusions to the unacceptableness of my "mulatto" features, the ugliness of which also unfitted me as a bride.

He paused as if for breath, and I spoke the first words I had dared to utter in his presence: "Love, affection of any sort, then, is quite out of the question? My fortune forms my sole—"

"Love! Affection!" interrupted Cousin John. He seemed astonished that I should dare to feel their want, let alone speak of it. "After giving way to the unnatural perversions which have reported themselves to my ears, Belle, you ought to be grateful for common civility."

He went on in this vein for some time. I confess that after a while I paid his lecturing scant heed. It put me in mind of my father's scolds to me when, as a child, I showed myself too prone to adopt the quaint customs of Yeyetunde and the other blacks about our place. As Cousin

John prated away, I seemed almost to see my parent stand before me in his linen stock and shirtsleeves, urging rationalistic empiricism upon a child of ten. Of course I was eventually brought to Reason's worship. But well I remember the attraction to me of the island's cult of magic, with its grandiose claims to control the forces of nature which my father sought only to understand. The brightly colored masks and fans and other ceremonial regalia, surrounded by highly scented flowers; the glitter of candles in dark, mysterious grottoes; hypnotic chants and sweetly chiming bells; all clamored at my senses and bade me admit in their train the fantastic beliefs with which they were associated. Then, too, I felt these practices to be connected somehow with my mother, of whom, as I told you, I have no true, clear, conscious recollection. Yet her presence seemed near when I was surrounded by these islanders, to whom the barrier between life and death was but a thin and permeable membrane.

Indeed, I can still dimly picture the altar which Yeyetunde instructed me to build in my mother's honor. It was a humble affair of undressed stone, with a wooden cup and a mossy hollow, wherein I laid offerings of meat, fruit and bread, and poured childishly innocent libations to her spirit.

My thoughts had wandered thus far afield when I was roused to my senses by the sudden seizure of my hand. Cousin John knelt, actually knelt on one knee at my feet, and held me in a grip firmer than was pleasant. Ere I had time to discover what he meant to be about, came a knock on the door, and the sound of its several bolts and chains being shifted about, in preparation for someone's entry.

My cousin with difficulty regained his feet, and the man Orson entered the room, bearing with him two chairs, followed by Martha, who carried a collapsed, brass-topped table.

I have not yet made you see these two, I think, fixtures though they are in my prison. Both are tall, stout, loose-fleshed, and grim of countenance. Did they for some reason of devilry trade clothes, one would be hard pressed to note the change, for they are distinguishable otherwise only by the female's slightly greater height, Orson's face being smooth-shaven.

In bringing in their burdens, this pair left open the door. I stepped round as noiselessly as I could to obtain a view through it, that I might determine what chance I had of making off. None, it appeared, for the door's whole frame was filled by a large, bony, yellow dog, a bitch. She eyed me suspiciously, and her hackles rose, and a low growl rose from some deeper region, it seemed, than her throat. Martha heard it. "Come away from that!" she ordered harshly, whether speaking to me or the bitch, I could not tell. I backed away anyhow, and the bitch held her place.

I realized that in this apparition I had an explanation of the tiresome barking which plagues my dark hours here, and bids fair to keep me from ever obtaining a full night's sleep.

But my light and my ink both fail me, and I must postpone the telling of my thoughts and the rest of the day's events till morning.

***

I cannot recall exactly where I left off in my account. The door was open, I believe, and I had discovered it defended by the tawny bitch . . . yes, and I had just remarked how I believed her the source of the irksome barking which, together with the poorness of the pallet provided (Martha or Orson brings it in the evening, and it is removed on the arrival of my dish of gruel), and the uncomfortably chilly atmosphere, conspires to ruin my nightly rest. The barking goes on literally for hours: low, monotonous as the drop of water from some unseen, uncontrollable source. It is tireless, hopeless almost in its lack of change in tone, pitch or volume; in frequency just irregular enough that one cannot cease to remark its presence. With daylight it ends, but so soon as I am able to fall into a broken slumber, my gaolers appear, remove the pallet, and the miserable day commences. No wonder, then, that this animal and I viewed each other in instant and seemingly mutual detestation.

"Come away from that," cried Martha (have I already said?), and not knowing to which of us she referred, I retreated anyway. The two servants dropped their burdens and took turns in bringing in the food and other necessities, then shut the door and proceeded to set before us our dinner. This was much nicer than I usually get, consisting of a baked chicken, boiled potatoes, a side dish of green peas and a steaming hot pie, fragrant of fruit and cinnamon. I could not but imagine that Martha and Orson had designed this for *their* meal, and my mouth fair watered at the sight and smell of such good things. But Cousin John would have none of it at first and raised a fit, asking for soup and fish, jellies, cakes and such, and demanding that all be taken away and replaced with something better. However, there was nothing else, Orson told him, be it better or worse, so he was forced to make do with what was before him. But he did demand wine to drink, and two bottles were brought, and the servants then dismissed.

I made quick enough work of the portions on my plate, and surprised and pleased my cousin by requesting more. He helped me to it, refreshing himself with great draughts of wine between his labors. "That's the dandy!" he said, spooning forth a quantity of gravy. "Mustn't have you wasting away, merely because you are under a punishment."

Well fed, I felt an increase of courage. How long, I asked him, must my punishment continue?

"Why, till you repent your sins, little Belle, and show that you are truly sorry for them." As he said this he gave a heavy wink. Then he bellowed for Martha and Orson, who cleared the dirty dishes and broken meats, close-watched once more by the bitch, which confined itself, nonetheless, to the passageway. Orson would have taken the wine with the other things, but his master bade him leave it.

Then we were alone, without hope of interruption. I had not drunk my wine, but lifted my glass now as cover for an inspection of my cousin's face. I hoped to reassure myself by tracing in his blurred, reddened outlines some coarse resemblance to the beloved features of my father. I saw puzzlement there, and thick, unaccustomed lines bent the brow in frowning thought. I lowered my eyes, and when I looked up again upon setting down my glass, his expression had shifted to a false grin.

"Come, Belle," said he, "you are not so unseemly to look at when you smile a little, and let down your guard. Black but comely, a regular Sheba, one would say. As for your schoolgirl episodes, I could bring myself to set all that aside. Many a man would not have you, but for myself I say you're as good as a virgin, and a blood relative besides. Thicker than water, eh? You want no more than a proper bedding, which your little adventure proves you anxious to receive. I'm not proud, I'll take you to wife, let the world say its worst."

"No more you will," I muttered through hard-clenched teeth. In the next instant the table top was swept aside with a crash, and my cousin on his feet, dragging me to mine.

He seized me in a horrid, suffocating embrace, mauled me about with two fat, hairy paws and breathed into my shrinking face a thick, wheezing lungful of tobacco-scented, wine-soaked breath.

Half-swooning, I yet fought with ineffectual fists for my release. The monster loosened his grip, but only to change the angle at which he held me, leaving more of my frame subject to his inspection. And not with his eyes alone did he examine me! But with eager hands he sought to undo my bodice, and gain sight of what its strictures denied him. Busied thus, he failed to notice my slow recovery, until I made him know it! He stooped to bestow upon my bosom a noxious kiss and received a sharp bite on the nose! Alas, not sharp enough, for no blood flowed, but a torrent of curses and ugly expressions of wrath.

I took advantage of my attacker's pain and distraction to extricate myself from his hold, and with trembling hands tried to restore somewhat of my customary appearance. When he saw this, he laughed. "Don't bother yourself with that business," he sneered. "I've not finished yet." In a most sinister manner he advanced, and I retreated to the utmost corner of my prison, protesting uselessly. A bully and a tyrant I called him, and other fine epithets, but it must have gone hardly with me, if not for intervention of a most unexpected sort. A great noise arose at the door, a confusion of banging, barking, scratching, scraping, howling and I know not what else. Though loud enough to herald the arrival of a pack of hell-hounds, it proved, upon Orson's opening the door, to proceed solely from the tawny bitch. The beast rushed past him to a position which would have forced my cousin to engage with her in order to come at me. Though she is an ill-favored brute, I admit an obligation to her for this timely interruption. A few blows quieted her, and gave vent to most of my cousin's spleen. This was further relieved by cursing Orson, and demanding to know what he was about to keep such an unruly animal. And why had he not better control of it and what meant he by unlocking the door to it, and exposing my cousin to its attack?

As he restrained the barely subdued dog, Orson seemed somewhat puzzled to defend himself, and made out that the bitch was not his own, but his master's. Hadn't he seen it trotting up behind my cousin's carriage as he arrived that afternoon?

"Mine?" cried Cousin John. "Why should I saddle myself with such a wretched-looking animal as that? Put it out, have it whipped from the grounds!" And that he might supervise the execution of these orders, he left me to soothe my disordered nerves and recover from his attack as best I could on my own. No apology or inquiry as to my well-being came either that day or the next, today. Only I cannot think he was successful in barring the tawny bitch from the property, for again last night I heard her constant, irritating bark.

But perhaps it is not the same dog. These disturbances have gone on ever since my arrival here, and according to Orson, the bitch came with my cousin.

***

It is now afternoon, I think. Cousin John has not approached me all the day. Perhaps he may be gone away again. If not, if he should once more assault me, what shall I do? How defend myself? Should I agree to marry him in order to gain some measure of freedom? I do not think that in a case of coercion, the contract would be valid. Yet, I hesitate to take such a step, uninformed as I am of my rights here in England. Who could tell them to me? Who would deign to defend them? Escape is a better tack to try.

I contrived this morning to retain a damp cloth from amongst the meagre provision for my ablutions. With this I have been rubbing at the window panes, at least, as much as I could reach of them through the iron bars. Of course, a great deal of the dirt is on the outside, but I do think I have made an improvement. In one corner I can see a bit of the landscape. From this I judge that the house in which I am confined is in a hollow, for a dingy lawn sweeps up almost to a level with this window, topped by a row of dreary firs. A road – very rough, little more than a cart track – falls gradually along this declivity, till it disappears from sight around the house's corner. All is grey and forbidding, and altogether northern in its aspect.

Forgive me, my friend, I know you love this land, even its rural solitudes. You, in your turn, are as sensitive to my longing for the smiling skies of St. Cecilia, for the loss of which you comforted me so sweetly. But now, separated alike from my home and my dear solacer, and ignorant as to how long this separation lasts – oh, my spirits are abominably low. I cannot go on writing in this vein. Besides, it grows too dark.

***

Very low. No plan as yet. My situation seems very bad, though still without sign of Cousin John. Left alone to brood on my wrongs. The food is as inedible as formerly. If it continues so, I shall not have to weigh my promise to you. Starvation will put a period to my troubles.

I try to think on happier times. It is now five days since I have been here. Allowing time for travel, and for the effects of the drugs I believe to have been administered upon me, it is perhaps not much more than a week ago that we were together.

Do you remember the delight with which you caressed my hair, likening it to rain clouds and the weightless fluff of dandelions? How you loved to twist and smooth and braid the dark masses, remarking on their softness and compactability! And how I loved your touch there, so gentle yet so thrillingly luxurious . . . I had not known such tender attentions since the sale of my nurse, on my father's death and the breaking up of our household. It frightened me sometimes, your tenderness; it seemed but a fragile insulator for the energy of your passion. As if, the more delicate its outer expression, the deeper and more primordial its final essence. Exactly so did I find this essence, when at last it was unveiled to me. And in its echoing through the sad hollowness of my orphaned heart I heard, I felt, music, rapture, bliss! To hold with all my might this joy, and to enfold my own within it, to wrap myself around you and your fierce love, to feel you yield it to me with such voluptuous uncontrol, and in your pleasure afford me mine, oh my dearest, it was right, it was good and inevitable. My maiden hesitancies melted all away in these heated storms, as a summer downpour annihilates the hard pellets of hail strewn before it.

I know that you believe our separation to be a judgment upon us. So much I was able to divine from your hasty note, though I read it only a few times the night I received it, and could not find it on waking here. I understand your assertion, but I deny it. We have harmed no one, have behaved only according to our natures. This time of trial is troublous, but hold fast and it, too, shall pass. My cousin may confine, he may persecute me, but over the passage of time he can have no control. In a few short months I shall be twenty-one, and mistress of my fortune. Better if I spent those months free from this confinement, but however slowly they may slip away, whatever horrors or privations I may have to endure, I will live to come of age. Nothing, then, can divide us.

I will find you; I will

**

A carriage has come up along the road. A sound so unusual stood in need of investigation, so I ceased my writing for a moment, to see if I could catch a glimpse of the equipage. I just made out the closed top of a smart brougham, giving no hint of its occupant as it wheeled swiftly by.

I cannot contain my hope and curiosity. The sound of the carriage's movement ceased abruptly. Has it brought rescue? Another prisoner, perhaps? Perhaps – my love, could it be you?

I am agitated; I think I hear signs of an approach—

**

So very wretched a turn things have taken that I cannot bring myself to write for long. Dr. Martin Hesselius is the name of this new visitor; a proud, sparely fleshed man with a Continental accent, a cold eye, and an even colder heart. My entreaties for release engrossed him but as symptoms. He has been persuaded of my insanity, and sees in me a rare opportunity to exercise his theories on the causes of, and effective treatments for, mental disorders.

Upon examining me he was greatly surprised that I spoke the Queen's English, and never seemed quite possessed of the idea that I could understand it. He made many offensive remarks on my physiognomy and physique, as of their primitive nature, and was deeply derogatory of my mother, hardly less so of my father, citing his "degenerate lust" and her "cunning animality." Any protest I uttered against his infuriating statements was made to stand at no account, except that of proving my madness.

And then, my friend, Cousin John brought in his report of our doings. It was sickening to witness the happiness with which he made sordid-seeming all that I hold in my memory as sacred. And much worse was the light in which Dr. Hesselius received these tidings. I take it now that for a woman to love a woman is more than just a crime, it is the very definition of insanity . . . How shall I ever, ever win my way from here?

***

Distracted. Bitch barking throughout the entire night. Early in the morning, just at dawn, I detected the sound of a carriage leaving, but I take no heart from that. By something I overheard Martha to say to Orson, I believe Dr. Hesselius has left, but only temporarily, in order to procure some "medicines" and "instruments" for my torture – he would have it, for my cure.

***

Somewhat better now. I have had a meal, the menu of which was decided by the good doctor: boiled lamb, finely minced, and asparagus. I had some difficulty in eating this, as I am no longer entrusted with cutlery, nor any implement more dangerous than a wooden spoon, even under the watchful eyes of my guards. The meal was not ill-prepared, though, and I did it some justice. The whole washed down with great lashings of green tea, of which, I am told, I am to have any quantity I like, this dietary regimen being a part of Dr. Hesselius's recommended course of treatment.

Three other changes are to be instituted as a result of his prescription. I learned of them through indirect means, as neither of the servants will answer my questions, even now that I can call them by their names. But Orson complained to Martha of having to draw and haul the water for my baths, which I gather I am to be given daily from now on. Martha retorted that she was just as much put upon by the order to accompany me on my airings in the garden. Then there are "salts" to be administered, which I hope will prove harmless when they arrive. I believe there are other points in the doctor's program, with which I must wait to acquaint myself till his return.

The idea of being able to walk out of doors fills me with an almost unhealthy excitement! At last, I shall be able to look about me and form some estimate of possible means of escape. To abide in my cousin's power any longer than necessary, even though he make no further advances upon me, is an uncountenanceable thought. I am not mad to be so confined, nor a naughty, impetuous little girl. I have full and clear possession of all my faculties.

***

Just returned from my first, highly anticipated airing. It was not much in the way of what I had expected. Martha wrapped me round with a rough, woolen shawl and hurried me out to a dull little plot of grass divided by a gravel walk. Along this she proceeded to lead me back and forth, under skies in that irritating state of not-quite-rain, and between thick, tall hedges which retained just enough of last year's leaves as to make it impossible to spy out any significant features of the landscape barely glimpsed between their branches.

Still, I managed to obtain some intelligence from this outing. From the general air of dirt and neglect visible on my quick trip through the house, I am strengthened in my belief that it has probably no other inhabitants than myself, Martha, Orson, and (if he yet remains) my cousin. There is no one else, then, whose sympathies might be won to aid me in my plight. However, one may also say that there is no one else to hinder any efforts I am able to make on my own behalf.

***

My evening walk and meal differed slightly from those of earlier in the day. Celery stalks substituted for the asparagus, and a muffler made an addition to my walking ensemble.

As we stepped rapidly along the gravel, I noted a peculiar effect occasioned by the stems of the hedges which we passed. Lit now by the pale, watery yellow of the declining sun, they alternated with their shadows in such a manner as to produce the illusion of *something* – some animal, perhaps – keeping pace with us on the hedge's further side. It was most marked. My eyes were able to discern that the effect rose to a height somewhat equal to my waist, in a blurry, irregularly shifting mass. That it was an illusion, and not an actual animal, was proved by the precision with which it matched our speed and direction; pausing where we paused, hesitating, turning and recommencing along with us in an exactitude not to be explained otherwise.

I amused myself by imagining to which natural laws my father would ascribe this curious phenomenon, from the wisdom accumulated through his naturalistic inquiries. He had studied thoroughly many occurrences which our islanders saw in a supernatural light, always assuring me, when I became frightened at one of old Yeyetunde's tales, that there was a rational explanation for everything to be encountered in

***

Such an uproar as there was last night! No one thought to inform me as to the cause of the hubbub, and I wracked my brains in sorting out its details, trying to see how they might be made to fit together to accompany a reasonable sequence of events.

First came the sound of an approaching carriage. Or was the noise sufficient for two? I got up and strained my eyes to look through the dark, dirty windows. There were lights, as of coach lanterns, but briefly glimpsed and not steady enough for me to count their number.

The horses halted. Muffled shouts and cries for assistance came in coarse workmen's voices. Then a furious gabble of frightened screams, heavy crashes, and ferocious barks. Now canine, now human tongue predominated, till at length came a lull, followed by the sounds of a carriage in movement again. This soon ceased as well, so presumably the vehicle was just led round to the stables. Then came a long silence. Then the sharp report of a pistol.

Nothing further disturbed the night's calm, not even the customary plaint of the tawny bitch. I am left to surmise that she attacked the arriving carriage, or its occupants, perhaps dislodging some heavy piece of luggage, and for her sins was shot. The sadness with which I greet this conclusion surprises me. Dogs are lowly animals, as my father taught me, unworthy of their fame as faithful, noble creatures. "A wolf," he would often say, "is somewhat noble. A dog is a debased wolf; an eater of human waste and carrion, fawning, half-civilized, wholly unreliable."

The islanders, too, hold dogs in very slight esteem. Their use in the tracking of runaway slaves, perhaps, has led to their general abhorrence. I am not sure whether any were sent after my mother. She was not a slave, because married to my father. Somehow she wandered away from the plantation and became lost. The exact circumstances leading to her death were never spoken of.

Yeyetunde, with that patient obstinance so typical of the African, said only that my mother had met her fate deep in the forest, after being missed at home for more than a day. What was she doing there? Who found her? And how came they to know where to look? I could not induce her to answer me, save with the stricture that such things were for my father to tell me, if he would.

He would not.

Oh, he spoke of my mother, and that frequently enough. Almost, I could believe his memories my own. Her beauty; her skin described in a multitude of hues, such as amber, honey, and the pure light of dawn; her genius for discovering rogues and ill-wishers amongst his pretended friends; the portside hostelry where first they met; the speed and ease of her confinement and my delivery; with these I am more than familiar. They only serve to make the blankness following the less bearable.

In time I grew so used to my father's evasions and silences on the subject of my mother's death, I began to conclude that the occurrence had been excruciatingly painful, and that he omitted to recount it, not from any conscious design, but from his positive inability to do so.

Still, I learned to note one peculiarity in his responses, which, however, I am yet uncertain as to how I might interpret it. For hard upon his silences, or at the heart of any irrelevancies with which my father might choose to distract me, came the subject of dogs: their viciousness, their unruliness, and their unpredictability, especially when dealt with as a pack.

***

I grow weary of lamb. Asked of Martha if there were no other provision to be had. She answered me with stony and insolent silence. The tea is good, though, and very warming after my cold immersion baths.

If last night's arrival was the doctor, or my cousin, I have not heard from them, nor received any word of their coming. How annoying to be dependent on the doings of servants for my augury of what goes on around me! Orson has been absent, all my needs being met this morning by Martha, even the toil-some task of hauling up and filling the tub for my bath. Was he injured in last night's fracas? Or perhaps another was hurt and requires his attendance. That would make of the present an opportune moment for my escape. I wish I knew.

Gathered no further intelligence from my morning's excursion, save that the odd phenomenon of the shadow beyond the hedge seems not to confine itself to evening hours. Mentioned this to Martha, who took it just as she takes all I say: with no further notice than an evil, impertinent look. But I noted her eyes trained nervously on the blur as it accompanied us, and I believe our exercise was curtailed as a result of its effect upon her. I shall not mention it aloud again, for I grudge every step denied me. I must keep up my strength. It would not do to come upon a chance to flee and be physically incapable of taking advantage.

***

Languid all the day. This must be the consequence of my perpetually disturbed rest. The bitch is back. That expressionless bark, as of a monotonous lesson learned by rote. I cannot sleep, but I begin to think that nonetheless I dream, for words fit themselves to its untiring, evenly accented rhythms. Admonishments, warnings, injunctions to take up unclear duties, the neglect of which foreshadows danger, yet the accomplishment of which is impossible because ineluctable. The whole effect is one of unbearable tension. I rise and pace, barely able to keep myself from rattling the barred windows, the bolted door – I dare not give way as I should like to do. I must remain in possession of my faculties, that I may engage the belief and sympathies of whomever I first come across on breaking free of my captivity. It may be the keeper of a nearby inn, or some pious and upright local divine; for their sakes, I must retain a rational appearance.

I must escape while I have the wit to do so.

***

Violation! Oh, foul and unwarrantable assault! To live and endure such a burden of shame, oh, my friend, how? How can I? My hand shakes; I have not the strength to write. But if I do not, I may be moved to relieve my outraged feeling on myself, and I have sworn to you—

I have a further thought that these words, so poorly penned, will yet stand witness to my sobriety. In order that I might give the lie to my cousin's claims as guardian of an unhinged mind, I will recount here all I recall. The sickening details...

The bed – I cannot bring myself to rest there. It is a symbol of my humiliation, with its awkward headboard and thick, stiff straps. When it arrived in my prison this afternoon, I thought I might perhaps be able to recoup some of my lost sleep, and so fight off the half-dreaming state that recently has plagued me. The straps repelled, but the thick mattress was more welcoming than my poor, vanished pallet. I had just lain down to test its softness when my gaolers made an unexpected return, wheeling with them a strange apparatus. A large, inverted glass bottle hung suspended from a tall rack. At its neck dangled a long, flexible tube, and on the end of this – oh, it is of no use, I cannot . . . yet, I will go on – a hard, slick nozzle, fashioned of some substance such as porcelain: white, cold; horribly cold . . . I fought, but Martha and Orson together managed to restrain me to the bed, strapped in so that I lay stretched out on my side. Beneath me they tucked a piece of thick, yellow oilcloth. As they did this they lifted and disarranged my skirts and draped sheets over my head and shoulders, and also about my knees. Thus I lay with my fundament exposed, while I had no way to see anything further of what passed.

Imagine my sense of shame, then, when I heard voices approaching and recognized the tones of Dr. Hesselius and Cousin John! They entered the room, discussing my case as though I had not been there. Far from protesting this rudeness, I maintained a foolish, cowardly silence. A child with her head hidden beneath the counterpane, avoiding nightmares; that is how you must picture me.

Dr. Hesselius spoke of how a host of substances he termed "mortificacious" had deposited themselves throughout my inner workings. "I deduce that they have chiefly attached themselves to the lower end of the patient's digestive system."

My cousin cleared his throat. "Mmm. Er, how did you arrive at this conclusion, sir?" He sounded a great deal embarrassed.

"You intimated that the patient's studies progressed well, exceedingly well, in fact, for one of her primitive origins. This indicates that the head's involvement is only a partial one. As the mortificacious material tends to gravitate to its victim's polar extremities . . ." So much I am sure he said, and a quantity of other quackish nonsense besides. My attention was distracted by a clatter nearby, as of glass and metal rattling together. Then came a liquid sound, like water running into a narrow container. I cannot convey to you the sense of unreasoning dread these noises aroused in me.

Suddenly, gloved hands seized me upon – no. Seized me, I say, and I was forced – forced to accept the nozzle. My shame and confusion were such that not for several moments did I realize another's howls of pain and outrage were mingled with my own. As this was borne in upon my suffering consciousness, I subsided into sobs, listening. The other sounds quickly died down as well, though a low, near-constant menacing growl made evident their author's continued presence.

The good doctor had ceased his ministrations at the clamor's height. He now ventured to ask my cousin why he had not done as requested, and shot the damned bitch?

Cousin John replied that he had done so, "and at pretty near point-blank range. But the revolver must have misfired, for the beast got up and ran away. I suppose it was only wounded."

"A wounded animal is all the more dangerous," Dr. Hesselius informed him. "I have already paid to your hell-hound my tithe of flesh.

Better take care of the problem at once."

Only my cousin did not chance to have any weapon handy, so that these two brave, bold gentlemen were required to cringe in my prison with me while Orson was sent forth into the now-silent passage armed with a board torn from the floor. Meanwhile, I lay in my sodden clothes, half-naked, half-suffocating in a cooling puddle of noxious liquids. After some moments, the quiet continuing, Martha was ordered to unbolt the door again and go in search of the other servant. From her hallooing and remarks subsequent upon her return, I deduced that the house appeared empty. This filthy, *soi-disant* treatment is to be inflicted weekly. I do not intend to remain a captive here for so long.

***

The hedge-haunter is no specter, but live, flesh and blood. It is the tawny bitch who has followed me on my daily walks. I saw her outline quite clearly through the hedge this morning, despite the rain. Orson accompanied me; I fancy Martha has taken a dislike to her duties, or to my other escort. I know not why, for the poor beast cannot help her looks. As for temper, the only signs she has shown of that have come upon threats to my well-being. I could almost love her.

***

Walked again with Orson this evening. I made sure he noticed how marvelously close the tawny bitch was able to follow our various paces. He liked it not.

Barking commenced earlier, at sunset, long before dark. Text: 'How sharper than a serpent's tooth it is, to have an ungrateful child,' etc., etc. Well-laid arguments, but I cannot see anything apposite in the quotation. Does it contain some hint as to how I may make my escape? I must reflect on this.

***

Oh, my friend, my best and most beloved friend, soon now I shall be able to confide my heart unto your very bosom! I have quite a clear presentiment that it will be so.

This evening I was let out to accomplish my walk on my own. Martha's eyes were ever on me, it is true, as she stood in the entrance to the kitchen garden, with all the long gravel walk in her plain sight, but she could do nothing to prevent my plan.

It came to me because they would give me so much lamb. And the poor thing looked so thin, gliding along outside the hedge. And indeed she must have been quite wasted away, to have slipped through those tight-packed branches and come to me. I coaxed her to take the meat straight from my hand. Such a pet! I called her my honey and kissed her cool, wet nose, and collared my arms about her soft, smooth-furred neck. Goat's meat would have been preferable. I remember that from Yeyetunde's teachings. It was goat's meat I placed upon her altar as a child. But the lamb was quite acceptable.

Twice more shall I make my offerings. I can hardly contain my great joy, but soon the barking will begin, so steadying to my nerves. So reassuring to know that she is there.

***

Afternoon. This morning I have given unto her the portion brought to me to break my fast, and she has shown me the passage, preparing for my escape. Thin as I am, the hole will yet need widening. My feeble hands have not been of much help. I am to leave this evening. She says she can dig all the day and that it will be ready. Of course I shall have to crawl and become fearfully dirty. So much the better if my light clothes are thereby darkened as they will not so easily betray me to my pursuers.

Pursuers I shall have, but she says she can distract them. I do know that she can set up an awful cacophony at will. But would she actually turn back to attack them? If so, she shall no longer fight alone. Together we will tear, we will savage.

***

The preceding text has been assembled from a collection of fragmentary writings discovered during the demolition of an old country house. Their presentation is as complete and chronologically correct as my efforts could make it. The veracity of their contents, however, has proven somewhat difficult to determine.

Penmanship and internal references (Dr. Hesselius drives a brougham; oilcloth rather than a sheet of India rubber is used during the enema's application) lead to the conclusion that the events narrated took place between 1830 and 1850. This very rough estimate I narrowed a bit further by deeds and entitlements pertaining to the purchase of the property, in 1833, by a Mr. John Forrest Welkin, presumably the narrator's "Cousin John". Parish records show his death as occurring in 1844. He would, at this time, have attained forty-eight years; he was not young, but certainly he fell far short of the age at which one dies suddenly and without apparent cause, as seems to have been the case. He was single and had no heirs of the body.

Of the locations described by the author, only this house's "high garret" is of unquestionable provenance. The papers were found secreted beneath the loose flooring of just such a bare, comfortless room. The house itself had been uninhabited for half a century, commencing early in the reign of our Queen. The place has a bad reputation in the district, as being haunted, and reports of various canine apparitions are easily obtainable at the hearths of all the neighboring alehouses. Of course, such superstitious folklore can scarcely be credited. No two "witnesses" can agree as to the size or number of the pack, though as to coloring there seems a fair consistency. To the rational mind, however, the house's situation down in Exmoor, halfway between South Molton and Lynmouth, and its less than luxurious appointments, ought to be enough to account for its long state of tenantlessness.

Turning to those proper names revealed by the text, often so fruitful of information for the careful investigator, my researches became more and more problematic. Winnywood Academy may possibly have been located in Witney, near Oxford. A relevant document, a six-year lease, apparently one in a series of such contracts, has been uncovered. It stipulates an agreement between one Madame Ardhuis and the fifth Viscount Bevercorne for the use of Winny Hall. Contemporary records also indicate a pattern of purchases by this Madame Ardhuis at stationers, chandlers, coal merchants, and the like. Quantities and frequency are sufficient for the type of establishment sought.

Though the narrator writes of the "smiling skies of St. Cecilia," there is no trace of such an island in any atlas. Santa Cecilia is a small village in the mountains of Brazil (26 .56' S, 50 .27' W). Also, there is a Mount Cecilia in Northwest Australia (20 .45' S, 120 .55' E). Neither of these satisfactorily answers the description. We are left to make do with the uncomfortable knowledge that place names do change with time and that local usage varies.

In reference to most of the persons depicted above, none but Christian names are used: Belle; John; Martha; Kitty; Belle's old nurse, Yeyetunde. Four others are referred to only by title: Father, Mother, Madame, and the document's intended reader, "my friend." The research involved in matching all these references with actual historical personages is beyond the scope of a lone amateur. Belle may have sprung from the loins of the irresponsible Hugh Farchurch, a connection of Welkin's on the distaff side. In postulating this, equating "Madame" with Madame Ardhuis, as seems reasonable, and achieving the identification of "Cousin John" with Welkin, I have done that of which I am capable.

In the case of Dr. Martin Hesselius we have a surname, and corresponding historical linkages. The doctor was well known during his professional career (1835–71), and his presence would seem to vouch for the *text's authenticity. But Hesselius's character as represented here is quite at odds with his reputation. He was known as a layer of mental disturbances, not as one who raised them into existence. Moreover, the few details of his personal appearance given us do not tally. We are left with the distinct impression that in this matter someone has been imposed upon.*

Note from the Author

My story is rooted in cultural reminders of violence against marginalized people, and particularly marginalized women. It's a dual tribute to Louisa May Alcott's sensationalistic "blood-and-thunder" stories and that feminist classic "The Yellow Wallpaper" by Charlotte Perkins Gilman. From Alcott I draw the triumph of the oppressed woman, as presented, for instance, in her scheming-governess-wins tale "Behind a Mask." From Perkins Gilman I draw persecution by close family members and the terrible ease with which a woman is convicted of madness. The dog element comes from the shameful history of dogs turned on African American escapees and activists. The ambiguity and darkness are my own.

—Nisi Shawl

Happy Birthday Baby

Kelley Armstrong

"Happy birthday, Baby." Reggie hoists a fishbowl-sized cosmo glass and waits until I raise my matching monstrosity of a drink and clink it against his.

"She'd have hated this," he says, motioning to his cosmo, bedecked with a half-dozen umbrellas. "But that was always the point, wasn't it?"

"It was," I murmur.

Baby would have hated all of this. The fishbowl cosmos. The faux-fancy steakhouse with dim lighting that kept you from actually seeing your meal. The silly birthday hats bobbing on our heads. But, as Reggie says, that had always been the point. Birthdays were about embarrassing my little sister, and she'd loved it. Baby had been the kind of kid who'd make us swear not to tell a server it was her birthday and then be bitterly disappointed if we did not.

Reggie excelled at finding the line between delighting her and actually embarrassing her. They'd been friends since college. For her twenty-seventh birthday, he'd hired a *Dirty Dancing* impersonator to sweep her off her feet, quite literally. As an assistant professor, she'd been in the middle of giving a lecture at the time. She'd sworn she'd never forgive him, but she had glowed like she had the first time we saw *Dirty Dancing* together, when she decided she would henceforth be known as Baby, not Babette.

The next year, it had been my turn to surprise her, and I'd vowed to outdo Reggie. I never got the chance. My sister spent her twenty-eighth birthday in a coffin. When the date rolled around, Reggie and I had sat in these exact chairs, drinking silly cosmos and wearing silly hats and sobbing onto our untouched meals. With each passing year, we've cried a little less, laughed a little more. Now, for Baby's thirtieth, there haven't been any tears yet. No laughter, either. I'm not in the mood. Reggie senses that and stays quiet.

She would have hated this, indeed.

"We were supposed to have a party tonight," Reggie says as he takes a long swig of his drink. "She promised that for her thirtieth, I could throw her a surprise party."

I nod. I should make a joke about my sister not understanding the concept of *surprise* parties. I should talk about the party my parents threw for her sixteenth birthday. Or the drunken debauch I arranged for her twenty-first.

Dip into the shadow of memory. Conjure my sister to life. I owe her that much.

Before I can, Reggie says, "Have you heard anything from the police?"

I stiffen, and he makes a face. "Sorry, Lisette. I know you would tell me. I just keep hoping. . ." He smacks his glass down, pink liquid sloshing. "How the fuck did he get away with it?"

I don't answer. I don't need to. I can predict his next words well enough to recite them. I'd written the original script, after all. The drunken rants in those first few months, when I'd call up Reggie and demand to know how my sister's husband got away with murder. As if being a social worker meant Reggie was responsible for the system that let Leo kill her. Now Reggie makes the alcohol- and frustration-laced soliloquy his own, and I can tune it out.

I remember the first time Baby admitted that Leo was hitting her. Until then, she'd insisted the danger signs existed only in my head. If I said he seemed controlling, I was overreacting. If I questioned her eye makeup, she was just tired. She laughed off my concerns. Typical overprotective big sister. Then she stopped laughing and started withdrawing. And I stopped asking because that was the only way I could stay in her life. I needed to be there for her when she was ready to admit it.

She told Reggie first. Did that sting? A little. But he *is* a social worker. He knew how to handle it, gently working on Baby until she was ready to leave Leo. When the call for help came, it was my number she dialed. That middle-of-the-night cry for rescue that only her big sister could answer.

I got her out. And I still didn't save her. Couldn't save her, and I'll never forgive myself for that.

I make it through dinner as best I can. I push my food around. Take a few sips of my drink. Biding my time, because what I need to say cannot be said here.

***

We're in the alley, heading to Reggie's car. He's staggering a little. One hand goes to my shoulder, and I catch his arm, steadying him.

"I loved her," he says, his eyes glistening with tears.

"I know."

"Not just as a friend."

"I know."

"I just wish we had more time. I wish I could have told her."

"She knew."

"I should have been there, Lisette." His voice catches in a sob. "We thought it was safe. We thought *she* was safe. He hadn't contacted her in weeks, and she finally felt ready to move out on her own, and then. . ."

He doesn't need to say the rest. After Baby left Leo, she'd moved in with Reggie. A month of that, and she'd declared herself ready to fly.

To start a new life. Two days of freedom. That's all she got before I showed up to take her to lunch and found her in the bathroom—

I squeeze my eyes shut against the memory. Then I say, softly, "I hired a private eye, Reggie."

He stops walking, sobering instantly. "What?"

"When our grandmother died this spring, I came into a bit of money. I'd always told myself that as soon as I had extra, I'd spend it on Baby. On doing the police's job and getting evidence. Hard evidence."

"And?"

I shake my head. "I was a fool for thinking it would make a difference. She'd reported the abuse. She'd reported the calls and the threats. He has no alibi for the time of death. He'd texted her the day before her death, telling her she'd regret leaving him. The problem is that it's all circumstantial, and three years after the fact, there's nothing left for them to find."

"We know he did it. *They* know he did it. There's just nothing anyone can do."

I go quiet, and he peers at me in the darkness. A distant rain gutter drips one, twice, three times before I whisper. "There's something *I* can do. There's something I'm going to do. Tonight."

He goes quiet. Then he says, carefully, "Do you mean. . ."

I look up, seeing my wan smile reflected in his glasses. "I mean whatever you want me to mean, Reggie. This is your chance to walk away. The only reason I'm mentioning it is because you said . . ." I trail off, gaze dropping. "You were angry. More than a little drunk. So, it's probably best if we say goodbye here."

"I said I wanted to kill him." Reggie's voice is hollow with grief. "I asked for your help. You said you weren't ready."

"I'm ready now."

We're silent for a few moments, that distant drip echoing.

Reggie takes a deep breath. "All right, then. I wish I could have left you out of it, Lisette, but I need you to get close to him. He hates me." Reggie shoves his hands into his pockets. "Does he still drunk-text you?"

"Every month like clockwork. Telling me he didn't do it. Begging me to believe him."

"Asshole. He couldn't be helpful and confess, could he?"

"That'd be too easy. As for getting close to him, though, I know where he'll be tonight. Where he goes every night on her birthday. And it's the perfect spot for. . ."

I open my purse and show him the gun.

***

We're in Baby's favorite place in the world. Well, one of a dozen favorite places. That was Baby, endlessly and exuberantly delighted by the world around her.

When she graduated, she'd declared she was done being called Baby. She was going to be a professor, after all. *Babette* suited that version of her. Yet some of us, like myself and Reggie, never stopped calling her Baby, because it suited the real her: the wide-eyed and curious child. The innocent, good-hearted girl who'd met a controlling bastard and told herself she could fix him. She would show him kindness and light, and he would respond to it. Instead, Leo took Baby's goodness as a personal affront and tried to beat it out of her. He tried to drag her down to his level. And when that failed . . .

This specific favorite spot of Baby's is a park near the college where she went to school and later taught. A hundred acres of trails and forest that she jogged every day. Jogged at dawn and after dusk, no matter how many times I told her it wasn't safe. I'd been wrong. The danger she faced didn't come from a man lurking in the bushes.

When Baby died, our parents donated a park bench to her and put it along her favorite trail. As I listen to the roar of the nearby river,

Reggie walks over and stares down at the plaque.

"Here? Leo comes *here* on her birthday?"

"He told me in one of those drunken texts, as if it proved how much he loved her." I pull up my glove to check my watch. "He comes at one AM. That's the time they met."

"Oh, I remember. I was at that damned frat party."

I tell Reggie my plan. There's a thick stand of trees nearby. When Leo pauses to pay his respects, Reggie will come out and confront him. I'll take advantage of the distraction to sneak up and shoot Leo. Then we'll dump his body in the river.

Reggie agrees, and I lead him into the stand of forest.

"The best hiding spot is back here," I say. "I marked it with a— Oh, there is it. See the ribbon?"

He nods and heads toward it.

"Can you grab that, please?" I say. "We can't leave anything behind."

He pulls the yellow ribbon from the sapling. Then he turns to find my gun pointed at him.

"Lisette?" He looks behind him, as if expecting to see Leo there.

"I lied," I say. "I did hire a private investigator. Not to prove Leo did it. To prove you did."

"Wh-what?"

"Two years, Reggie. I guessed the truth two years ago. I took your calls and got you drunk on Baby's birthday, even putting something in your drink last year. Praying you'd let something slip. But you didn't. So, I hired a private investigator. Tonight, you joked about Leo drunkenly confessing. That's what you did, isn't it?"

"I don't know what—"

"The private eye found this." I pull a printed sheet of paper from my pocket. "Your confession. You were drunk, I presume. The next morning, you deleted the file but not well enough. The investigator pulled it off your hard drive."

"Then he made it up, Lisette." Sweat beads on his forehead. "Concocted a story to convince you to keep paying him. I didn't kill Baby. I loved her."

"So you said. And I told you she knew that. How could she not? You wouldn't stop telling her! She always knew you had a crush, but she thought you'd gotten past it. You were so good, giving her a place to stay when she left Leo. But then you wouldn't leave her alone. And when she moved out, you killed her."

Reggie shakes his head. "It was an accident. She didn't understand! I loved her. I'd always loved her. She *needed* me."

"She needed a friend."

He starts to cry, shaking his head. "It was an *accident*. She just wouldn't listen. I'd never hurt her on purpose, Lisette. Never. I'm not Leo. I'm the good guy here."

I lower the gun and walk over to him. He spreads his arms for a hug, his face contorted with grief. I step into his arms. They close around me. When I step away, he's holding the gun.

"Reggie?" I say. "What are you doing?"

He blinks down at it. "What? No. I-I didn't—"

The gun rises, pulling his hand up with it.

"Reggie! Don't!"

"I-I'm not." His voice squeaks. "I'm not doing it."

The gun points at his temple. His eyes bulge. His mouth opens. And I smile. I let him see me smile. Then I flick my hand, and the gun fires, and the silenced gun gives a soft *pfft* as the bullet slams into his brain. He only has time to gasp, and then he's sliding to the ground, gun falling by his side.

I glance around. The park stays silent and still.

Another flick of my hand slides Reggie's printed confession into his pocket. I stand there, watching him, watching and wishing I could have done more. That I could have used my power to save my sister. But it's

213

such a little thing, more of a parlor trick, really. Not enough to save her. Just enough to avenge her.

I stand there, and I breathe. I just breathe. Tears prickle, but I blink them back. Later. Those will come later.

Before I go, I walk to the bench and let my gloved fingers graze the plaque commemorating my sister's life.

"Happy birthday, Baby," I whisper, and then I walk away.

Devil's Hollow

Errick Nunnally

Mike held his son's shoulder, looked around the campus, and said, "So much better than a state college." He poked his son in the chest. "A man's gotta get out and take a few shots to the balls, to learn a few things."

"Dad. . ."

Mike grinned at his wife and surprised Davey with a light slap in the crotch.

Karla cringed, but only inside. Outside, she maintained a stoic facade and made no comment. There were actions she could take, however, small things she could do to break the momentum without drawing her husband's ire. She stepped between the two and hugged her son, congratulating him on his first day and wishing him well. She held his face and blocked her son's embarrassed eyes from his father.

"We have a flight to catch. You two should say your goodbyes," she said, wiping at the corner of her eye.

Mike thrust his hand out for a shake. "Don't forget, m'boy, you're here because of my hard-earned dollars. I never took it easy on you, because I knew you could make something of yourself. Just like your old man. Make me proud." Despite going soft around the middle, Mike was still a strong, imposing man. A successful salesman forever eyeing a dealership of his own.

Davey's jaw muscles rippled as his father grasped his hand and squeezed. He preferred *David*, but his father insisted on infantilizing his name. He treated his son like a smaller version of himself, an offshoot, a product.

David was at college on a full athletic scholarship—the same as his father—but he wasn't planning on becoming his father. Football was the old man's preferred sport, and David had chosen lacrosse. His father understood how rough the game was and begrudgingly accepted it.

Karla watched as her son leaned in to meet his father's hand. David had learned long before to meet his father's handshakes aggressively, to thrust his hand forward so that their palms met at the crook of thumb and pointer. If he failed at the move, it meant getting his knuckles ground together. He was nearly as tall as his father and entering the physical prime of his life. Karla knew that David squeezed back just as hard.

Mike released his grip and slapped his son's shoulder. Karla waved, a sad smile on her face.

On the way back to their rental car, Mike massaged his fingers. Karla maintained the silence, encouraging her husband's reverie.

Mike ordered whiskey and sodas on the plane until the attendant gently deflected his requests.

"Do I seem at all drunk to you?"

The flight attendant, a young woman half Mike's size, smiled and said, "Not at all, sir. It's our policy to limit drink service for everyone."

"Bulldung!" Mike barked, a sly grin on his face. He winked at the attendant.

Karla sat in the middle seat, studiously avoiding involvement.

When the attendant met her eyes, Karla offered a weak smile.

"I can show you our policy if you like, sir." The airline worker exuded good humor and professionalism.

Mike held his hands up in surrender and leaned on his charm. "Okay, okay, I know when I'm beat. How about just a club soda for me, then?"

He did that with women mostly, a sort of reverse play where he came on strong, then caved easily. It'd worked on Karla. Worked until she'd said yes to the ring. Until she got pregnant. Even when the drinking increased.

Karla felt a strong nudge. Mike nodded in the attendant's direction. The nametag on her lapel said *Rachel*.

"Anything for you, miss?"

"Oh, no, I'm fine, thank you."

The attendant nodded and turned to leave.

"No, wait," Karla said, "I'll have a cola. Whichever brand is fine."

"Yes, ma'am."

"No, I'm sorry—"

Mike said, "Jeez, make up your fuckin' mind, Karla."

Karla stared at the back of the seat in front of her and said, "Water, please."

"You're makin' this lady's job way harder than it needs to be. All she's gotta do is bring you a drink." Mike grinned at Rachel. "It's not a thousand-piece puzzle; I mean, if you're thirsty, you should know what you want to drink—"

"Actually," Rachel interjected, "you wouldn't believe the training we have to do in order to bring drinks."

"Oh?" Mike said. "Do tell." He leaned forward a bit, the better to beam into Rachel's face.

Rachel briefly met Karla's eyes and a jolt of emotion passed between them. Karla felt a sudden sense of safety and calm. The attendant launched into a brief of technical requirements, medical training, safety regulations, and more. Mike forgot about his wife, pleased to have Rachel's full attention. And that was the flight. When they deplaned, the attendant stopped Karla and handed her a folded piece of paper.

"That book on Italy I mentioned."

"I don't—" Karla's train of thought derailed when their fingers touched and a pop of static electricity zapped her. Smells of flowing water and wet stone hit her nose, out of place for any jetway. The corrugated walls rippled, making a sound like windblown grass.

"Sorry! You mentioned Italy early in the flight. When I asked about your travel interests, remember? It's a good one; you can check it out at the library."

"Oh, right."

"Chrissakes, Karla, let's go. Thank the lady," Mike said.

"I. . . Thank you, Rachel, I'll look into it, next time I'm at the library." A feeling of subterfuge swept across her, international spies and forbidden meaning. It was a moment of unexpected joy, a bit of fun that she indulged in the moment.

They drove home with Mike leaning hard on the gas and cursing other drivers.

Before the garage door could close all the way, Mike yanked the bags out of the trunk and dropped them in the foyer. He stalked into the dining room and pulled out a bottle of bourbon. They'd had dinner before the flight, but Karla knew her husband well and went into the kitchen. She pulled out the fixings for a sandwich.

Mike swallowed a mouthful of whiskey and said, "What are you doing?"

In the midst of washing her hands, she replied, "You're headed back to work tomorrow. It'll be early. We had such an early dinner, I thought some food now would help you sleep well and get a fresh start."

"That's what you thought, huh? That I looked hungry?" Mike leaned back, a thoughtful look on his face.

Karla didn't answer and he didn't ask again. She focused on the task at hand. By the time she brought the sandwich over to the table and set it in front of him, he looked melancholy.

"Davey's gone," he said.

She nodded, refusing the bait to disagree with his statement. Instead, she gave a tight smile and said, "Our little boy's off to college."

"That he is." Mike eyed the sandwich and took another drink of whiskey. "But he ain't little anymore."

"Right. Well, I'm going to unpack and shower. Airports, you know?" She shivered a bit.

"Yeah."

Karla walked into the kitchen and froze when he called her name. Mike said, "I love him, you know? I do."

Then you should've told him once in a while. Karla thought. "I know," she said, over her shoulder.

"Thanks for the sandwich," he said to her back. She heard him take a bite.

"You're welcome," she answered, and walked into the foyer.

Upstairs, Karla unpacked, disrobed, and ran a hot shower. Afterward, she toweled off, moisturized, and pulled a large tube of aloe vera from the cabinet beneath the sink. She ran the hot water while applying balm to the bruise on her tricep. When the water steamed, she filled a small rubber bottle and placed it against the five purple marks for several minutes.

She looked down at her body and her flat stomach. Strong cheekbones, even features, wavy hair in a short cut that framed and accentuated her deep brown eyes. She put the effort in, worked out more often than she didn't. Mike insisted; he liked it that way. Like the bruise on her arm, Mike left an imprint on whatever he thought was his.

Karla took a ragged breath, forcing her thoughts to stop unreeling. She put everything away. Before leaving the bathroom, she peeked into the bedroom to see if Mike had come upstairs while she was in the shower. The bed was empty. She turned on the light on Mike's side of the bed, turned hers off, and crawled under the covers, listening. After ten minutes, she could hear her husband's heavy steps on the stairs. She curled up, tense, struggling to keep her breathing even. The noise of blood rushing in her ears couldn't drown out Mike's puttering before bed.

Dresser drawers opened and closed, his wallet *clack*ed on top. The clatter of his watch on the nightstand, shoes thumping on the floor, the light metallic jangle of his belt.

The bed creaked and shook as Mike sat on the edge. She could smell a cloud of alcohol around him. Like a light fog or the rush of energy preceding a storm. His breathing heaved. He sighed and the sound of skin on skin raked her nerves as Mike rubbed his face. She held her breath as he pulled the covers back, flopped over, and snuggled up behind her. He ran one of his thick hands through her hair and down her side. She didn't react, maintaining deep, regular breaths. He dropped his heavy arm over her, settling into the pillows. Blasts of hot, whiskey-tinged air tickled the back of her head. It seemed as if Mike's breathing triggered the flash of a terrible idea in her mind. She buried it, more concerned with the present.

Karla didn't fall asleep until Mike's snores rumbled through the air and she'd managed to put down the wicked thought.

***

Karla rose first, starting the coffee and a shopping list. The remnants of Mike's sandwich and an empty bottle remained on the table. She disposed of the crumbs and recycled the bottle.

Mike thumped down the stairs, finishing his tie. He grabbed some bread for toast and ran his hands through his short hair. As he poured a travel mug of coffee, he asked, "Shopping today, right?"

"Yes," she said.

"Be sure to get me another bottle of bourbon."

"Devil's Hollow," she said, and wrote it down.

"Yeah, duh." The toaster popped and Mike swiped butter on the browned bread. "Gonna be a good day; I can feel it." He grinned and took a large bite of toast.

"That's great," Karla said. "Good luck."

Mike slipped his sportcoat on and spoke around the last of his toast between his teeth. "Don't need luck, babe; I got skills to pay the bills. Gotta go."

Mike traveled to work light, taking only his coffee mug. No briefcase, no lunch, nothing but his phone to keep track of clients and his wife. He preferred it that way, focusing on seizing the day ahead. It was his focus and determination that made him a good athlete, a great salesman, and little else.

It wasn't until she entered the club retail store that Karla realized she was only shopping for two. Without their son at home, the usual volume of food wasn't required. The giant portions available there would go to waste. As she passed the alcohol aisle, she saw what wouldn't go to waste. The endcap was a bright red display featuring 1.75-liter bottles of Devil's Hollow bourbon.

This was new to the store and it was a huge bargain on the price of the usual 750-milliliter size. She placed two bottles in the cart and finished the rest of her errands without acknowledging that she often wondered when Mike's drinking would put him out of her misery. Even though she hadn't completed her nursing program, she had enough experience to know what alcohol did to the body. What it could do. His doctor had already warned him about the slight swelling of his liver and jaundice.

On the way out of the building, while digging for her keys, she came across the paper the flight attendant had handed her. She still couldn't remember the conversation that sparked the note. She unfolded it and looked at the unfamiliar title. The library was on the way home, so even if Mike were checking her location, it wouldn't be suspicious. He'd witnessed the exchange while deplaning, and reading wasn't a problem.

The librarian—Janet, an older woman with greying locs and a warm personality—directed her to the stacks where the book was. Karla saw Janet frequently. She pulled one of three copies down and flipped through. Dust swirled from the pages and hung in the air. It was a dry account of seventeenth-century Italy. A musky, sweet scent hovered in the book along with smells of wine and tepid water, straw and wood. Amongst pages dedicated to the plagues and wars troubling the country, there was a slip of paper with a phone number printed on it and the words *Help is here.* Curious, she flipped through the other two books and found the same slip of paper and old scents. Sunlight from the tall window nearby blinded her, and she startled, seeing the silhouette of a woman watching her. She shifted her weight to get the sun out of her eyes and there was no one there, just the warmth of the late-afternoon sun. An urgent feeling swept through her and she checked the time. Best to get moving. She took the book to the counter, where Janet paused at Karla's choice.

Karla said, "You know there's a piece of paper in there? With a phone number?"

The librarian licked her lips and said, "Oh. I do. Are you going to call it?"

"I don't know. Seems like a not-safe thing to do."

Janet looked left and right before handing Karla the library phone. "I . . ."

"Honey, I know someone's not treating you right and I know someone pointed you at this book. You can use this phone and see what it is, and if you want to talk privately, call them back later."

Karla swallowed hard and ignored the little zing of static from the phone's plastic shell. She felt exposed. Taking a deep breath, she dialed the number, listened to the message, and disconnected the call. She pushed the phone across the counter, back to the librarian.

Janet put the phone on the cradle and said, "You can call later."

"No," Karla said, "I can't do that."

Janet sighed and said, "If it's a matter of privacy. . ."

Karla nodded—a small movement, a hesitant gesture.

"You don't have your own phone." Janet said it as a matter of fact, intuiting Karla's situation. She pulled her purse from beneath the desk and counted out two twenty-dollar bills. "You can buy a burner phone with this and at least a hundred minutes. Untraceable."

Karla stared at the bills on the counter, her mind a frenzy of the good memories she clung to, the ones before she became pregnant with her son. Memories that tangled with what followed during the pregnancy and the years after. Threads that had been corrupted. She couldn't quite remember herself anymore, what life was like before nursing school and before Mike had courted her. She placed one hand slowly on the money and whispered, "Thank you."

"You're welcome," Janet said, "The book's due in two weeks."

In the car, her mouth dry, Karla turned the ignition, rushing through the motions to get moving. If she hurried, a quick stop at Target wouldn't be noticeable.

***

Karla dialed the number.

It had been a race to put everything away, tidy up, start dinner, and carve the temporary phone out of its fused-plastic prison. Her armpits prickled with sweat as the line connected. There'd be no turning back if she confessed her situation to a stranger.

Now is the time, she'd told herself. *David is out of the house and Mike is off his game.* She'd resigned herself to further years of this existence because she'd need help and none was forthcoming. Both her parents had passed; she had no siblings and no best friends. Now this.

On the second ring, she realized that the refuse of the phone's package sat at her elbow and Mike would be home soon.

Shit.

It had to be disposed of where Mike wouldn't notice.

Shit, shit, shit. . .

She tucked the phone to her ear and gathered up the plastic bits and paper. Someone picked up on the third ring as she shoved the detritus into a small plastic bag.

The woman who answered ran through her short spiel with a pleasant tone and identified herself as "Caroline." Karla answered, sounding close to breathless. The operator's tone shifted, immediacy entered her voice, and she asked if Karla were in any sort of danger and if she needed assistance.

"No," Karla stammered and took a deep breath. "No. I was just. . .throwing something away that I'd forgotten."

"Okay, that's no problem," Caroline said. "What's your name?"

"Karla." She went to the garbage can beside the garage and moved some bags around. Then she tore a bag on the bottom and slipped the packaging debris inside.

"Got it, thank you. Let me tell you something real quick before we continue." Caroline explained the confidentiality of the call and the legal protections, a scripted spiel. "What brings you to call us today?"

Karla dropped the phone into the garbage. Frantic, she rooted around, found it, and put it up to her ear. "I'm sorry! I dropped the phone in the garbage!" She huffed a nervous laugh.

"That's okay, not a problem. What can you tell me about why you're calling today?"

"Well, um, someone recommended me."

"I see. A friend or family?"

"A friend. I guess? Yes, a friend." Karla made her way back inside.

"That sounds like a story. Can you tell me more about that? Oh! Sorry, before that, are you able to provide any contact information? A phone number or address?"

"I. . .think so. This is a—a new phone."

"I understand. Is it disposable?"

Karla drummed her fingers hard on the counter. "Yes."

"Okay, so it's a temporary number. But before you give me the number, I want you to make sure you can silence the phone. We'll only schedule a call with your permission, and the caller ID will be masked like a doctor's office. If you don't answer, we won't leave a message and you can call us back. Is that okay?"

Karla checked the side of the phone and flipped it to silent. She said, "Yes," and gave Caroline the number.

"All right, thank you. How are you feeling? Have you had any thoughts about hurting yourself?"

"Hurting myself? No, I haven't thought of. . .that. Not hurting me, anyway."

And just like that, the thoughts she'd been burying felt real; they'd been given air and life outside of her mind. All the fear and suppressed feelings unfurled, a sinuous, dark shape.

"I understand that. Do you want to tell me how you came to be recommended?"

Karla relaxed a bit and told her about Rachel the flight attendant and Janet the librarian.

"That's something, all right," Caroline said, "What was it, you think, that made Rachel share that with you?"

Karla recounted Mike's behavior on the flight and how Janet had diverted his attention.

Caroline made encouraging sounds as Karla spoke, and asked, "Where were you coming from?"

Karla explained the purpose of the trip.

"Congratulations on getting that done! How'd your husband handle the drop-off?"

Karla told her. Then she heard the garage door opening. "Caroline,

I have to go. My husband's home."

"Will you call us back, Karla?"

"Yes," she whispered. With that admission, she felt like there was a crack in the walls keeping her in this marriage.

"You can ask for me or speak to anyone else. Okay?"

"Okay." She ended the call and put the phone in a pocket of her purse, beneath her emergency pads. Another small act of rebellion, of subterfuge. The phone could come in handy other ways, as well. In an emergency, she reasoned. If Mike—

Mike opened the door and boomed, "Winning! Big sales today. *Big. Sales.*" He chuckled as he strode into the kitchen.

Karla stood at the stove, stirring a stew, and Mike grabbed her shoulders before kissing the back of her neck.

She smiled.

"You look good today, babe." Mike patted her backside.

She smiled again.

He didn't spend much time on her; it wasn't but a few seconds of interaction before he headed to the cabinet in the dining room. The bottle wasn't inside the cabinet, however; it wouldn't fit.

"Holy shit. The size of these things. . . What the hell'd you do?"

"They were on sale," she said, "the warehouse had them, it was cheaper overall, and I know you like it."

Mike walked back into the kitchen, carrying one bottle, appraising it thoughtfully. "I mean, thank you. I guess. That's a big bottle, huh? Yeah. Really unexpected."

Karla could feel his size, how he was taking up the room like he couldn't bear to share the air. The cracks in the walls were filling back in. She turned off the burner and twisted her hands together. "You're unhappy with it? I can take it back."

Mike shook his head. "Yeah, no. I just didn't expect. . . What, you tryin' to drink me to death?" He laughed, a braying double bark. A sound that drew attention wherever he was.

She flinched but then smiled.

"Too loud? You used to be made of sterner stuff. Huh. Yeah, no. I guess it's fitting, after today. Big sales, big bottle. I earned this." He cracked the top and went back to the cabinet for a glass. He spoke from the other room. "Today's sales are going to bring me close to Girard's record. I might match it or, I dunno, if I get lucky. . ."

Joe Girard. Guinness World Record holder for car sales and author. Mike used Girard's sales record as his gold standard, she recalled.

"Wasn't there some other fellow who broke that record?" she asked.

"Ali Reda," Mike answered. "But that's impossible. I bet the fuckin' raghead got his family to buy half those cars; there's just no way."

Karla flinched at the slur. Then she relaxed by a measure, content that Mike's scorn landed elsewhere for the moment. She brought supper to the table. Beef stew and biscuits. One of Mike's favorites. They sat. There were two rocks glasses at the table; each had two fingers of whiskey in it.

"Celebrate with me," he said, salting his stew before shoving a mouthful in around a bite of biscuit. "Big man, big appetite," he liked to say.

Karla grinned and sighed. She scooped up the glass, went back into the kitchen, and dropped a few ice cubes into the glass.

"Hey!" Mike said. "You don't ice this bourbon. That's not how you drink it; it's gotta be neat to enjoy the flavor, the *heat*."

"Mike. . ."

"C'mon, Karla, you don't bring snow to the Devil's Hollow." He grinned, holding up a glass to toast. "Next one's gonna be neat. Right?"

She smiled and nodded before taking a sip. "Sure, I guess this is appropriate because. . ." She paused, chewing on the words. "I want to go back to nursing school."

Mike took a long pull on his whiskey and sat back. "You want to go back, huh? I thought you were done with that."

She shook her head. "When I got pregnant, you convinced me it'd be better to focus on David. And family. You were doing so well—still are—it just made sense. But I loved it and I miss it. Now that David's off to college, I thought—"

"I thought we might have another baby." He finished his whiskey and poured a second that was taller than the first.

Karla couldn't mask her shock.

Mike smiled and shivered in a dramatic gesture. "What? You're in great shape, not even forty yet, we got some years left, and. . . I think it'd be good for you. Give you something better to focus on. Dragging yourself through school with women half your age. Homework, late nights. What's the alternative? Empty nest syndrome? Like you said, I'm doing great; there's no reason for you to go back to that or change bedpans."

"Mike. . ."

"Hey, what? Is this why you were at the library so long today? Huh? Research, I guess?" He emptied his glass and poured another.

Karla folded her hands and looked down at her bowl. "No. I picked up a history book. About Italy."

A book that smelled of ancient clay and slow-moving water.

Mike sighed, took a sip of whiskey, and said, "Okay, okay, I get it. You want to get away from me, the house, empty nest, and all that."

"No," she said, "it's not like that; I just—"

"No, no, it's fine, whatever. Hey, look, let's sleep on it. Okay? We both want something, they're both"—he wiggled his fingers together— "intertwined and messy. I don't want to argue. Today was a big win, so we celebrate. Okay? I earned this moment, I *earned this*. Right? Like you said, I'm doing great. Now drink up, and second one's gonna be ice-free!"

Mike's charming capitulation that wasn't capitulation at all, his easy grin, the laser focus he seemed to bring on her, the attention. It all reminded her of how they got there—how she got there. How she got pregnant, by not thinking of her own future, the way Mike's trajectory eventually smothered her own. All because she stopped thinking of herself. No. That wasn't right. She never stopped thinking of herself, but she stopped believing in herself. She kept putting Mike first, and that had to stop or she might never have a life of her own.

A blast of anger surprised her. A lightheadedness fogged her brain and her hand trembled as she ate some stew. The routine of eating hid the sudden emotion, smothering it for Mike's sake. Fury took her again as she stared into her bowl.

"C'mon, Karla, don't be like that."

She smiled, raised her glass, and said, "Sleep on it."

"Yeah"—Mike beamed—"that's the ticket." He downed his whiskey. Before he refilled both glasses, he dumped her remaining ice and served them both three fingers of whiskey.

Mike nattered on around mouthfuls of food about his sales that day, while Karla chewed and sipped. The more she drank, the less the Devil burned and the angrier she felt. She took larger gulps and barely noticed Mike refilling her glass. She thought of Caroline's question earlier that day. Did she think of hurting herself?

Yes.

Another gulp of whiskey.

No.

This wasn't the pain she wanted.

This isn't my pain.

The room tilted as Mike's stories wound down.

I shouldn't be feeling this pain.

"Whoa, there," Mike said.

Karla put both hands on the table and heaved her body up. All she had left was anger to guide her. "I'm going to bed. I have to lie down," she said, her words sounding distant to her ears.

Then she was sitting again and Mike's hands were under her shoulders. His voice was in her ear; it was always in her ear. He was helping her to bed. She stumbled on the stairs and his bulk held her up. She touched the side of his face, the numbing bourbon making the motion seem affectionate. He cupped her ass and pushed her up the stairs, laughing.

They stumbled into the bedroom together. He pawed at her and the room spun. She reeled in confusion, not understanding how they'd gotten there. She tried to remember the man she'd loved, the one who'd convinced her to be a stay-at-home mom, to drop out of school, to commit herself to family.

Family. Families supported each other, didn't they? *Family* meant to love *and* respect, didn't it?

Mike peeled Karla's clothes away and she lay on the bed, pushing at him. He was too heavy; she made a strangled sound and Mike huffed back, a man in passion. He thrust, one arm awkwardly pinning her arm by the crook of her elbow. He attempted titillation and clumsily nibbled her lip before biting down in a spasm as he finished.

She tasted blood but felt little pain.

***

Dark was all Karla could see. It was cold, but sweat ran down her temples and between her breasts. She was uncovered. One leg was tangled in a sheet. Mike's grinding snore and the broad expanse of his back consumed her senses.

Mouth thick with mucus and lips dry, she struggled to untangle herself. Mike didn't stir. She pulled harder and rolled to her feet, stumbling to the bathroom. The light sent a shock of pain to her head, and she remembered dinner and afterward. Her lip hurt, and when she looked in the mirror, she could see the teeth marks and swelling. Dried blood glued half of her mouth shut. She sighed, a shaky, reedy sound, and ran warm water across her mouth until she could pry her lips apart. The wound came alive to send a bright jolt of pain from lip to chin. Her stomach heaved and she lunged for the toilet. A violent surge of stew and bile fled her body. The scent of alcohol and half-digested food floated like a cloud at the back of her throat. She shivered at the toilet long enough to wonder how much time had passed. Cold and stiff, she had to get up.

I need to do more than get up, she thought.

Anger drove her to her feet again. She pulled on a bathrobe, slipped her feet into slippers, and stepped out of the bathroom. Mike lay like a felled, snoring log. He was half-naked, wearing black socks and a white T-shirt soaked with sweat.

Every dark thought she'd held back the past few years uncoiled and rose, a jumble of rage and frustration. She'd shared her story with Caroline earlier, given it air. Now it was real, she'd loosed it, this thing, and it whipped around her brain like an open firehouse. It was the basest kind of clarity. She padded downstairs, drew the longest knife they had from the block, and went back up the stairs. In their bedroom, she stood over her husband, clutching the blade. She pressed it to his neck and pushed—just a little.

He didn't react.

Her blood hammered at her temples, each pump a dull shock of pain. She trembled, telling herself to push harder, that she didn't have anything to live for, anyway.

That's not true, she thought.

There was David and there was *herself*. She withdrew carefully, going back downstairs to return the knife to the block. She rinsed and refilled the coffeepot and set the timer, her mind a swirl of terrifying thoughts. Her fingers trembled from sheer adrenaline or anger—she couldn't tell which. With the pot set, she curled up on the couch, twisting into herself within the robe, and cried until she fell asleep.

***

Karla awoke to Mike's phlegmy voice in the kitchen.

"Coffee! Thank God."

The clatter of the pot and crack of the travel mug on the counter brought her to a sitting position. Mike called her name.

Without a thought, she answered, "I'm in here."

"Damn, the kitchen's still a wreck. I thought you came down here early to deal with that or something?"

Or something. She ground her teeth.

Mike peeked into the living room and said, "Wow, you look like shit." He froze, taking in what he was seeing of his wife. "Oh, no! Did I do that?" In two strides, he was next to the couch, sliding to a knee and cradling her face.

She didn't meet his eyes.

"Oh, my God, I'm so sorry. I didn't mean to do that; it was just passion. We were so hot and heavy and. . . I'm so sorry. Oh, God, I bit you, didn't I? That's. . .not me. I wouldn't do that. Did you put some ice on that, baby?"

She shook her head no.

"Here, I'll get you some." He left, rummaged in the freezer, and returned with a towel wrapped around shattered cubes of ice. He pressed it to her lip and she flinched.

"Sorry," he said, "I'm so sorry. I swear I'll make it up to you."

Karla smiled. As painful as it was, she smiled and nodded. And Mike left for work. She walked into the kitchen, holding the ice to her lip, and looked at the mess. She dumped the ice, picked up a curved plate, and hovered over the sink. She put the plate on the counter, dug beneath the pads in her purse, and dialed the number that had so serendipitously fallen into her lap days before.

She asked for Caroline, and before anything but the basic pleasantry of *hello* could be exchanged, she told Caroline what had happened from the day before.

"That's awful," Caroline said. "Can you see a doctor or I could send someone to help? I have referrals in your area, if that'd help."

"No," Karla answered, "thank you. I. . . I have a little medical experience. I know I'm okay, that I'll be okay. Physically. I'm just. . . I'm so angry. . . I can't— There's nothing. . ." She growled, a guttural sound that kicked off a gasping flood of teeth-grinding tears.

Caroline held the line the entire time, offering consolation and reassuring Karla that she was there and could offer other kinds of help if Karla wanted.

"Thank you, Caroline." Karla rubbed the scalding sensation out of her eyes and sniffed, believing she caught a whiff of roses and wondering where it came from. "I just needed to vent some. Y'know? I have to clean up now. I'm a mess, the kitchen's a mess." The depth of her emotion had taken her by surprise. It made her feel ashamed, and using the atrophied muscle of self-interest left some soreness. With the discomfort came air, however; she could breathe again.

"Right, sure. I understand," Caroline said, "Will you call tomorrow or tonight and let me know you're okay? Or I can call you back?"

"I'll call."

"Good, that's great. Uh, listen, Karla?"

"Yes?"

"I think— I'd like to recommend you to someone that might be able to do you one better than I can. She's sort of a specialist in situations like yours."

"I don't know. . ."

"If you choose not to, I understand, that's fine. Her name's Giulia, if you change your mind. You can ask for me or her when you call, no problem. Today, tomorrow, whenever, day or night. It's totally up to you. I trust your judgment."

***

The amount of malice humming through her veins disoriented her. She had to get straight. First, she gulped down a pint of water, then set to her exercise regimen. An hour later, she cleaned the kitchen and attended to the laundry. Her lip throbbed in time with her heart, but she couldn't stop. The thoughts wouldn't stop—the ideas, what it would take.

Mike called from work—noting that he could see she was still home—to check in on her. It was a brief "I'm fine" conversation. Karla barely concealed her surprise at the timing of the call.

Karla put the clothes in the dryer and straightened up the garage, removing the remnants of David's childhood. The dark thoughts that had been bottled for years bubbled to life again and loosed rivulets of plans to infect her mind. She couldn't escape the vileness of her own ideas.

Her phone rang again and she tensed. It was David, however, not her husband. She took one deep, calming breath and answered.

"Hi, David; how's school?"

It was another brief call. David was between classes and wanted to check in. She let him know that she was fine and asked if he'd spoken to his father.

"No," David said in a flat voice.

"Okay, well, you two should talk. Let him know how you're doing."

"Yeah, okay, Mom. I gotta go; love you."

"I love you too, son."

There was nothing left to do but fidget with her phone. She rummaged in her purse for the other phone. She held the cheap plastic, believing she should feel remorse about her thoughts and finding none, before dialing the number.

A woman answered within a few rings.

"Hi, I've been talking with Caroline?"

"She's free. I'll connect you right—"

"No, wait! Um. Can I speak to Giulia?"

"Oh, sure, I'll connect you."

The line clicked and rang once.

"This is Giulia; how are you today?"

"Hi. Um, this is Karla. Caroline recommended me to you?"

"Yes, she did. Are you safe today?"

Giulia's voice wasn't as chipper as the others'. She had a no-nonsense tone. There was an edge to her voice, a surety. Giulia had a light accent that Karla couldn't place, something European, Spanish or Italian maybe. In the background, she could hear the low, rhythmic murmur of voices, chanting. It had been quiet with the others, no distractions. This felt different. She didn't feel like there was any other choice but to answer the question. *Yes,* she was safe. For now, Mike was at work.

"You're not thinking about hurting yourself, are you?"

It was an odd way of asking the question, Karla realized. She tensed, wondering if she should ask to speak with Caroline instead.

"Hello, Karla, are you still there?" Giulia oozed confidence.

"No. I mean, yes, I'm still here. The answer to your question is no, I'm not. . .thinking of suicide."

Karla's own words surprised her. She worried what Giulia might say next, what she might think. What was this feeling? They'd barely traded two sentences, and already she felt both safe and nervous with this woman.

"Then what are you thinking of, Karla?"

With this sharp *woman,* Karla thought. She sighed and said, "I, well, I've been. . . I've been having some thoughts I don't think are. . .healthy."

"About your husband? I know your story from Caroline."

Karla straightened. She began worrying about a record, some sort of trail that led back to her. "That doesn't sound right. I don't think she's supposed to do that."

"She didn't tell anyone else, just me. There's no written record."

"That's fine, but—"

"Tell me what you're thinking, Karla; let's walk through it together. We can't do that if I don't know what you're thinking."

Karla panicked; this woman knew too much already, this "Giulia" who she'd never met. Caroline too. The promised protection regarding their interactions felt flimsy at the moment, something ready to break off and fly to Mike and whisper in his ear. She could smell the book again, a dizzying swirl of sweet and pungent, like rubbing alcohol without the acidic bite.

"Karla," Giulia said.

A prickling current flowed through the phone. Karla felt dizzy for a moment and infected with Giulia's apparent resolve.

In a flood, Karla shared what she thought she could do to escape the situation with her husband. The *how* and *when*, the experience she had that would help, what could go wrong, why she couldn't do it—why she shouldn't, and the missing pieces.

After a moment's reflection, Giulia said, "You need a venipuncture kit."

Karla swallowed audibly, struggling with the last bit of a leash on her mind's worst instincts. "Only part of it."

"The needle, then. And you need to get it without anyone knowing."

She trembled, holding a thread of the past. "Yes," she whispered.

"You already have everything else you need. Give me your address; I'm going to send you a sweater. What size is your husband?"

"A. . .sweater?"

"Yes. Size?"

"XXL."

"It'll be there within two days, by Friday."

"But he'll. . ."

"See it, open it? Sure, maybe. But all he'll find is a sweater. Hand-knit. With a gift receipt. You'll find what you need, however, embedded in the cardboard."

This was a plan, not a thought; it was alive. The feelings within Karla writhed and pushed all common sense out of the way.

***

Karla had set the crockpot of lamb earlier in the day and brewed a large pot of tea. It had taken some care to make sure its color matched Devil's Hollow bourbon. She still had time for an errand to pick up trash bags, laundry detergent, and a few other items.

Yesterday had been quiet. Her husband had been chagrined about the damage he'd done to her lip—her face. For him, it was truly a mistake. He'd been cordial, mostly quiet, and still had several glasses of whiskey before bed. At her suggestion to call David, he'd been reluctant and expected his son to call first. Regardless, she'd cherished the respite and stuck to her routine. With luck, today wouldn't be any different, but she knew that time and drink quickly eroded her husband's softer edges.

The package hadn't arrived when she left for her errands, but by the time she got home, Mike was there. Home from work early. A rare occurrence. She pulled into the garage and stared at his car before gathering her resolve, and the bags, to enter the house. Mike sat in the living room, the open package on his lap. In one hand he held a rocks glass half-full with whiskey; in the other hand he held the handwritten receipt. In the natural light, she could see the sallow edges of his skin around his neck and ears.

Karla stood in the doorway and stared at him, unsure what to say or do. He stared back.

"C'mere," he said.

She walked over.

"There's this package for you; I. . .thought it was. . .weird. So, I opened it and— What is this? A gift? For who?" He pulled the brightly colored sweater partially out of the box.

"It's for you," she said. "Handmade."

Mike looked at the tag; it was his size, after all. "Huh. I don't remember seeing a charge for this." He set the box and drink aside, stood up, and placed both of his large hands on her upper arms. He squeezed and pulled her off-balance, looming over her.

In one shaky breath, Karla said, "One of the ladies at the library knits. She was working on one of those. We got to talking and I mentioned your birthday was coming up. She gave it to me. For you."

"Oh." He released her and looked down at the sweater. He ran his palm over it. "Feels nice. Kind of fag colors, though."

Karla looked down at her shoes and chewed her bruised lip.

Mike knit his brow and looked out the window, taking a quick drink from his glass. He squirmed, pushed the sweater back into the box, and said, "I ruined your surprise. I'm sorry, I didn't mean to—I just. . . Shit." He swayed, nudged the package on the chair, and left the room.

Karla stood in the room a few minutes more, feeling the cold air pass over the back of her legs and neck. Breathing evenly, she wondered where the lie had come from so quickly and eased past her lips like oil.

Karla heard the clatter of a bottle and glass in the kitchen.

She closed the door to the garage and looked at the box. The top of the gift receipt said, *Tofana's Threads.* Beneath that, a note of authenticity and guarantee of exchange. The sweater was nice, but she wasn't interested in that.

Mike's heavy footsteps went to the media room, where he turned on the television perennially set to sports news.

She placed her purse and phone on the counter, gathered the package and detergent up, and went to the basement laundry. On the clothes-folding table, she set the sweater aside and ran her hands along the bottom of the box. The faint scent of jasmine and rose hovered around the box. She imagined it was Giulia's perfume or lotion. There was a slight impression in the cardboard. She peeled it up, revealing a plastic tube and bag, with a catheter and needle at its center. It lay there, coiled like a serpent. Her heart jumped hard against her sternum. She'd done nothing wrong. The feeling of warm hands against her skin caused her to flinch away. The warmth remained, a steadying influence. She closed her eyes and held her clasped hands against her chest, over her heart. The scent of the box billowed and the drumbeat beneath her sternum slowed. She again reminded herself that she'd done nothing wrong.

Yet.

These tools didn't mean anything until she had an opportunity.

Nothing I do would be anything Mike wouldn't do to himself, she thought.

Her phone rang and rattled on the kitchen counter upstairs. She placed the sweater back into the box and left it in the laundry room—a place Mike never visited. As she went up the stairs, she heard his voice.

"Hey, Davey."

He answered my phone, she thought. *He's home early. David wouldn't have known.* The reality that her burner phone sat inches away in her purse sent lightning shocks of anxiety through her stomach.

"Yeah, o' course your mom's here. She's fine, jus' in the basement."

Mike's voice was sloppy. If he kept drinking, from this point, he'd quickly slip into incoherency. It was too early for the plan, this wasn't right, it wouldn't work. She held back a shock of panic and let out a little groan on the steps.

"Hey, yeah, tell me 'bout school, son. How's the lacrosse goin'? Any o' those chumps givin' you trouble? . . .Huh, wha's that? The fuck? 'Slow start'? Tha's bullshit, boy; you better get your ass in gear—"

Mike drew up short when he saw Karla in the doorway to the basement. He shook his head slightly and continued.

"Ah, fo'get that, you're my boy. You'll get your feet un'erneath you soon enough; tha's why you got that scholarship, right? Got my good genes; gonna kill it like your old man. Right. Okay, yeah, how 'bout them coeds, huh? Meet any pretty girls yet? What? Yeah, I said you mom's here, she's fine. How come you don't wanna talk to me, huh? You ain't called me yet. You a momma's boy? Guess so, here. . ." Mike thrust the phone in Karla's direction. "Get your skirts ready for your boy."

Karla caught the phone as it slid from Mike's hand. Her husband had already turned away, frustrated.

"Hello, David? Sorry about that. I was in the basement," she said.

"What the fuck you got to be sorry about?" Mike yelled from the other room. "He's jus' talkin' to his old man. Jesus fuckin' Christ. . ."

"No, sweetheart, I'm fine—"

"'No, sweetheart, I'm fine,'" Mike mocked as he walked back to the living room, his glass refreshed.

She squeezed the phone hard enough to hear the plastic crackle and assured their son that everything was fine. She traded some empty banter with David long enough to get him off the phone. She didn't want her son involved in this anymore. She couldn't bear any further heartbreak. The frayed line of happier memories from the past snapped. There were tasks that needed doing.

***

During dinner, Mike didn't let up on the bottle, and Karla accommodated him. He insisted that she join him, however, so she gave in and offered to fill two glasses. He'd left the whiskey in the kitchen. It was the perfect opportunity for a test. There'd have to be some other arrangement later, though.

Karla returned to the table with two nearly indistinguishable glasses. Mike had been complaining about his son and wound down to muttered, incomprehensible words. She sipped her drink. The bitter, lukewarm tea matched her mood.

Mike downed the last of his whiskey and banged the glass on the table much harder than he'd intended. His head looked like it was too heavy for his shoulders and he slurred, "I'm goin' t' bed. Fu' this and y'all. Fug id all. . ." He rose and stumbled, knocking the chair over without noticing, and moved to exit the dining room.

Now. It's now. Tonight. Her thoughts crackled.

Karla slid from her chair and nimbly got in front of him.

This is wrong, she thought, *I can't do this.*

"Whaddya doin'?" he asked.

I shouldn't do this.

"I need to get a pad from the bathroom," she answered, and hustled forward.

"Ew, that time o' monf," he said too loud as they mounted the stairs, "that'd 'splain your shitty mood."

A hard line of clarity washed away any hesitation. At the first landing, where the stairs turned, Karla placed one hand on the riser's rounded cap and pulled hard. It came loose and she shot backward into Mike's chest, her head smacking into his mouth. He made a surprised sound and they fell. She tucked her arms and legs in and put her chin to her chest, letting all of her weight push backward. Mike's soft middle cushioned her fall while his back absorbed them both. They hammered down the stairs until they hit the floor. She rolled off of him and he crumpled in a heap with his ass and legs in the air.

"Mike! Are you okay? Are you hurt?" The words fled from her mouth reflexively. She questioned her own actions. Seeing him on the floor like this, however, set some steel to her mouth.

He groaned in response and rolled to his side, moaning. He was trying to speak, to draw air into his lungs, but he couldn't. The best he could manage was to cradle his bulk and make soft hissing sounds.

Adrenaline flooded her body and she shook with nervous energy, shocked at her own decisiveness. She had to make the call now, while he couldn't object. There'd be no choice for him. There would be a trip to the hospital.

The ambulance arrived ten minutes later. They spent several hours in the emergency room. Follow-up appointments were made. Blood was drawn from Mike for analysis and saline bags were set up to provide fluids. His doctor would warn him about his drinking—same as he'd been warned before—and the cycle would continue.

***

It had been a grueling, long day for Mike. He was hungover and agitated from lack of sleep. A lump like a golf ball swelled at the back of his head where he'd impacted the floor, his nose was red and sore from banging into Karla's head, and he squirmed in his chair because of the bruising from neck to tailbone. He wriggled and stared at the bottle of Devil's Hollow on the table next to the empty glass on his left.

"Jesus fuck, these doctors," he grumbled, fingering a bottle of oxy in his right hand. He read the container again. "Four hours and still pain." He eyed the liquor bottle.

Karla set the table. She'd already palmed two of the pills earlier, crushed them, and dissolved the powder in a shot of whiskey. The rest of the day had been spent working on a roast. Mike's second-favorite meal. As she set the table, she watched her husband. His fingers trembled when he wasn't twirling the glass or the bottle. He had small bandages over several injection points from all the prodding of the last twenty-four hours.

She licked her lips, tasting oregano and rosemary. The herbs willed steel into her spotty resolve. Something sweet like blackberries caressed her tongue and she said, "They told you not to have any drinks if you're taking the pills, Mike."

He responded so fast, it was barely a breath after the words left her mouth. "I know. Fuck. I'm not a junkie. This shit doesn't work, anyway." He slid the pills across the table and drummed his fingers near the bottle of whiskey. "I bet one shot wouldn't hurt."

"Mike, you shouldn't," she said, putting a thick slice of beef on his plate.

"Hey, don't tell me what I can't do. Okay? I saved your ass last night. You ain't a nurse; you don't know."

She smiled and nodded. "You're right."

Mike's eyes narrowed and then widened slightly. He stopped moving for a second, taken aback by his wife's words and how sincere they'd sounded. "Oh, am I?" He sneered. "You know a guy my size can handle it."

"You're right," she said, "you earned it."

"Damn right I did— Hey, what are you doing?"

Karla took the bottle and glass off the table and put them on the bar. With her back to him, she said, "I meant, you're right about the other thing." She pulled out two shot glasses, unscrewed the cap on the bourbon, and poured one shot. "There's something we should celebrate."

Mike leaned back when Karla put the shot of whiskey in front of him and kept one for herself.

"We should have another baby."

She sat and Mike stared at her, incredulous. "Really?"

"Really." She raised her glass and smiled. "This might be the last time I can drink for a while. One shot can't hurt."

"Well, hot damn." Mike picked up his glass and toasted her with it.

They drank and Karla said, "You're probably feeling it now. You'd better stop." She turned back to the bar and feigned pouring whiskey while filling her glass from a container of tea stashed for this purpose. She walked to the freezer for some ice.

Mike, his skin flushed and taking on an orange hue, watched his wife and said, "Naw, I'm fine. I can have one more; I feel fine. It's been four hours, anyway."

"But your doctor—"

"Oh, fuck him. Fuck all of 'em. They can't tell me what to do or when to do it."

"Mike—"

"Hey, I am a God-damned man. I have earned everything I have, and I didn't do it by letting other people hold me back. I'll get it my damn self." He moved to get up.

"No, no, Mike!" Karla rushed to the bar. "I'll get it. You relax, okay? You're pretty banged up."

Mike barked one laugh. Karla could see his heart drumming against his sternum. "Banged up, my ass; I feel fine!" He spread his arms and flexed, grinning like a child. Then he winced, feeling his shoulders. "Ouch."

"See?" she said, and placed a rocks glass of bourbon in front of him.

"*Please.* That was nothing."

He launched into an oft-told story about a horrific knee injury he'd suffered during college, one that he'd come back from. It was a long story. Long enough for Karla to top off his drink mid-telling. More than once.

Mike wound down and struggled to sip his drink as if his arm wouldn't obey his commands. He dropped his hand and the glass shattered on the edge of the table. His head lolled and he spoke in a syrupy slow motion. "How come. . .Davey. . .doesn't love me?"

"He does," Karla said. She watched her husband as his breathing came in shallow blasts, an audible rush of air as if his chest were constricting.

"You. . .lo'e me, don' you?"

"I think I did, but it's been a long time since."

The hot, diminishing flow of Mike's rancid breath touched her nose and she cringed. That she didn't love her husband anymore was a thought she'd never given air. The declaration lit a fire of anxiety beneath her. It felt as if the ground would split at any moment and she'd slide down into Hell where the Devil himself would welcome her.

If she called an ambulance right now, they might be able to save Mike. It would be an accident, a result of his poor judgment. Maybe the moment would change him for the better; maybe he'd stop drinking after a near-death experience.

Mike's head sat heavily on his chest. Karla stood and saw that the glass had left a terrible cut in her husband's hand. He felt no pain. Between Mike's heavy breaths she could hear the drip of his blood pattering on the carpet.

The thick silence in the house settled on her shoulders as she picked up the kitchen phone and dialed the first of three numbers. In her memories, Mike screamed and hit her.

She dialed the second number. She'd become an extension of him, an organ that autonomically did what was required of it. But sometimes, organs malfunctioned. Sometimes, there was cancer and it moved fast. Sometimes, it couldn't be stopped.

Her finger hovered over the third number, and she considered David and wondered if he'd miss his father. Then Karla thought of herself and placed the phone back in the cradle.

She gathered the intravenous materials for setup and filled the bag with Devil's Hollow before hanging it from the chandelier over the table. Peeling one of Mike's bandages back, she saw that all of his insertion points looked terrible and obvious. Her fingers trembled. A warmth, like a gentle hand, spread between her shoulders, calming her. She slid the needle into his arm and replaced the tape. At the clamp holding back the flow, she hesitated again. Once more the warmth spread and surety came to her fingers. She opened the clamp and the

Devil flowed directly into Mike's veins.

The bottle on the table beckoned and she tipped a splash of bourbon into her empty glass before bearing witness to her actions. Mike's actions, really; she was an extension of him to the end, an organ that did what it was programmed to do until it malfunctioned. She wasn't grown inside Mike, though; she could survive outside of his influence.

She grabbed a handful of ice and watched over her husband's last breaths. It wasn't hard to imagine that the sound of the ice in her bourbon was the last thing he heard.

Karla raised her drink and said, "I earned this." The whiskey tasted of sweet oils and old wood, of fire sparked by lightning.

Note from the Author

I've always liked Marie Shear's definition that "feminism is the radical notion that women are people too." It's the first thing I think of whenever I hear a man use his wife, sister, or daughter in their reasoning to support stopping violence against women. Men shouldn't need an excuse to support a woman's right to exist without fear. The vast majority of harm is being caused by men against women. Too often, it is intergenerational violence that sets boys and girls into a horrific cycle. It's not up to women to break this cycle, however. It's up to men. I implore any man reading this to seek help and break this cycle. It's never too early, it's never too late, and the people we love deserve a future without violence. Monsters are created, not born.

—*Errick Nunnally*

The Little Thing

Christina Henry

Maura knelt in front of the altar—a tiny thing, tucked in the corner of her bedroom on a shelf. If her mother saw it, she'd probably flip out, but her mother never came into her room anymore. Maura's mother hardly even looked at her these days, and when she did, her eyes would be huge and liquid and confused and full of words she didn't know how to say. Maura liked it better when her mother kept her words inside her mouth and her eyes.

She'd heard more than enough words and seen more than enough eyes with words inside them, words that weren't true, but it didn't matter, because Maura didn't talk back anymore. She didn't say any words of her own to anybody. She saved all of her words for the altar.

The altar was rickety and probably half-baked and deep down she knew it, knew that it was made of ideas that might not be true. She'd gathered all of the objects on the altar based on things in books that she'd stolen from the library. Stolen, not borrowed, because she couldn't face the librarian looking at her askance over the stack of books, books she never would have even looked at eight months before, books with about magic and demons and curses.

Part of her thought all these rituals and spells couldn't be real, that there weren't demons and spirits and devils waiting to be called to hand. It couldn't be real, because if it was, then it meant that God and the angels and the saints were real, and if they were real, they hadn't helped her; they'd left her alone even when she screamed and cried and told those boys to stop.

But maybe God and the angels and saints were real and they just didn't care about what happened to Maura that night, the night she tried never to think about but was somehow never far from her mind. And that meant there might be demons out there, demons of power, demons who would help her because no matter what she said or what she did, no one else would.

So, she knelt before the symbols and the signs at the altar, lit the candles, said the words. And waited for something to happen, for a great being to appear, but there was nothing, only the *drip-drip-drip*ping of the candles and the distant sound of dishes clattering downstairs in the kitchen. In a moment, she would have to leave, pick up her school bag and go downstairs and pretend to eat something and then get on the school bus. She clenched her hands together, her fingernails digging half-moons into her skin.

"Please," she said. "Please help me. Please help me hurt them."

The candles flickered. The symbols stared. Blood ran down the backs of her hands, where her nails had dug in.

"Please," she said, and she felt the word deep in her throat, in her lungs, in the pit of her stomach, and she tried to put everything she was into that *please*.

But there wasn't much left of Maura, really, wasn't much left after the boys had taken what they wanted and everyone else had chiseled away at her with the words in their mouth and their eyes, words like *whore* and *slut* and *probably her fault* and *what was she wearing* and *deserved what she got*.

There was so little of her now, just a little thing, a little thing made of hate and rage, but she put it all into her *please* and sent it out into the world.

But nothing came back, nothing to help her, nothing to save her. She stood then and knocked over the stupid altar, blew out the candles, spilled their wax on the floor, and the blood from the back of her hands touched everything, stained the symbols red.

***

It had started with a little thing, a smile that didn't mean what she thought it meant, but she was just an ordinary Maura and he was an extraordinary Jason. Afterwards, she thought that of course she'd gotten confused, because his smile was the sun and moon and she'd been blinded. Who wouldn't be blinded when in such a presence? She took that smile, a casual expression thrown her way during algebra, took it to mean that he knew her and saw her, and that smile curled up inside her heart and made a home there.

She was only fourteen, only a child, and she didn't know how dangerous smiles could be, how they looked like stars in the night sky, but they were made of teeth that bit.

She didn't know that when he offered a ride, it wasn't a ride home, that it wouldn't just be her and Jason in the car, that two of his friends would come along, that they would snigger about things she didn't know about or understand.

She didn't know that it was all a game to them, that she wasn't a person to them, that the way home would mean taking a detour into the woods, that they would think it was funny when she cried, even though it wasn't funny at all.

But it wasn't what happened in the woods that was the worst part of it. It was the way everyone looked at her like she was the one who'd done something wrong, that she must have asked for it by agreeing to get into the car that day. She felt herself shrink into nothingness when she tried to tell the doctors, the police, her parents what happened— like all she was or could ever be was made of pain, made of this terrible event, that there was nothing left of her except a victim. It was the way the judge said it was just a little thing, that it wasn't worth ruining those boys' lives over. They shouldn't go to jail. They shouldn't have to pay forever just because she said something that she shouldn't have said. She should have kept her words inside her mouth.

No one asked about her life. No one worried about how her future was ruined.

Her mother never hugged her again after that day. Her father never even acknowledged her presence in the house. She had made them pariahs, had brought them shame.

And so, she went to the library, and she bought candles, and she said words and she begged and pleaded for someone to help her, but no one came.

No one came until they day her blood fell, because blood is always needed and required if you want blood in return.

***

When Maura returned home from school, she did just what she always did—walked wordlessly past her mother, who hovered in the kitchen like a nervous mouse afraid a cat will notice it. Maura thought she heard her mother's intake of breath, the breath before a word was spoken, and she hated herself for thinking *Please say something please tell me you care that I'm still here.* But the indrawn breath was just a breath, just the habitual sucking of oxygen, and no words followed it, and Maura felt then that she hated her mother, that she hated her almost more than Jason and the boys that hurt her.

Her mother was supposed to love her no matter what. Her mother was supposed to shelter her from harm. Her mother wasn't supposed to stare at Maura, that stare full of blame.

Maura climbed the stairs and pushed open her bedroom door. She threw her school bag in the corner without looking, threw it at the pile of worthless junk that was supposed to be an altar to summon demons.

"Ouch!"

Maura paused in the act of shutting her door, shutting out the world that hurt her and didn't care that she hurt. She glanced in the corner, her heart pounding.

There was nothing there except the candles and the symbols and the fallen shelf and her bookbag. She'd imagined the voice, conjured it out of her want, just like she'd hoped for that stupid pathetic moment that her mother would speak to her, would hold her, would cry with her and make her feel like she wasn't alone.

Maura slammed the bedroom door and threw herself facedown on her bed, her booted feet dangling over the edge. She should have taken her shoes off downstairs, but she didn't care anymore about rules, about treading dirt into the carpet, about doing things that might make her parents angry. She almost wanted them to be angry. If they were angry, that would be proof that they noticed her, proof that she still existed.

Something rustled in the corner of the room, the corner where she hadn't heard the voice because she'd imagined that voice.

Maura determinedly pushed her face into her pillow because she didn't hear that rustling. She didn't hear what sounded like grumbling and muttering and cursing and the sound of her bookbag being shifted aside.

"That was rude."

She grabbed the ends of the pillow and pulled it up around her ears. She didn't hear that. There was no one speaking.

"I'm talking to you."

The sound was muffled but she could still hear.

You can only hear it because it's in your head it's not really there it's not really there it's not really there because if it is then it means something worked and I don't want to get my hopes up I don't want to start dreaming that I can hurt them back.

"Hey!"

The voice was small, like mouse-small, but it was also clear and strangely deep. There was no rodent squeakiness. It could almost be the voice of a grown man, except that it came from the floor.

From the corner of the room where she'd kept her altar and had prayed every day.

She pushed the pillow away, rolled over, and sat up.

There was a demon in the corner of her room.

It was very small, small enough to put in her pocket, or perch on her shoulder, but it was undeniably a demon. It looked like every movie depiction of a demon Maura had ever seen, just on a significantly smaller scale. It had red skin and curling black horns and protruding fangs and yellow eyes with slitted pupils. It even had tiny hairless wings.

It was just a little thing.

"Well?" it said.

"Well, what?" Maura said. Part of her couldn't believe it was there, in her room, the way she'd wanted. Another part of her couldn't believe that this minute creature would be able to help her.

"Well, where's my apology?" it said.

The expression on its face could only be described as *truculent*. Maura was a good language arts student and vocabulary was one of her favorite subjects, and she always scored well on tests. She'd never had a chance to use *truculent* before, even in her mind.

"I'm sorry," she said, though she wasn't sure what she was apologizing for.

"You threw your bag on me, and then you ignored me while I struggled to get out."

"Did you just read my mind?" Maura said.

"No, I read your face," the demon said, and this time, it appeared a little smug. "You definitely had that 'I'm only apologizing because I should' expression."

"Okay," Maura said. "I'm sorry I threw my bag on you. I didn't know you were there."

The demon narrowed its eyes at her. "And then—what? You didn't believe I was there when I made the noise?"

"Well. . ."

"Well, yes," the demon said. For a moment, it appeared to consider continuing the argument, then apparently decided against it. It rubbed its clawed hands together. "Now, let's get on with the business at hand. We need to make an agreement and then I can assist you."

"An agreement?" Maura vaguely remembered something about this from one of the books she'd read. She needed to form a pact with the demon in order to get it to do things for her. But the book had been very careful to warn against making pacts lightly.

"Yes, an agreement," the demon said. "Do you just repeat everything everyone says all the time?"

"No," Maura said, sitting up straighter. This was weird, undeniably weird, and not at all what she'd expected, but she'd asked for a demon and a demon had arrived. She needed to clear her head and pay attention before she ended up accidentally consigning herself to hell.

The only people who should be consigned to hell are Jason and Matt and Noah. They're the ones who deserve to suffer.

Remembering them, thinking of the possibility of their suffering, made Maura feel strong for the first time in months. She looked the little demon in the eye and said, "What's your name?"

"Bogmaroth," the demon said. "And you are. . ."

"Maura," she said, and was careful not tell him the rest of her name. She definitely recalled that names had power, and if she gave her whole name to the demon, then it could have control over her.

Bogmaroth looked a little disappointed, which let Maura know that her instincts had been correct.

"Maura," it said, rolling her name around in his mouth. "You spent many hours speaking to us, calling for help. What is it that you want?"

"I want revenge. I want those who hurt me to suffer." Maura paused, then added, "Why did it take so long for you to come if you could hear me?"

"You didn't offer anything in exchange until today," Bogmaroth said, and pointed to the tiny splatters of blood on the symbols that she'd had on her altar.

253

"Blood," Maura said. "Of course."

"And blood is what is required if you expect my help," Bogmaroth said.

Maura eyed him warily. "How much blood?"

"That all depends on you," Bogmaroth said. "The more blood you give, the more power I can share."

Maura thought for a moment. "If I give you three drops of blood, what can I get in return?"

"Three drops?"

Bogmaroth was distinctly disgruntled at the suggestion, and Maura was sure he'd been hoping she'd open a vein for him. But Maura wasn't stupid, even if she'd stupidly believed Jason was interested in her. Just talking to the demon for a few moments made her feel better than she had in months, as sharp as she used to be. She would not be alone; she could make them hurt as much as she had—even these newly planted seeds of possibility seemed to renew her spirit.

"Well?" she asked, when Bogmaroth didn't respond to her proposal.

"One drop will let you lure one person to you under an enchantment. A second drop will let you fly. A third drop will allow you to flay the skin from their bones."

"All of that?" Maura said, unable to keep the skepticism from her voice. "All of that for giving you three drops of my blood?"

"Just imagine how much more you could do with more blood," Bogmaroth said, his eyes gleaming.

For a moment, Maura felt the temptation, felt the pull of power. Then she shook her head, freeing it from dangerous thoughts. She wanted Jason and Matt and Noah to pay. She didn't want to give any more of her own pain than she already had done.

"Three drops for each person I want to hurt. Nine drops altogether," Maura clarified.

"Yes."

"Very well," she said.

She pulled one of the badges off her bookbag. She had lots of these pinned to the outside of the bag, with pictures or funny sayings. She'd bought them before, when she still was somebody, before she'd been ground down.

Maura sat on her bed and took the edge of the pin to her finger and pushed it in until blood welled under the tip. Bogmaroth flew to her and perched on her knee, kneading his claws into her thigh.

"If you draw blood from me, it doesn't mean you get to keep it," Maura said, and Bogmaroth ceased, looking sulky.

She extended her finger toward the little demon, and he licked the drop of blood. At the very same moment, something surged in her own blood, something she couldn't describe but felt a little like the rush of adrenaline.

"One," she said, and repeated the process.

"Two," she said, as Bogmaroth's tongue darted out.

"Three," she said, and she felt in that moment that she could do anything, anything at all, and she truly understood then just how dangerous it was to be strong.

"The bargain is sealed for one person," Bogmaroth said.

He smiled, a dangerous smile that would comfort no one, and Maura smiled back exactly the same way.

***

Nobody seemed to understand what had happened to Matt and Noah. Rumors ran rampant through the town after their bodies were found. Matt was missing for two days before a search-and-rescue volunteer came across his remains in the woods, in the copse where he and his friends had raped Maura. That copse was isolated, far from any neighbors that might hear noise and come to investigate. It had been perfect for the purpose Jason and his friends had in mind. And it had

255

been perfect for Maura's design, too.

But it didn't occur to anyone to connect what happened to that boy to what happened to Maura. The idea that Maura—or any teenager, really—could have done that kind of damage seemed incomprehensible.

Matt's bones were broken—*pulverized* was one of the words Maura overheard—as if he'd fallen repeatedly from a great height. And of course, he had done exactly that, because one drop of blood given to Bogmaroth had allowed Maura to fly.

Much of Matt's skin was gone, peeled off in strips. Between the lack of bone structure and the flayed skin, it would have been nearly impossible to identify him, were it not for his clothes and personal items.

The search-and-rescue volunteer retched for an hour after finding him.

The horrifying state of his body had people talking about serial killers, and satanic cults, and about town curfews.

When Noah was found in the same place and the same condition a week later, there was a full-blown panic. Parents started keeping their children home from sports practice and refused to drive anywhere after dark. Theirs was a small town. Bad things weren't supposed to happen in places like that.

And still, nobody seemed to connect what had happened to Matt and Noah to an assault of a teenage girl that had taken place almost a year before.

Nobody, that was, except Jason.

Maura caught him looking at her more than once when they passed in the hallway. Before Matt and Noah died, all three of them would snigger and whisper when she passed, so she'd glue her eyes to the floor and walk faster, pretending not to hear.

Now she walked with her head up again, and when Jason walked by, she'd stare at him until he looked away, his face pale.

She saved him for last, because he was the one who'd started it all. He was the one who'd smiled at her and made her believe.

Six days after Noah's punishment, Maura was putting her books away in her locker before lunch. She sensed someone standing behind her and turned around slowly.

Jason stood there, shifting his weight from one foot to the other, one hand half-outstretched like he was going to tap her on the shoulder. Maura looked at him and then at his hand, and he hastily shoved it into his jeans pocket.

"Maura. . ." he said, the second syllable of her name fading off somewhere as his voice dropped.

She waited, saying nothing, giving him nothing. He deserved nothing from her. She felt the fear and uncertainty coming off him in waves, like a palpable force, and she felt her own strength growing in response to it.

It didn't have to be this way. You didn't have to hurt me. You chose it, she thought. *And then you lied about me, about what really happened, to save your own skin.*

"Maura," he said again. He was thinner than he had been two weeks before. "Maura, you seem different."

She raised an eyebrow at him.

"Maura, listen, I'm sorry about what happened," he said. He blurted the words out in a hurry, each one piling on top of the last.

"You're sorry?" she said. She wanted to scream, to yell, to leap on him and pull each one of his teeth out by the roots.

How dare he say he's sorry. How dare he say he's sorry now, *when he's scared and he thinks I'm the reason he's frightened. How dare he think that* sorry *can fix everything now.*

"Yes, I'm really sorry," he said. Sweat rolled over his temples and down his cheeks. "So just, please, just please don't. . ."

"Don't what?" Maura said.

He leaned a little closer, his eyes darting from side to side.

"Don't do what you did to Matt and Noah. I don't know how you did it, but I know it was you."

The hallway was empty now except for the two of them, all the other students gone to their classes or their lunch period.

Maura said, "Do you remember what I said that day?"

Jason stared at her, and if anything, he seemed paler than before, his lips bloodless.

"What did I say?" Maura said, and there was force behind her question, a demand that he respond.

"You said. . ."

"Yes?"

"You said, 'Please don't hurt me, please stop.'" His voice was barely above a whisper.

"And what did you do?"

A tear fell from one of his eyes. "I laughed."

"That's right," Maura said. "You laughed. Remember that."

***

Maura sat in her room the next night, her own wild laughter ringing in her ears, mixing with the memory of how he'd screamed and cried and pled, how he'd asked her to stop.

Bogmaroth sat on her knee again, his wings fluttering like a restless moth.

"They aren't the only ones, you know."

Maura frowned. "The only ones, what?"

"The only ones who've hurt girls like you. There are lots more of them, and they all need to be punished. They're almost never punished."

"No, they aren't," Maura said, and looked at the demon.

She knew what he wanted. He wanted more blood from her. He was

258

already bigger than he had been when he arrived—not too much bigger, but not as small as he'd been. And the more powerful he became, the more power he was able to give to her.

She could help other girls, other women. She could make sure the ones who harmed them were punished. And all she had to do was give the demon three drops of blood.

It was such a little thing to ask in exchange for the strength to right wrongs, to listen to the weeping of bad men.

Maura put the tip of the needle to her finger again.

Violence Against Women:
Learning More and Getting Help—A Starting Point

If the stories in *Giving the Devil His Due* have inspired you to take action to stop violence against women (VAW) in your community or help someone you know who is a victim, here are a few starting points:

To learn more about violence against women and how to help victims worldwide, visit www.thepixelproject.net

If you are in Asia, you can find a list of crisis helplines for women at https://asiapacific.unwomen.org/en/focus-areas/end-violence-against-women/shadow-pandemic-evaw-and-covid-response/list-of-helplines

If you are in Australia or New Zealand, you can find a list of crisis helplines for women at https://matebystander.edu.au/support-service-information-australia-and-new-zealand/

If you are in Europe, you can find a list of crisis helplines for women at https://www.coe.int/en/web/istanbul-convention/help-lines

If you are in North America, you can find a list of crisis helplines for women at:

- **Canada:** https://dawncanada.net/issues/issues/we-can-tell-and-we-will-tell-2/crisis-hotlines/
- **USA:** http://domesticshelters.org

If none of the list above covers your country or area, follow the Pixel Project on Twitter at @PixelProject (https://twitter.com/PixelProject). We tweet out helplines for victims of VAW in over thirty countries twice daily at ten AM and eight PM Eastern Time.

For domestic violence and sexual assault helplines and resources in every UN-recognized country and territory in the world, visit https://nomoredirectory.org/. This resource hub was created by the NO MORE Foundation in partnership with the United Nations and the World Bank.

Acknowledgment

All anthologies are collaborative projects, and *Giving the Devil His Due* is no different. Yet this anthology is so much more because everyone who has contributed to making it a reality is united by the collective aim of ending violence against women and girls.

And so, The Pixel Project's humblest and sincerest thanks go out to:

- Stephen Graham Jones, whose story "Hell on the Homefront Too" inspired this anthology in the first place.
- Rebecca Brewer, our wonderful anthology editor, who believed in this anthology from the moment we were introduced to her. We could not have done this without her invaluable guidance and superpowered editing expertise, which she generously donated to the cause. You're one of the Pixel family, Rebecca!
- Guy Gavriel Kay, who suggested Rebecca and introduced us to her in his unfailingly gracious and generous way.
- Kelley Armstrong, who gave us a 101 lesson in what makes a fair and straightforward contract for authors. . .and who was the first author to get on board the anthology and patiently waited for us to pull it all together.
- Dana Cameron, Hillary Monahan, and Leanna Renee Hieber, longtime Read For Pixels authors who got on board the anthology with zero hesitation. You promised us powerful stories. . .and you delivered in spades.

- Angela Yuriko Smith, Christina Henry, Errick Nunnally, Jason Sanford, Kaaron Waaren, Kenesha Williams, Lee Murray, Linda D. Addison, Nicholas Kaufmann, Nisi Shawl, and Peter Tieryas, your individual and collective generosity in writing original stories or offering your most powerful reprints for the anthology has been instrumental in bringing this project to life. We are so proud to have you as Read For Pixels authors.

- Lisa Kastner, founder and executive editor at Running Wild Press, who immediately said yes when we pitched the anthology to her.

- The Running Wild crew, including Nicole Tiskus and Lisa Montagne, who worked with us to get the book out for reviews, promotions, etc. Y'all are the best!

- Taylor Grant, who performed a serendipitous spot of literary matchmaking by introducing us to Running Wild.

- Richard Shealy, copyeditor extraordinaire and longtime Pixel Project supporter, who said yes without missing a beat to volunteering his time and expertise to copyedit our anthology.

- Jessica Brewer, attorney-at-law, who kindly volunteered to help with the Letter of Agreement.

- Clarence Young (Zig Zag Claybourne), who tirelessly supported us behind the scenes by recommending suitable authors to us, then introducing them to us.

- Paul Tremblay, for writing the awesome blurb for this anthology and his years of steadfast support for our anti–violence against women work in his capacity as a Read For Pixels author, as well as introducing us to Stephen Graham Jones.

- Charles de Lint, for helping with everything from suggesting potential authors to offering to help spread the word about the anthology.

- Subterranean Press and *Space and Time* magazine, who each very kindly offered to promote the anthology.
- Sara Megibow, who generously shared her advice and expertise as a veteran literary agent when we consulted with her about how to choose the right publisher.
- Steve Drew, head of r/Fantasy, and his mod team, who have supported our work over the years by hosting all our Read For Pixels author AMA sessions.
- All our Read For Pixels authors past and present who have supported our Read For Pixels program, working with us to take it from strength to strength with each passing year.
- The Read For Pixels community of supporters who have stuck with us and believed in our work for years—donating to keep our anti–violence against women programs alive while helping spread the word about stopping violence against women in their families and communities.

And last but never, ever least:

- The Read For Pixels team (Anushia Kandasivam, Denishia Rajendran, Juliana Spink Mills, Samantha Joseph, Suloshini Jahanath, Tan Shiow Chin), our senior editor Crystal Smith, and our secretary/CFO Bridget Hudacs, who have always been on standby to pitch in with everything from doing emergency proofreading to figuring out solutions for the bumps in the road on the way to publication.

Author Bios

LINDA D. ADDISON

Linda D. Addison, award-winning author of five collections, including *How To Recognize A Demon Has Become Your Friend*, the first African-American recipient of the HWA Bram Stoker Award®, received the HWA Mentor of the Year Award and the HWA Lifetime Achievement Award. Addison is a co-editor of *Sycorax's Daughters*, an anthology of horror fiction/poetry by African-American women.

KELLEY ARMSTRONG

Kelley Armstrong believes experience is the best teacher, though she's been told this shouldn't apply to writing her murder scenes. To craft her books, she has studied aikido, archery and fencing. She sucks at all of them. She has also crawled through very shallow cave systems and climbed half a mountain before chickening out. She is, however, an expert coffee drinker and a true connoisseur of chocolate-chip cookies.

DANA CAMERON

Whether writing SF/F/H, noir, historical fiction, thriller, or traditional mystery, Dana Cameron draws from her expertise in archaeology. Her work has won multiple Agatha, Anthony, and Macavity Awards and earned an Edgar Award nomination. The Emma Fielding archaeology mysteries were optioned by Muse Entertainment; the most recent, *More Bitter Than Death*, debuted in 2019 on Hallmark Movies & Mysteries.

LEANNA RENEE HIEBER

Award-winning, bestselling author Leanna Renee Hieber writes historical fantasy novels for Tor and Kensington Books such as the *Strangely Beautiful* saga, *The Eterna Files* trilogy and *The Spectral City* series. A classically trained actress featured in film and television, Leanna created and tours a one-woman show portraying nineteenth-century designer Clara Driscoll.

CHRISTINA HENRY

Christina Henry is a horror and dark fantasy author whose works include *Near the Bone*, *The Ghost Tree*, *Looking Glass*, *The Girl in Red*, *The Mermaid*, *Lost Boy*, *Alice*, *Red Queen*, and the seven-book urban fantasy Black Wings series. She enjoys running long distances, reading anything she can get her hands on and watching movies with samurai, zombies and/or subtitles in her spare time. She lives in Chicago with her husband and son.

STEPHEN GRAHAM JONES

Stephen Graham Jones is the *New York Times* bestselling author of nearly thirty novels and collections, and there's some novellas and comic books in there as well. Most recent are *The Only Good Indians* and *Night of the Mannequins* and *My Heart is a Chainsaw*. Stephen lives and teaches in Boulder, Colorado.

NICHOLAS KAUFMANN

Nicholas Kaufmann is the author of six novels, the most recent of which is the bestselling horror novel *100 Fathoms Below*, co-written with Steven L. Kent. His fiction has been nominated for the Bram Stoker Award, the Shirley Jackson Award, the Thriller Award, and the Dragon Award. In addition to his own original work, he has written for such properties as *Zombies vs. Robots*, *The Rocketeer*, and *Warhammer*. He and his wife live in Brooklyn, New York.

HILLARY MONAHAN

Hillary Monahan is a *New York Times* bestselling author of twelve novels, her books spanning the gamut from young adult horror to contemporary romance. Her next novel, a gothic retelling of Miss Havisham's younger years, is forthcoming from Penguin Random House Delacorte.

LEE MURRAY

Lee Murray is a multi-award-winning author-editor from Aotearoa-New Zealand. Her work includes military thrillers, the Taine McKenna Adventures, supernatural crime-noir series The Path of Ra (with Dan Rabarts), and debut collection *Grotesque: Monster Stories*. She is proud to have co-edited *Black Cranes: Tales of Unquiet Women* with Geneve Flynn. Read more on her website: www.leemurray.info.

ERRICK NUNNALLY

Errick Nunnally was raised in Boston, served in the USMC, graduated from art school, and studied Krav Maga. He has published three novels, *Blood for the Sun*, *All the Dead Men*, and *Lightning Wears a Red Cape*, and several stories in anthologies and magazines. Visit erricknunnally.us to learn more about his work.

JASON SANFORD

Jason Sanford is a two-time finalist for the Nebula Award who has published dozens of stories in *Asimov's Science Fiction*, *Interzone*, *Apex Magazine*, *Fireside Magazine*, and *Beneath Ceaseless Skies* along with appearances in multiple "year's best" anthologies. His first novel, *Plague Birds*, will be released by Apex Publications in late 2021. Born and raised in the American South, Jason's previous experience includes work as an archaeologist and as a Peace Corps volunteer. His website is www.jasonsanford.com.

NISI SHAWL

Multiple-award-winning author and editor Nisi Shawl has taught for Clarion West, Viable Paradise, Centrum, and Hugo House, and spoken at Duke University and Spelman College. They contribute reviews to the *Washington Post*, *Ms. Magazine*, and *The Cascadia Subduction Zone*, a literary quarterly. They cowrote *Writing the Other: A Practical Approach*, a standard text on inclusive representation. They live in Seattle and take frequent walks with their cat.

ANGELA YURIKO SMITH

Angela Yuriko Smith is an American poet, Stoker-nominated author and co-publisher of *Space and Time* magazine, a publication that has been printing speculative fiction, art and poetry since 1966. Join our Flash Battle leagues, compete as an Iron Writer and help raise an Exquisite Corpse at SpaceandTime.net.

PETER TIERYAS

Peter Tieryas is the award-winning internationally best-selling writer of the Mecha Samurai Empire series (Penguin Random House), which has received praise from places like the *Financial Times*, Amazon, *Verge*, *Gizmodo*, *Wired*, and more. The series has been translated into multiple foreign languages and won two Seiun Awards, and the Mandarin version was one of Douban's Top 10 Science Fiction Books of 2018. He's had hundreds of publications from places like *New Letters*, *Subaru*, *ZYZZYVA*, *Indiana Review*, and more. His game essays have been published at sites like *IGN*, *Kotaku*, and *Entropy*. He was also a technical writer for Lucasfilm.

KAARON WARREN

Shirley Jackson award-winner Kaaron Warren published her first short story in 1993 and has had fiction in print every year since. She was recently given the Peter McNamara Achievement Award and was Guest of Honour at World Fantasy 2018, Stokercon 2019 and Geysercon 2019. She has published five multi-award-winning novels (*Slights, Walking the Tree, Mistification, The Grief Hole* and *Tide of Stone*) and seven short story collections. Her most recent book is the novella *Into Bones Like Oil*.

KENESHA WILLIAMS

Kenesha Williams is an author and Founder/Editor-in-Chief of *Black Girl Magic Lit Mag*. She loves speculative fiction and writes in the horror, science fiction, and urban fantasy genres. Kenesha lives in the DC Metro area with her husband, children, and finicky cat.

Past Titles

Running Wild Stories Anthology, Volume 1
Running Wild Anthology of Novellas, Volume 1
Jersey Diner by Lisa Diane Kastner
The Kidnapped by Dwight L. Wilson
Running Wild Stories Anthology, Volume 2
Running Wild Novella Anthology, Volume 2, Part 1
Running Wild Novella Anthology, Volume 2, Part 2
Running Wild Stories Anthology, Volume 3
Running Wild's Best of 2017, AWP Special Edition
Running Wild's Best of 2018
Build Your Music Career From Scratch, Second Edition by Andrae Alexander
Writers Resist: Anthology 2018 with featured editors Sara Marchant and Kit-Bacon Gressitt
Frontal Matter: Glue Gone Wild by Suzanne Samples
Mickey: The Giveaway Boy by Robert M. Shafer
Dark Corners by Reuben "Tihi" Hayslett
The Resistors by Dwight L. Wilson
Open My Eyes by Tommy Hahn
Legendary by Amelia Kibbie
Christine, Released by E. Burke
Running Wild Stories Anthology, Volume 4
Tough Love at Mystic Bay by Elizabeth Sowden
The Faith Machine by Tone Milazzo
The Newly Tattooed's Guide to Aftercare by Aliza Dube
American Cycle by Larry Beckett
Magpie's Return by Curtis Smith
Gaijin by Sarah Z. Sleeper

273

Recon: The Trilogy + 1 by Ben White

Sodom & Gomorrah on a Saturday Night by Christa Miller

Upcoming Titles

Running Wild Novella Anthology, Volume 4

Antlers of Bone by Taylor Sowden

Blue Woman/Burning Woman by Lale Davidson

Something Is Better than Nothing by Alicia Barksdale

Take Me With You By Vanessa Carlisle

Mickey: Surviving Salvation by Robert Shafer

Running Wild Anthology of Stories, Volume 5 by Various

Running Wild Novella Anthology, Volume 5 by Various

Whales Swim Naked by Eric Gethers

Stargazing in Solitude by Suzanne Samples

American Cycle by Larry Beckett

Running Wild Press publishes stories that cross genres with great stories and writing. RIZE publishes great genre stories written by people of color and by authors who identify with other marginalized groups. Our team consists of:

Lisa Diane Kastner, Founder and Executive Editor
Andrea Johnson, Acquisitions Editor, RIZE
Rebecca Dimyan, Editor
Andrew DiPrinzio, Editor
Cecilia Kennedy, Editor
Barbara Lockwood, Editor
Chris Major, Editor
Cody Sisco, Editor
Chih Wang, Editor
Benjamin White, Editor
Peter A. Wright, Editor
Lisa Montagne, Director of Education
Pulp Art Studios, Cover Design
Standout Books, Interior Design
Polgarus Studios, Interior Design
Nicole Tiskus, Production Manager
Alex Riklin, Production Manager
Alexis August, Production Manager
Priya Raman-Bogan, Social Media Manager

Learn more about us and our stories at www.runningwildpress.com

Loved this story and want more? Follow us at www.runningwildpress.com, www.facebook/runningwildpress, on Twitter @lisadkastner @RunWildBooks

Made in the USA
Coppell, TX
07 November 2021

65330774R00164